THE FAMILY WAY

THE FAMILY WAY

AN ORIGINAL ANTHOLOGY

Edited by
Peter Kendell & Darren Everett

Illustrated by
Meghan Hawkes

chalk path books

CHALK PATH BOOKS

Published by Chalk Path Books
www.chalkpathbooks.com

First published 2013

ISBN: 978-0-9574711-2-2

10 9 8 7 6 5 4 3 2 1

Interior art copyright © 2013 Meghan Hawkes
http://www.meghanhawkesillustration.com

CONTENTS

MRS THATCHER'S MOLECULE

Margaret Thatcher, that clever, energetic, ambitious woman, once said – or so it is often reported – that "There is no such thing as Society." This quotation has been used to harry her reputation all the way up to and, indeed, beyond her death.

That is fair enough so far as it goes, but it does not tell the whole story. What she actually said (in a 1987 interview with Douglas Keay printed in *Woman's Own* magazine) was, "And, you know, there is no such thing as society. There are individual men and women, and there are families."

Without getting too deeply into politics – apart from noting that the quotation clearly expresses the Lady's support of small-statism – it is possible for anyone of whatever political persuasion to see what she was getting at. Because, although we may operate as individuals, our motivations are directed in support of what is called the family unit. Or, in other words and taking a somewhat dubious scientific analogy (which Baroness Thatcher, the trained chemist, might have appreciated), the family is the basic molecule of humanity and human individuals the atoms that go to make up that molecule. Wider society often has to take its chance and when its needs are in conflict with the needs of a family, it is never a surprise when the family wins. It's easy to point out how much harm we do ourselves by confining our mental scope of operation to such small groups and also how family responsibilities can be used to justify selfishness. "I did it for my family/children/wife/mother" sounds much better than "I did it for myself" however untrue it may be.

It is also true that family issues dominate daytime television and the columns of agony aunts the world around. It's as if we can't live without our families, but we can't live with them either. To take another well-known quotation, "All happy families are alike; each unhappy family is unhappy in its own way." (Leo Tolstoy, *Anna Karenina*.)

The title of "family" is so important to us that we allow it to be appropriated left, right and centre. At the top end of the size scale, the British Commonwealth considers itself a "Family of Nations" with, presumably, the Britain that once ruled an empire sitting comfortably in the position of parent and onlie begetter. Commercial enterprises like to call themselves "Family Firms". Care homes for the sick and elderly will tell you they have a "family atmosphere", as will such hierarchies as private schools and military units. In all these organisations there is the implied understanding that here is a place where you can slot in quite naturally, as secure in your place as a wolf in his pack.

All the stories in this collection are set in families of one kind or another. Some are happy, more are not. Some are intact, others are fractured. In some cases the family is entirely conventional, in others less so, but it's fair to say that the more they differ, the more they remain the same.

There is a tradition in fiction of the child who can only grow to full adulthood after he or she has left home and made their way in the world. When a character leaves a family it is as likely as not that he or she will eventually return to it because, after all, a molecule without its constituent atoms is no longer the same molecule and a family that is missing one or more of its members is no longer the same family. It is, perhaps, only when the straying child, whether prodigal or otherwise, comes home to his or her family that he or she truly becomes part of it, and Mrs Thatcher's molecule is complete once more.

Peter Kendell, Summer 2013

SAMANTHA

Peter Kendell

Peter Kendell writes stories, mostly when he's supposed to be doing something else. He is the author of THE BOY AND OTHER STORIES *(also available from Chalk Path Books) and you can find his website at www.cereswunderkind.net.*

Peter lives with FW and Minor in the south-east of England, where he works as an engineering consultant. Although he usually kills any plant he touches – not intentionally, it just happens – this year he has been notably successful with his geraniums.

SAMANTHA

S AM'S MOTHER IS THINKING OF KILLING HERSELF AGAIN. SHE CAN BE heard, downstairs, on the phone, speaking with her counsellor. To Samantha, solitary in her attic bedroom with its open door and clear path to the first floor, the conversation sounds strangely upbeat. Her mother's voice is pitched manic-high, not depressed-low, and she talks like someone seeking advice. How should she go about the task this time? Samantha believes she hears the unheard part of the conversation. It consists of a how-to guide, a handbook to oblivion. Which method would give the quickest result? Would be guaranteed to work? Is there an FAQ I can read?

When the phone pings back onto its rest, and her mother goes into the kitchen, possibly to make a brew – whether of hemlock or coffee is yet to be determined – Samantha gets up from the bed where she has been sitting stiffly upright, exactly half-way between the headboard and the footlocker. The mattress follows her as she rises, slowly filling in the hollow her weight has dimpled in it. She walks the three steps to the dormer window. It overlooks the back yard, giving a private view of grass, flowers, trees, shrubs and barbeque pit. To one side there is a hedge, to the other a fence. At the end stands a paved area with wrought-iron tables and chairs and, loosely hidden behind a screen of woven willow, a shed. Below the window, a twenty-foot drop to the decking her father constructed three summers ago. Twenty feet is a long way to fall, but the outcome is not guaranteed to be fatal, not onto wood. Concrete would be better.

Sam wonders if her mother is considering throwing herself from this window. Should she be warned about such an act's uncertainty? To live on, crippled or brain-damaged by an awkward fall – or to suffer the humiliation of surviving completely unhurt – would not give her mother the outcome she is seeking.

The attic is a pretty room, brightly lit all day even when it is cloudy outside, and wallpapered with pink and blue roses. Samantha chose the wicker chair and the antique bedstead – so hard for the delivery men to carry upstairs – herself, while her mother and father picked the blue velvet drapes and rich maroon rug. Even now, with its beauty age-faded, it is a pleasant place to be. Perhaps, then, Mother should come here, despite the window's easily released safety latches and tempting screen of blue-white sky. Perhaps her mood will be correspondingly elevated as her feet lift her step by step to the top storey of the house.

But, to repeat, Mother does not sound sad. She is excited, as she was when she was looking forward to going on vacation – to Florida, say, or their friends' house in Maine – when Samantha was younger, and the climb to the attic a bright ascension to a starlit realm. It would be to fall into a trap, then, to invite Mother here in the hope of regulating her mood. Opportunities are there for the seizing, they say. *Carpe Diem*, and so on, but they carry risk with them.

The house has a basement, but Samantha does not go there and neither does Mother. The door is locked and a curious odour permeates the air around its frame.

Mother worries about Sam. She is a quiet girl and subject to night terrors, which she has always endured in silence. A little fish, creeping trembling into their bed. One hand thrust into her mouth to still the screams. Another hand, chilled, put out to be held.

Samantha does not come to her mother's bed these days. She a big girl now, much too big to be a scaredy-cat. Big enough to endure bad dreams on her own and not bother her parents. Samantha does not appreciate that grown-ups – proper grown-ups, with houses and cars and mortgages and health plans and 401(k)s – have nightmares too.

So now there is a night-time moratorium. Doors remain shut. The family meets on the landing outside the bathroom, or downstairs in the kitchen, over coffee and, if there is time, pancakes. They come together again in the evening; and so their temporal country is divided into bleary morning east coast and tired evening west coast, and its heartland is separation. Father has work, and Samantha has school and Mother... Mother has herself, and the company she shares in town or mall or at the thrift store – once a chapel – where she stands behind the counter three days a week and disburses her time charitably. She meets other charitable ladies over the once-used gadgets and twice-turned sheets, while pretending she doesn't recognise the customers who come pinging through the street door to riffle through the bins and shelves. Unless, of course, they want to be recognised. For every shopper who is ashamed to be seen rummaging through other people's cast-offs there is another who is proud of her enterprise and economy in seeking out a bargain. While the women consider drapes and doormats, their men turn rusty kitchen appliances over in their hands, fancying they could make them work again if they could only get hold of the right components, or had the right tools to take them apart and find out what's really wrong with them.

'Made in the USA,' says one, once a motor mechanic with his own shop. 'That's the sign of quality. That's reliability. That's fixability. Built to last.'

'It's all disposable Chinese crap now,' says his white-moustached friend. 'Doesn't matter if it says Honeywell or Westinghouse or Philco on the outside. It's Chinese crap on the inside. Made by slave labour. Not worth fixing.'

'Dam' right. Buy you a beer.' They leave. There is a bar down the road, not far, where it is warm and they will be welcomed by other, equally dispossessed men.

Mother sighs to see them leave. The place is untidy now, and she will have to sort it. Then home, and quietness, and her thoughts. And, perhaps, death.

Father has a desk job. Were a stranger to ask him what this job entails, he would reply that he makes calls, and signs papers, and goes to meetings and speaks with clients. At the appropriate times he tells the appropriate people that he has a passion for this line of work. He says he is committed to its success and to the increase of shareholder value. He observes all the strictures of due diligence. He does this to insure that he is included in the upper quartile of employee assessments and thereby not placed at risk of dismissal for underachievement. He makes certain that his contribution is appreciated.

In the morning he unplugs the Prius and drives it to the office. In the evening he drives it home again and plugs it back in. He buys very little gas; something of which he frequently boasts to his colleagues. 'Zero pollution at point of use,' he says, proudly. 'Three hundred miles to the gallon. What does yours make?'

After making sure that current is flowing into the car's batteries he goes indoors to check on his wife.

What will he find? Will the kitchen be full of the smell of cooking? Or not? Will it be warm? Or not? And will his wife be waiting for him; dressed in a pinafore, holding a busy skillet in her right hand and wearing a Doris Day smile? Or will she be lying cold in the hallway, dead again?

Samantha has had a bad day at school. Or a good day, depending on your point of view. She has fallen out with her friends Melissa Goldstein and Mary Klovac over some silly matter in the cafeteria. Some boy or something-whatever-why-should-I-give-a-shit. Ryan, his name is. But Miss Meyer has praised her history essay and her grades are holding up well this year.

She sometimes wonders what it would be like if that boy were to carry her books home for her, tied up with string and flung crazy-man over his shoulder. That boy would call Father "Sir" and Mother "Ma'am". There is, thank God, no boy. The essential uncertainty of her quotidian return home makes such a consideration impossible ever to consider. She has the same anticipations as Father.

Today turns out to be one of those days. As before – they have a routine now – there is no ambulance ride, no credit check, no magazine-strewn waiting room, no Kleenex box waiting ready on the table. There are no names to sign or bills to be paid. Merely a cruiser parked outside in the falling dusk and a tired deputy and a notepad to sign and an unlit house. And a spreading stain on the decking and a slow drip-drip onto the well-nourished weeds beneath.

The funeral is cheap. You might, were you indulging in a morbid form of humour, say it was obtained at wholesale rates. Mother is not a believer, so there is no call for minister, music or prayers. No beds have to be made, no rooms need to be reserved at bed-and-breakfast or hotel, as there are no mourners coming from out of town. In fact, nobody attends other than Samantha and her father – no neighbours, acquaintances, colleagues or friends. Everyone is sick of death.

Afterwards, father and daughter get into the Prius and drive slowly home.

'Hi Ben, hi Sam,' says Mother as Father opens the front door and enters the hallway, followed reluctantly by Samantha. 'Did you have a nice time?'

'You know, Iris,' says Father.

SNOW

Raphael Kabo

Raphael Kabo loves words. He hunts for them in the streets of dream cities, shouts them into microphones, and argues with them in notebooks until they turn into stories. Raphael's words took him to the 2010 Australian National Poetry Slam finals and the 2012 National Folk Festival, and have now landed him on the banks of the Thames, where he hopes to write many a strange tale and read many a twisty poem.

SNOW

F OR THE FIRST FOUR MONTHS AFTER MOVING INTO THE NEW FLAT, WE didn't have a television. There wasn't anywhere to put it, because what wasn't taken up by mislabelled cardboard boxes was full of things for the baby. Then, when we had settled down a little, we didn't have any money to buy it with; and then, dad was just too busy with his new job and mum with the baby. I thought I'd be considered some sort of freak not to have a TV but nobody at school really seemed to mind.

Finally, though, my parents succumbed, and we got a second-hand one at Cash Converters for fifty quid. Dad brought it in, grunting and panting up the stairs, followed by mum with the shopping. He cleared a space on the table with his elbow and put the TV down. We all appraised it. It was made of matte black plastic and had rounded corners, so it looked sort of ageless – not an antique with a silver clicky wheel, nor a silver monster with no buttons at all, but something unspecific from the 90s. It was a Kanashi, which was a brand I had never heard of before, but dad said Japanese TVs are always good. Hannah was very excited about watching Fairly OddParents. Fairly OddParents is rubbish. I was excited about watching Star Wars. Hannah and I don't see eye to eye about many important things.

We set the TV up in the living room, on the floor by the bookshelf, because we didn't have anything to put it on yet. 'If it works,' said mum, 'we'll get a stand.'

It didn't work. I connected up the antenna and the digital tuner box, because that sort of thing confuses dad, and mum doesn't even know where to start. I turned it on and flicked it to AV, but all I got was snow – fuzzy hushy black-and-white snow that hurt my eyes. There were things in the snow that were like lost ghosts.

'That's all static is,' I said, staring at the snow, 'ghosts of TV signals you can't properly catch, right?' Anyway, it was rubbish. I tried connecting the antenna straight to the TV, to get the normal channels, but it was still the same snow. I tried all the buttons on the remote, and got snow with green letters over it.

'They promised me it'd work!' fumed dad, waving the dog-eared manual in the direction of the city. 'Now I bet they'll say we've broken it, and I'll be surprised if I get so much as a sorry from *them*.' He waved the manual some more.

'It's only fifty pounds, dear,' said mum soothingly. She always soothes dad, except when he soothes her. They're a soothing couple, my parents.

'Fifty pounds of my – of our hard-earned money!' he raved, and stomped around the room, though there wasn't really enough room to stomp around in, what with the couch and the TV and the bookshelf and the baby-changing table clogging it all up. I sat on my chair and looked at the snow. I felt sort of forgetful, like I wasn't sure if I was supposed to fix the TV or just stare at it forever, until I became all thin and empty. The snow made a *tissshhhhhhhhhhh* sound, like a wave stuck on repeat.

'Come on, Tony,' said mum. 'Turn it off. You can tell it's broken.' I did, then went to the study to play Team Fortress. Team Fortress is wicked. Even Hannah likes it, but she only gets to play until her bedtime and that's really early so I get to play heaps. That night I didn't really want to play for long, though, because I kept thinking that something was creeping up behind me as I sat at the computer. It wasn't a monster-under-the-bed feeling. You know exactly where those monsters are. It was a going-to-the-toilet-by-yourself-in-the-middle-of-the-night feeling. That's when the monsters can be anywhere.

'That TV messed with my mind,' I told mum. She was reading in bed.

'Oh, sweetie,' she said. 'I bet it's dangerous. It's probably leaking radiation, like the microwave.'

'The microwave is *fine*,' grunted dad from the other side of the bed. 'Just don't stand near it when it's on.'

'We'll take it back tomorrow,' she said. 'I don't want it near Hannah or Suzie. Or you.'

I went to bed. I didn't dream much, but what I did dream about was a castle made of baby-changing tables, stuck far out in the sea, and the waves hit it and washed the baby-changing tables away, and there was something inside the castle that was appearing slowly with every wave. It felt all faded and sour, like the sticky spot from a sour lolly if you take it out of your mouth and put it on the table. It was really scary, and I woke up in the middle of the night, my throat raw with thirst.

The TV was on. I could hear it as soon as I opened my eyes, exactly the same sound, just a quiet sort of steady sound, like rain on asphalt or kettles before they boil. I climbed out of bed – my legs felt foggy – and opened the door, and I could see its white glare all down the side of the door frame, and along the living room wall, and on one leg of the baby-changing table.

'Mum?' I called out, really quietly, and felt sort of stupid when nobody answered, because mum was asleep, of course, and so was dad. I looked back into the bedroom, and Hannah was asleep too, in her stupid pink bed. She looked sort of cute when she was asleep. She's got a funny nose. Then I tiptoed into the living room, where the TV sat in the middle of the floor. *Tshhhhhhhh*, it said.

'You're weird,' I replied, and pressed the power button to turn it off.

It didn't turn off. If anything, it got a bit brighter. The static looked at me, and sort of through me, and sort of into me, and sort of laughed. I pressed the button again, then a few more times – nothing.

I tried turning it off with the remote, and then again with the switch. Then I went round to the power board and pressed the power button there. With a sort of *dzing*, the TV turned off, and the room turned pitch-black and scary, so I leapt up and hurried out and climbed into bed and went straight back to sleep, and forgot completely about being thirsty.

The next morning, everything was sluggish and late and broken and wrong. Dad had a meeting at work but woke up late, so he yelled at things in the kitchen while wearing a dressing gown and clutching a slice of toast, and then mum had to soothe him. That meant mum had almost no time to do baby stuff for Suzie, and of course Suzie started bawling her tiny eyes out for no good reason, so mum was late taking me and Hannah to school, so she started shouting at things in the kitchen and dad had to soothe *her*, and eventually I just sat on my bed with my bag all packed and smelling of tomato and ham sandwiches, and felt sad and knotty and worried. Worried that I hadn't told anyone about the television last night, but also just worried, like when you suspect you didn't do well in a maths test. After a minute of that, I got up and had a peek at the TV. Hannah was sitting in front of it, kind of tiny and pale, just watching the snow.

'Turn it off,' I said, sharply. 'Mum said we can't use it. It's broken. And it turns on by itself. It did last night.' *There*, I thought. *Now I've told someone*. I felt better all at once. But Hannah didn't reply.

'Come on,' I said again, almost pleadingly, just as mum yelled for us to get moving. Hannah looked at me, and for a second her eyes were all big and empty like wells. She blinked, and they went bright blue again.

'Okay,' she said, and ran to the bedroom to get her stupid pink bag. I have a Star Wars bag. It has a stormtrooper on it. I was distracted from thinking about stormtroopers when I felt this tingle up my spine, and realised that I was alone in the room with the TV again. I turned to it, and felt like I was being slowly, slowly swallowed. I was going to turn it off but just then mum rushed in and pulled me out and rushed me down the stairs to the underground car park.

School was boring, because it's school, but half-way through English I got a really horrible headache and went to the sickbay for an icepack. I have a nice teacher, Miss Morris. She lets kids go to the sickbay when they're feeling any sort of sick, not only when they're bleeding all over the floor or something.

Hannah was in the sickbay, too. We hugged.

'I have a headache,' she declared, in a miserably small voice.

'Curse come upon the Whyte family?' asked the sickbay lady, smiling. I couldn't remember her name, but she was nice too.

'Maybe,' I said. 'Is it just a headache?' Even with the sickbay lady there, and the disinfected safe small smells of the sickbay around, my head felt like it had a bag of iron attached to it, with the handles digging into my skull.

The sickbay lady chuckled. 'Just a headache,' she said. 'I won't give you a Panadol unless your mum says so, so hold this ice pack to your head and just have a lie down. I'll go ring her.'

Hannah and I lay in beds next to each other and waited quietly. The bell rang for recess, but it felt sort of exciting in the sickbay and I didn't mind missing it. After a bit, a girl came in with a grazed knee, and the sickbay lady along with her.

'Do you want to lie down?' I asked the girl. I knew her name was Miranda, and she was in the other year 6 class.

'No, you keep lying,' said the sickbay lady, and got a chair for Miranda. 'I tried calling your mum but I couldn't get through – is she at work?'

'She's with Suzie,' I said, feeling a knot tighten in my stomach again, the sort of knot I felt when I couldn't tell anyone about the TV.

'Suzie's the baby,' added Hannah.

'That's odd,' said the sickbay lady. 'I'll try again.' She walked back into the office.

'Where's your mum?' asked Miranda.

'I don't know,' I said. I didn't like her, all of a sudden. 'She'll find her.'

'Her name is Mrs Higgs,' said Miranda.

'Okay,' I said, and rolled over in bed. It was a long while until Mrs Higgs came in again. At one point, I thought Hannah had started crying, but she was just whispering to herself. I couldn't tell what she was saying.

'How's your head, Han?' I asked her.

'Still hurty,' she said. 'How's yours?'

'Yeah, mine too.'

'Where's mum?' she asked.

'Maybe Suzie's sick too,' I suggested. 'Maybe we've all got some… flu or something. And she took her to the doctors. You know how it is with babies.' Miranda looked at both of us.

'Apparently—' she started, when Mrs Higgs came into the room, with my mother right behind her. She looked tired and thin. Her hair was frazzly around the edges. But she was my real mum. I felt my headache lift instantly, like a spaceship.

'Mummy!' yelped Hannah. 'I missed you!'

'I missed you too, mum,' I said, looking sidelong at Miranda, who was staring out the window awkwardly.

'Goodness, my babies!' she said, a little hoarsely. 'Is everything okay? Mrs Higgs had to call the building manager to find me!'

'You weren't answering the phone,' said Hannah. 'And our heads hurt.'

'Apparently there's some problem with it,' she said. 'I can't hear a dial tone. Come on, I'm taking you both home. Is there anything I need to sign, Mrs Higgs?'

Mrs Higgs led her off to the sickbay office. Hannah looked at me and grinned.

'Get off early!' she said. 'Yes!'

'It's not properly early, dolt,' I replied. 'There's like one class left.' Mum led us out into the car park and drove us home. I got to sit on the front seat, and Hannah had to sit in the back with Suzie, who was surprisingly quiet. I fiddled with the air conditioning knobs.

'Now, Suzie's not feeling well either,' said mum, 'so you two have to stay out of the way and behave yourselves. Okay? And no playing the computer, if you've got a headache.'

'I don't have a headache anymore,' said Hannah, instantly. I rolled my eyes, but I couldn't feel my headache either.

'You still can't play the computer,' said mum. 'Do your homework.'

'I'm still sick, though,' added Hannah hurriedly. But as soon as we got up to the flat, our headaches returned – and Suzie started bawling her eyes out.

'Like clockwork,' sighed mum. She looked really unwell. 'Maybe it's the altitude or something.' As I wandered up to my room, I saw the flickering from the living room again.

'Mum, you left the TV on!' I shouted.

'It's not turning off,' she shouted back, over Suzie's crying.

'Weren't you going to take it back today?' I asked. I wished they had.

'Dad's held up at work. He'll have to stay till after five. And I can't leave Suzie.'

'You can leave her with me,' I said.

'Not when she's like this,' replied mum, and made shushing noises. The crying got louder. Hannah came in and peeked over my shoulder at the TV.

'It's creepy,' she said, with relish.

'Yeah, it is,' I agreed. 'Let's just leave it.' We closed the door and went to our room. We tried to play Uno, but Uno's no fun with two people and my head was still hurting. Eventually, Hannah got out her dolls and started organising a jewellery shop with them, which was so sickening I had to leave.

I wandered through the house. Suzie was quiet in her cot. Mum was sitting at her laptop in the kitchen, holding her head in her hands. She looked like she didn't want to be disturbed. I walked past the living room door three times, and eventually made up my mind to go inside and turn the TV off.

The door opened silently, even though I swear it usually creaked. The whole living room seemed too quiet. The static was flickering softly on the TV, but this time, there were definite shapes in it, like when you've almost got the station. Except I knew these weren't station shapes. They were hungry shapes. And they were eating all the noise out of the room. I felt my blood pumping slowly in my ears. I felt the little hairs on my arms standing up.

'You have to go away,' I said, and closed the door. My words sounded like they were drifting up through cotton wool. 'I'm going to turn you off!' I shouted, muffled. The TV looked at me. The shapes moved in closer. They were small and sharp and liked the taste of my words. I tried the power button, but nothing happened, as I knew. Then I went to the power board.

The switch was off. I had turned it off last night, and nobody had turned it on again. But the TV was still on. It was on by itself. The hairs on my neck all stood up. I pulled out the AV cable, but the screen didn't go black. The snow wasn't in the reception. It lived inside the TV. I yanked out the power cord, so hard that I fell over on my side in front of the screen. The TV was still on. The shapes sniggered at me. I looked around in despair. I pulled the TV away from the powerboard, right up against the other wall of the living room. I looked at the static. It was so deep and so hungry. I felt my eyes with my fingers, and they were like wells. My fingers went right into them. Into my head.

I jumped up, ripped open the door, and ran into the bedroom. Dolls went everywhere. I slid on a plastic toy and almost fell over. All the sound in the world suddenly came back to me, and I realised that my ears and heart and lungs were all pounding like drums.

'*Hey*!' shouted Hannah. 'Look what you've done! You ruined my shop!' She started to cry.

'Wait, wait, Hannah, I'm sorry,' I said, grabbing her by the shoulders. 'Hannah, what are my eyes like?'

She looked at me in teary confusion.

'…they're normal?' she said.

I collapsed onto the bed in relief. Hannah looked upset. I didn't tell her about the TV, because I didn't want to scare her. After a few minutes, my breathing calmed down, and I helped her fix up her dolls. The pounding in my head didn't stop for hours, though. When dad finally came home in the evening, I ran up to him.

'Dad, dad,' I said. 'Dad, we *have* to get rid of that TV. It's the creepiest thing ever. I'm not kidding.' He looked at me. His eyes were like wells.

'*Dad*!' I screamed. Mum ran into the hall.

'What's happened?' she asked. She looked like she hadn't slept in weeks. Her hair was tangled and grey. Her clothes were crumpled. Her skin was saggy.

'D—dad,' I managed to say, pointing at his face.

'You don't look well, love,' she said, lifting his face up. 'Tony, settle down, he's just tired.' Dad looked from me to mum with his empty black eyes. He didn't say anything.

'Are you alright, love?' asked mum.

'We're hungry,' said dad. It wasn't his voice saying it. Something had stolen his voice.

'Well, I'm making pasta,' said mum. She went to the kitchen, and dad followed her, soundlessly.

'We're hungry,' I heard him say, through the door.

'Yes, dear,' said mum. 'It'll be ready soon.'

'We're hungry,' said dad. The voice that had stolen his voice was flat and tinged with static. It was broken, like other voices were interfering with it. I knew exactly where it had come from. I looked at

Hannah, and her blue eyes were the best thing I had seen all day.

'We have to destroy that TV,' I said.

'Alright,' she replied. We held hands and walked up to the living room door. I opened it and we walked inside.

The living room seemed bigger than it had been before. And it was emptying. There had been boxes of clothes and books. There had been chairs. They were all sort of transparent now. Not properly transparent. Like they were half in the world and half out of it. Like something was pulling them further and further away. The only thing that was really there now was the TV. I had pushed it against the wall, but it was in the middle of the room now. It was sharp and glittery and black. The snow kept falling inside its glass screen. But it was also leaking out, spreading along the carpet like the oil from a broken radiator. The walls were turning grey and transparent, too. I looked behind me and saw all the way to the other end of the house. Mum was stirring a pot of pasta. Dad was standing in the corner of the kitchen, his head on a funny angle. He was watching Suzie. He looked hungry.

'We don't have much time,' I told Hannah, my voice distant. She nodded. We went up to the TV, still holding hands. The TV spoke to us. It told us what it wanted. It told us what we should do. But we didn't like that one bit.

'You won't,' I said.

'Not on our watch,' added Hannah. We picked up the TV – it was almost too heavy to lift, but we put our shoulders up against it, and I took most of the weight. It tried to squirm away. It nipped at our fingers and all its surface turned to static and snow. We carried it, stumbling, over to the windowsill. Hannah wrenched the window open. The outside world looked like a painting. There was no sound of any traffic, no wind, no air at all really. I looked straight down. There was a balcony there, with a dead palm tree in a pot.

'Let's do it,' I said. The TV screamed a horrible scream. The screen cracked and bulged, and static started dripping out of it.

'Don't get any on you!' I shouted to Hannah, but I could no longer hear myself. I lifted up one finger. *On the count of three,* I mouthed. I lifted up two fingers. We tilted the TV out of the window. Faces pushed themselves against the screen. They were the faces of things that shouldn't have happened. They yowled at me like cats being drowned. I lifted up three fingers. We tipped the TV over the edge. It fell through the air silently, and smashed onto the balcony far below. It cracked and exploded and fell into itself, and a brilliant fountain of glass shards sprayed high into the air. There was a stir and a noise as if something enormous rushed past us and away. The sound came back to my ears; cars and planes and the wind, the best sounds ever.

'Did we do it?' asked Hannah. She wasn't quite tall enough to look straight down over the windowsill.

'We did,' I said. All I could see was the empty wrecked shell of the TV. No static. No faces. In the room behind us, the chairs were coming back. Most of the boxes were too, though some of them had gone missing. Hannah made a sort of crying laughing sound and half-fell against the windowsill.

'I was scared,' she admitted.

'Me too,' I said. I gave her a huge hug. I decided she wasn't such a bad sister after all. Still hugging, we left the living room and wobbled into the kitchen. Mum was chopping onions for a sauce. Dad was reading the newspaper. They both looked tired, but normal. Like normal parents, and not possessed.

'How are we going to break it to them that we smashed the TV?' whispered Hannah. This gave me pause.

'I suppose we'll just tell them the truth,' I said. 'That it was evil and wanted to kill us.' Hannah nodded sagely.

'How are you feeling?' I began, diplomatically.

'Fine, fine,' said mum. 'Suzie's being a darling. Not a peep!'

I went over to Suzie's cot and peeked carefully over the rails, so as not to wake her. Not quietly enough, though. She opened her eyes slowly. They were very dark. Almost too dark. Almost like...

'Funny thing in the news,' said dad, crinkling his paper. 'It's, what, only September? But they're saying it's going to snow tomorrow. Snow everywhere.'

MOTHERLAND

Duncan Atkinson

Duncan Atkinson is a struggling chemist from Bristol, UK, and still the author of that story with Anne Frank and the She-Wolves, written as "Danny Barefoot". He finds that tragic stories are a lot more useful and easy to write than positive ones, but would like some happiness as well, perhaps a little more time to write, and a lot more of God around in his world.

MOTHERLAND

T HE SKY BROODED OVER UNEVEN SNOWFIELDS LIKE A SHROUD OVER dead faces. This is a country that swallows fire and death in dull expanse. While the Celestial invasion had levelled the great cities of Nova Muskovia with atomics and spread mechanised death across the heartland, this northern province had preserved a solitary quiet. Wind flew across the snow like glass shards from a blast, tearing at the soldier's legs and neck as she tramped for a low dome in the middle of the fields.

The soldier walked and watched. The wireless Mil-Net implant buried above her ear passed data streams between distant servers and her audio-visual cortex. GPS location, distance from friendly units – predicted weather was snow. Tactical software lit up potential cover or ambush sites green and red, in her eyes. From its shape (the implant reported) the dome ahead was a Model 03.17 Farm-Habitat, the cheapest means of preserving un-cyberised life through winter on this vast, cold planet. Her military cybernetic muscles doubled as internal heaters – heat retained by the tough polymers that replaced her blood and skin. Cold still gnawed at her bones, as Cyrillic text scrolled across her steel-blue eyes.

The fanfare for Mil-Net news (noon) sounded in her ear – disabling the news feed outside combat was a treasonous offence.

<... last Celestial forces in full retreat from the Motherland... several

deserters detained by the PSG... our Royal correspondent states that his Blessed Majesty the Tzar will return to the rebuilt Summer Palace in Alexigrad by Rosemonth... statue promised of the devoted patriot, saviour of throne and Motherland, Sophia Susanin...>

A strange smile broke the cyborg soldier's grim face. There was joy, but not the happiness shared by peaceable humanity. Reaching the Habitat, she hammered a numb fist on the airlock.

'Oy! Friend! Open!'

A black-bearded face appeared on the intercom. With no help from any implant, the soldier could sense a weapon levelled at the inside door.

'Ivan Pytorovich Susanin? You've never met me, but I was a friend to your daughter, Sophia. I remember her favourite food was parsnip stew with extra pepper.'

The door slid open; the soldier stepped in. Before the air had reheated and the inner door squealed back, she'd pulled off her gloves, goggles, *ushanka* hat and olive greatcoat. A forty-ish woman with a tight blonde bun. Her body was thickset with cyberware, but beautiful through sheer mass and force; something wild sparked in her eyes when she spoke. An officer's uniform looked grubby enough to be her only clothes.

'Major Roza Vronsky, 44th Cyberised Infantry.' Ivan Susanin put his rifle aside (an antique caseless round M106, Roza's Mil-Net obsequiously noted) and hesitantly took her hand. Synthetic skin felt like warm leather.

'Well-met. The Holy All-Father bless you. You... fought in the war...?'

'And lived through it. Following your daughter.'

'Sophia. Sophia Ivannova Susanin.' In her own father's mouth, it was already one of the singular names made vast by a vast country's devotion, echoing with the cadence of sainthood. 'Our girl. We... we heard that she'd died. We get barely any news here, but we heard.'

'Yeah. After Zhokov Ridge, she asked me to come up here. Once everything was over. Tell you how it was. Who she was, in the end.'

'You'd better come in and eat. Uh... do you, I mean do His Majesty's cyborgs...?' Roza nodded curtly, 'Oy, Wife! A friend of Sophia, a guest!'

A thin woman emerged from an inner chamber, her face even more weathered by peace than Roza's round cheeks by war. Without speaking, she embraced Roza tightly. The cyborg stiffened in her arms – as they broke away, both women's eyes were warier than they'd been.

The three of them sat round the table in the Habitat's central kitchen. The controlled environment warmed incoming air before exchanging with the outside; it kept in the heat just as efficiently as the smell of cattle in their winter stalls next door. But the kitchen was dully clean, like the Susanins' clothes. Almost everything a farming peasant family would earn through the two-month Muskovian summer would go to the Noble Princes from Alexigrad or St Stephanyar that leased them their Habitats, farm robots and fields. The Susanins didn't have computers or communicators; they wouldn't have heard of anything like Mil-Net. They had a barely winter-sized larder, a family pew in the local church, and three cheap holograms above the worktop.

There was the Imperial Family Hologram, naturally. Another where the Holy All-Father reached from the clouds to lay a blessing on the Royal throne. The last image showed two burly, grinning young men, with a beautiful young lady and a dark-haired little girl in dungarees who Roza couldn't help staring at.

'Sophia was eight that summer,' Ivan told her, voice flat. 'She already helped her brothers with the work, anywhere she could. It was before her sister, Joan—' His wife gave him a brief look, and he shut up.

'Don't worry, Sophia told me about Joan.' Roza glowered at the table. 'Of course, she wanted to find her. But as soon as the Tzar made Sophia General of the Armies, the Public Security Guard wiped all records on her inconvenient sister. You're the only ones who can say Joan Susanin ever lived.'

Ivan and his wife nodded. Old griefs and long winters had put iron in their hearts.

In silence, Madame Susanin set out three small portions of meat and turnip stew. Producing a hip flask, Roza swigged its remaining contents, and glanced between her hosts with wicked innocence.

'Anything to drink round here? Vodka, strong kvass?'

'A little coffee.' Madame Susanin stated. 'As Old Believers, we take no alcohol.'

'Sophia must have told you,' Ivan muttered. 'She could never tolerate so much as the smell of drink. She was always a good girl.'

'Always? You certain of that?'

A very fraught silence preceded Roza's bark of laughter. Her mirth might have been as great as her miseries, before cyberisation, but years of service had made it bitter and hollow. 'Oh, don't worry, your girl was good. I liked her anyway. Neither of us saw quite the same world as other folk.'

'Tell us more when you've eaten.' Everything Mil-Net was telling Rosa about Madam Susanin's tiniest body movement said there was sadness, but no agitation, no eagerness. She might've been built to outwait the seasons. 'As our guest, would you say Grace?'

'Very well.' The military cyborg dramatically clasped her hands and screwed her eyes up. 'Dear All-Father. Please do for Roza Vronsky and this family what Roza Vronsky would do, if she were the All-Father and you were Roza Vronsky. And, Father's sake, do it *soon*. Amen.'

Careless of the Susanins' stares, she wolfed the stew down.

It had been four years since invasion ships had filled the iron skies above Novoroburg, St Stephanyagrad and Alexigrad. Two years since the giant Celestial battlesuits had broken the last Muskovian field army. The ancient, glittering cities had been flattened with nuclear weapons at the first exchange; no one had counted the dead. The heartland's fields and factory-cities were filled with white-armoured Celestials and Muskovian slaves. The Imperial Family was in hiding. Somewhere in the middle of the steppe, a small landskimmer was spotted by a party of deserting Muskovian soldiers. A few blasts from their plasma rifles aimed ahead of the craft were enough to stop it.

Jogging up faster than a horse would run, the deserters surrounded the landskimmer. Several farmboys stumbled out, a few clutching caseless rifles. Then two elderly veterans with barely a dozen cyberparts between them. And Sophia Susanin. A black-haired girl, small for eighteen, with eyes brown as a hawk, and lips like soft steel.

Defiant as the group looked, they could do little against six cyborgs. All had the scars of amateur surgery above one ear; disabling their Mil-Net implants prevented the Guards from tracking the signal. Though most looked wild-eyed and desperate, their captain's dull face was quite calm. As if national collapse were a happier state than the national order he had lived in.

'Hand over your guns, food, and money, all of it. And the dark girl—'

'—is heading off with the rest, right, Comrade?' The deserter ex-Lieutenant Roza Vronsky grinned without humour at the captain, who stared back like a snake. 'Come on children, hurry up and shove off.'

'Sirs, we have little money or food. We are Muskovians. I am travelling to speak with His Highness the Tzar, for our suffering Motherland's sake. Please,

join us.'

The deserters laughed, but barely. The dark girl's eyes were unworldly – spy-holes to some vast realm of divine certainty – yet still warmed with strange, grasping love for the whole frail world outside her. Not quite inhuman, very nearly something more. Roza tried to laugh and couldn't.

'This country went under six years ago, Missy,' the deserter captain growled. 'Come and warm all our bedrolls, if you want to do some good, but the All-Father, the Tzar – they don't mean anything now.'

'Did they ever mean something to you, anything good? You are alone, without a purpose. Without family. But the Motherland still suffers, and calls us her children. The All-Father himself has sent us to rescue his people – I would give my life to save them, with joy. You can join me, if you prefer honour and love to the cold solitude of the plains.'

In the Southern wars, the Dymitros mutiny and against the dreadful Celestials, Roza had heard some oratory. The dark girl wasn't even orating. She did nothing but say what she saw and believe what she said. The captain would have shot her down to save his face on that road, if Roza hadn't shot him first.

Still looking mildly bemused, she blasted another deserter before he drew. Plasma bolts shrieked past – she was beside another, thrusting with her palm and nearly taking his head off. She shoved a spitting rifle aside, flung the shooter into the final cyborg by his waist, and fired down at them both on the ground.

None of Sophia's party had been quick enough to twitch. The bubbling flesh-metal slag left by plasma bolts turned most of them pale. Sophia was visibly shaken, but not greatly moved, or surprised.

'Ha! By the devil and his great-aunt, are you some witch?' Without waiting, Roza strode back to her bike. 'They were ignorant pigs, anyway. Good luck with saving the Motherland and that.'

'What about the next lot of bandits?' a dark youth who resembled Sophia called out. 'You must come with us!' Roza glanced back into Sophia's unflagging gaze.

'The Tzar is in hiding, from the Celestials. How do you plan to find him?'

'The Holy All-Father will guide us. Just as he has provided for us today.' Her face had such peace that Roza almost felt like shooting her as well.

'Missy, you've never seen a war. You can't imagine how… Ach, forgot it. What about me? Before I fell in with that rabble last month, I was travelling north, to my parents' village. Don't you have a family somewhere, girl?'

It took cybernetically enhanced perception to catch the flicker in Sophia's gaze. Then she met Roza's eyes and indicated the group at her back.

'These are the ones who believe in my visions. My brothers and sisters, my comrades – at this time, you are all my family.'

Eyes warm and irresistible, she offered her hand. Laughter burst from Roza as she seized it.

Roza sat back. The Susanins had noticed that she grew still as an idle engine in repose, with a faint glower of potential for violent action. For a moment, they had nothing to say themselves.

'Well… thank you, Madame Vronsky,' Sophia's mother said firmly. 'The Holy All-Father will bless you—'

'Ach.' Ivan finally spoke, 'She told us about visions of saints from the Holy All-Father, like you, but we never believed her. When she said wanted to leave the farm and seek the Tzar with soldiers… I beat her.'

'Of course you did – of course it didn't stop her,' Roza grated. 'You'd feel worse if you hadn't, and nothing would've changed how she felt.'

'She left us behind. She left a message saying it was the All-Father's will, she hoped we would understand. What could we do? Pytor, our younger son, went with her. I believe George would've gone too, except we still had the year's harvest. After the Blessed Tzar gave our daughter his army, and she beat the Fatherless Celestials at Molmsk, she could send us money. So George could leave us too, and go to her.' Pain finally shone through Ivan's gruff voice. Madame Susanin sighed and cleared the bowls from the table. 'Ach. It was the Holy All-Father's will.'

Roza wondered how Sophia Susanin could have possibly come from such frozen, stoical peasants. They had no more power to change their world or even preserve their children than the cattle they tended themselves – but they had human hearts, perhaps as strong with emotion as their girl's, only helpless. Cyborgs couldn't shiver, but in Roza's mind, she felt very cold.

'Well – your son Pytor died at Zhukov Ridge. He was a good boy, the bravest soldier. He was Sophia's brother. He died quick. I haven't seen George since then…?'

'He came back here. Then one day he went away again, without a word. He could never speak to us about Sophia, his sister.'

'Oh well, the boy might've run off anyway.' Roza gazed brazenly round the bare kitchen, 'I ran off to join the army when I was eight.'

'You said your parents lived north of here?' Madam Susanin broke

32

in. 'Did you ever go back there?'

Roza gave the bright, mechanical smile the Susanins were learning to fear.

'Yeah, before I met Sophia, I was travelling to my parents' village. I'd spent four months in a Celestial prison camp before getting away – and all the stories you've heard are true. Then two months getting Mind Probed and roughed-up by the Guards for getting treacherously captured. I was ready to die, after blasting my father and mother first.'

'By the Father and angels, no—!'

'By the fallen angels, yes!' The Susanins drew back. Pale fire danced in Roza's eyes. 'I could tell you all about war – torture, meatgrinder assaults, freezing death in the snow. But I couldn't ever speak of the things done to little children in some solitary Farm-Habitats. When they made this machine of my body, I was ten and I was glad. My old body had fear bound under every scar... the Devil's aunt, why am I telling you any of this?' Viciously, she shook out her hip flask for a single drop. 'They're dead now – my parents died in a yellow scalp fever epidemic, months ago. I finally went home last week and found out. Then I came here.'

'You went home, to be reconciled with your family, this time?' Madame Susanin spoke rapidly. 'Our Sophia could make people change themselves, since she was the tiniest girl...'

'Maybe I was. *Maybe.*'

Roza's eyes were bright and hard. Madam Susanin looked away, and tense silence returned.

'Yeah, she changed folk,' the cyborg finally went on. 'Muscovia had a flock of spineless milk-bloods hidden in caves – she made it into an army of soldiers. She made drunks and rapists wail for salvation, and find it. She changed generals, princes, maybe the Tzar himself. Maybe – for a while. She was who she was, and asked all of us to be something else – I'd have died for her a hundred times. But she asked folk to change themselves, that was the trouble. Not everyone can do it. And it's not the way of generals, Tzars, or your blessed All-Father either. They all move our bodies and souls whatever cursed way they like. Well, I'm sick of talking, and I never got used to doing something for nothing. What was Sophia really like? When she was a child?'

There was a pause; the idea visibly intruded on the Susanins that Sophia might have stopped being a child at some point. Ivan took a minute clearing his throat.

The Family Way

* * *

It was a summer Sixthday in the northern province. The wind was still frosted, but fields of cold-weather maize shone in the bright-sharp sun. GM winter cattle like shaggy-haired yaks winked peacefully at the distant hills. The streets of the province's principal town were even emptier than they were in the rest of the week. If a man falls off a ladder here, they talk about it for a month, whenever they actually talk. When the Public Security Guard had driven into town, dragged an escaped political convict from the barn he'd been hidden in, and burned him to grease in the town square – no one had ever talked about it at all.

The next Sixthday, the Old Believers' church in town was filled with slab-bearded farmers and families, in their cleanest clothes. Joan Susanin looked beautiful as ever, but grim and tense, until Sophia clung to her waist in front of everybody and begged her to smile. Though everyone liked Sophia Susanin, she didn't seem to seek close friends that would draw her from her All-Father, her parents, her brothers or her beloved Joan. Indeed, the two sisters often seemed more obviously loving than their reticent parents. Most townsfolk would only say the youngest Susanin was diligent, outspoken when she spoke, a good girl.

The church's darkened naves were filled with holo-icons of angels, martyrdoms and demon-slaying heroes. The great Communion Message Board was above the altar; the Royal Hologram above the door. When Pytor was frightened by the bloodier icons as a child, his mother would always lift him up to that portrait and ask if the blessed Imperial Family didn't look like the wisest, most caring people? No one had known his younger sister to be afraid of anything, least of all the holy sacrifices of the saints.

The people rose as the Priest entered, the Prayer-Net implant glinting under his wide, black hat. There were solemn hymns, a prayer order for the Grand Duchess's pregnancy. A sermon on the divine appointment of rulers, the duty to love and honour the Father of the nation. Sophia shifted, impatient for the Communion – though she couldn't take the nanobot-treated metal Wafer until her confirmation next year, it already drew her heart.

'Though we are many, we are one body. Though we are scattered, we are one Family; one supreme Tzar, one Father in heaven. We are on earth but the Father is here. Share in His spirit, lift him up to heaven!'

The adult Susanins all placed the Wafers on their tongues. Their flickering eyes rose to the white Message Board above the altar. Across Nova Muscovia, the devotional ecstasy of a thousand priests flashed through Prayer-Net onto

34

the Board of every church. As the short-lived wafer nanobots settled into brains, images of angels and thrones flashed into visions of heaven. The Communicants began to receive and transmit – every prayer in the Motherland downloaded direct to every praying mind, at once.

In Sophia's town, a few old women collapsed in fits. Tears poured down her father's weathered face. All the softness out that trouble and winter had callused. They wept out praise to the All-Father until their knees shook. And His blessings on the Tzar, as their distant ruler's single dignified line of prayer finally scrolled across the Board.

<'We pray for the Motherland. We pray our people will serve with their lives, and rise to receive their reward.'>

Then it was over. The dismissed believers filed out to converse for an hour in the town square, and then return to their farms, their ill-paid drudgery, days like tomorrow and yesterday. The week's human devotion had been acceptably released, like every other Sixthday. There was nothing else to be done.

As her family talked, Sophia nipped back into the empty church. Gazing at the silent Board, she prayed her ordinary prayers, without cybernetic aid. Whatever her desire was, she must have prayed hard for it.

It was a Sixthday like any other, except that when Sophia met her family in the square, Joan was no longer there. Her mother had been crying, but she wasn't anymore. Her father and brothers, still dazed from Communion, wouldn't say anything. Sophia didn't ask again. In the north, people died all the time from winters, accidents, resistant TB and smallpox, but there was only one cause that people never talked about.

There was a Royal Hologram above the door of the schoolroom as well as the church. Sophia had been a bright, diligent student, until she was sent home that winter from asking inappropriate questions. Why did the Public Assembly even exist, if the Tzar could veto any of its resolutions? How was it certain that all prisoners in the Outer North were enemies of the Motherland, when not all had been tried in public, or at all?

'It's for your own good that I do this now,' Susanin father had told her, after he'd finished beating her with a rough belt, as his own father had beaten him. 'If you love the All-Father and your family, you will not question the laws of the Blessed Tzar. Understood?'

'I'm sorry, Papa.' Sophia seemed strangely calm, empty of tears, 'I just thought, if his Highness the Tzar is a just ruler because he seeks the All-Father's will, if, if I understood His holy will, and the law, I could be a better subject, a better Believer. I'm sorry…'

'Don't think about being better. It leads to pride.' Her father gazed from above his beard, distant sympathy burning in his eyes. 'All of us have a place. The best our family can do is to work, and not make trouble for each other.'

Sophia had much more time after that to sit out alone in the fields. She might have been trying to comprehend the whole sweep of the cold, beautiful plain, the endless sky. The tiny humans under it with their fervent, monotonous prayers. There were nights when she knelt outside the Farm-Habitat in the snow, still as the cattle and praying. She fell ill for days and her mother scolded her, but she still went out and prayed. Her brothers and the girls in the village stopped talking to her, there were rumours she could cure frostbite with prayer, rumours she could cure it with magic. Her father's drinking comrades advised him that a single beating was only enough to make a child fight, and Susanin ought to keep beating his daughter until there was no fight left in her. But he couldn't see that his daughter was fighting him. She was just silent.

She finally walked into the Farm-Habitat and told her father she no longer wanted to be Confirmed.

'You want to reject the All-Father's sacrament, His gift to you... damn yourself forever.'

'Worshipping the All-Father is all I want to do, Papa. He wants me to listen to Him, and do something, myself, though I don't deserve it. But if my mind was buried in all the prayers of Muskovia every Sixthday, I don't think I could hear Him anymore. I do love you Papa, so I'm telling you I believe – I've been told – I will speak with the Tzar, one day. The Motherland is in danger and filled with terrible acts. The ruler appointed by heaven must do heaven's will, and save his people.'

'Ach, where did your mother and I go wrong?' Limp in his chair, Ivan shook his head. 'How did we raise such a child...?'

(But he couldn't deny it. Her eyes looked just like her mother's had, in the bitterest hours of their life together, filled with endurance and nothing else.)

'Papa – this isn't happening because of anything you did to raise me. It isn't happening because my sister brought food to an escaped political, and was sent to the Outer-North work camps by the PSG for it.'

'How do you know—?'

'I know, Papa. You wanted to protect her... but you couldn't, without putting all of us in danger. It's all right. It's only the All-Father's will that sets a place for us all, and a task. I'm going to fight for the Motherland, Papa, to change this country. In ten years there will be freedom and justice. So you don't ever need to change, Papa...'

Tears leaked from Susanin's eyes. Sophia was in his arms and he was weeping over his little girl.

'Ten years…' Roza smiled like a cat, rocking on her chair. 'A prophesy?'

'She told the Tzar what the All-Father had spoken to her – but not me.' Susanin sighed. 'I don't know if she was a prophet. She was a brave, good girl, who loved her family…'

'Ha! You Susanins come over stoic for a while, but you do really say too much.' Madame Susanin peered at Roza's grim smile and humourless eyes. 'Say someone was out to discredit Sonya, or the Tzar, whose throne she died to raise from the ash-heap – one those revolutionary dissidents. They'd drag you all round Nova Muscovia with those stories about refusing Communion, and changing the country like some revolutionary – Sophia Susanin, the Tzar's holy saviour! If a PSG man ever heard about the "real" Sophia Susanin you knew, he'd shoot you, no questions. No joke. The whole Motherland's will to rebuild and unite depends on her. And she honoured the Tzar, so his people love him more than ever. His Highness wouldn't even tolerate a rumour that she wasn't a complete Royalist.'

'She was! She was a good Believer, who wanted to save Tzar and country from the invaders—!'

'Yeah. That's the story. At least that Communion of yours explains what she did with the cybernet. That was – still is – her real genius.'

' "Still is?" ' Not a flicker of hope showed on Madame Susanin's face. 'She's dead, Major. At rest.'

'Yeah, dead. But not resting, never.' Roza grinned, and gently tapped her Mil-Net implant.

The Tzar's decree, appointing the young girl sent to him by heaven to leadership of his remaining forces, was passed quickly across Nova Muskovia by the cybernets. The military Mil-Net, the Public Security Guard's Pol-Nets, the private Networks for Noble circles and families. In Muskovia, an 'internet' communicating across all classes and institutions would have been considered an obscenity; wireless cybernetic networks had been originally developed as a military tool. Combat information and commands could be passed by the second between generals, strategic computers and every cyborg soldier's brain. In theory, it was a strategic cornucopia. In practise, centralised micromanagement of soldiers trained to await orders whenever orders could be given had produced armies of ponderous automatons, paralysed by excessive data. *So much for the army that had been smashed by the Celestials' fast moving Battlesuits and skimmer-tanks.*

Sophia's use of Mil-Net was different. Her first act as leader was a Mil-Net broadcast to every receiving implant of the broken units scattered over forests and hills.

<...the All-Father has told me through his saints – he will restore the Tzar's blessed throne through me, if I go and do not fear. So if I must go alone, I will go, and holy fire will burn the Fatherless aliens to ash, before they harm a single Muscovian girl. Trust in your All-Father, fight for your Tzar, and you need just to stand and believe to have victory!>

It was unbelievable, but she believed it, and it was more than words. The Mil-Net implant poured directly into every stubborn, beaten mind, without any veil, all that Sophia thought, felt and longed for. It poured through Roza's body like medicine – like nothing she'd felt for years. Standing before princes and generals with Sophia, she wept for the first time since she'd been six. Soldiers swept in around the Tzar, eager to give away their lives and terminate the enemy.

Sophia's second action was to insist on an amnesty for deserters. The generals had insisted that cowardice and treachery must be punished – anyway, the All-Father's scriptures prescribed that mere peasants should obey His divinely appointed authority. Sophia had responded that she was delivering the All-Father's, words and not a peasant's – anyway, if they hanged every deserter they would have no army left. Eventually a surgeon repaired Roza's Mil-Net implant, a Mind Scanner was plugged into it, and her absolute loyalty to Sophia and the Tzar, established beyond doubt. Thanks to her new leader, she was a soldier again.

Sophia made more broadcasts, using external field-communicators as well as BattleComm; moving all the time in case the Celestials managed to break the adamantine Muskovian network encryption. Across the vast expanses of the nation, troops began to collect themselves, gather together, and prepare. In the ravaged backwater city of Molmsk, where the gathering army actually had Sophia's presence, the soldiers seemed barely less possessed with conviction than her. Sophia herself – though as leader rather than commander, she had no official duties – worked almost without rest. The Nobles were pressing for negotiation; the generals could only imagine low-level nuisance warfare. The All-Father apparently wanted one direct battle to restore the country's spirit; Sophia was constantly in contact with field officers to plan partisan raids that might lead to a battle with hope of victory. On top of all these concerns, the discipline, morale and holiness of the troops was her first passion.

'You seem even grimmer than usual today, Roza.' It was a typical day; she and her bodyguard were inspecting the tents and gloomy blocks where the army was barracked, 'Are you impatient for battle? I surely am.'

'If you knew what you're wishing for, Missy... but, yeah, that's it. There's going to be blood and death, so I want it in front of me to fight. And I can make myself more useful than knocking a few heads together here. The grunts might kneel to the Tzar when he drives round, but you're the only one holding this mob together.'

'Dear Roza... you should look for rest and joy, while you can. There's nothing like them on the battlefield.'

'Look for them at a prayer meeting? Ach!' Roza swigged from her hip flask. 'I've prayed some desperate, hopeless prayers – if the All-Father was doing anything for me, he would've done something already.'

'In all love, I order you not to give up so easily. Without hope, what are we...?' Sophia's quick brown eyes flashed towards two shadows in an alley mouth. She marched over, seized an arm; coins flew away. One of the figures was a soldier, who roared brief abuse until Roza stepped up, and knocked him out against the wall. The other figure was a pinched girl who looked no more than sixteen, with barely enough clothes to cover herself. 'Roza, I told you to clear out all criminals, hawkers and harlots from the camp. We are fighting a desperate war as the army of heaven itself; there can be no impurity among us.'

'Most of them are refugees, Sophia. They haven't any other way to live. And the men aren't saints; most of them need to have a girl or get raging drunk sometimes – '

'Those are lies from the devil – the lies this nation has already been judged for! As a handmaiden of the All-Father and the Tzar, I will not pity the servants of sin!'

'Excuse me... Madam Sophia?' Trembling, but almost dignified, the young girl sunk to her knees, and looked up with pale blue eyes. 'My name's Sonya Marmaladov... and I believe in the Holy All-Father, and his saints. I pray every morning and night, for forgiveness... I have the 119th Song by memory, and love to read all the scriptures. I know that it's wrong, to sell my body – but my mother's too sick to work, my brothers are young, my father is dead. I have to earn money so they can eat.'

Sophia sighed. She stooped to Sonya's eye-level, and placed a hand on her shoulder.

'Sonya. The All-Father commands us to live by faith. You must have faith that he will supply your needs himself, if you obey his law – in this life, or the next. But if you persist in your sin and distrust of His grace, you will certainly go to the Outer Darkness, with your family.'

Roza had seen men tortured to the point of death; after the invasion, she'd spent four months in a Celestial prison camp. But she couldn't remember anything like the horror in Sonya's soft, tear-stained face. Sophia stood up, and walked straight off. Sonya stared at Roza for a moment, then ran – the soldier never saw her again.

When Roza went back to the flat where Sophia worked and occasionally slept, she saw the girl's eyes were swollen and red. Somehow, she was hugging her with machine strong arms, careful and tight.

'I can't pity that girl,' she gasped, 'but my father, my mother... honest, god-fearing people, and I left them, to do the All-Father's will. I can weep for them. That girl – I will pray for her. It would be terrible if she loved her family so much and wasn't ever saved.'

Roza's unit spent the first hour of the battle of Zhokov Ridge crawling through a forest under thermal-scan resistant scout cloaks. There were five still seconds as Roza's cybernet flashed up a virtual arrow between the engine vent of a distant Celestial Battlesuit and her rifle barrel. She sighted along it carefully, and blew out the back at a thousand feet. Then there were more shots, faster, as Celestial infantry in their full-body armour and more eight-foot plasma-spewing Battlesuits came sweeping through into the trees at them from three sides. Then the breakout charge that took almost an hour of screaming and boiling flesh right in the nostril, blasting the enemy from an arm's length and snapping bones. Then the flank attack finally crested the ridge and blasted the main Celestial force away. In less than three hours, the war and the nation had changed.

Roza gazed down at the brown, slit-eyed face of a barely living Celestial footslogger. Foreign alien and enemy of the Motherland that he was, the pain in his eyes was the normal human kind she'd stopped noticing years ago. She aimed her rifle at those eyes, before Sophia pushed past her, took the young man's head between her hands, and spoke to him softly in Muskovian until he died.

'Feel good about that?' Roza sniffed, looking over the grassy ridge with its swathes of broken flesh and metal under a smoked-stained blue sky. Muskovians were roaming across the field, burning any survivors; after the nuked cities and prison camps, they weren't inclined to mercy. 'Is this where you thought your All-Father was leading, sister? Or not quite how you pictured it?'

'I shot four of them, the enemy,' Sophia's voice was faint, but firm. 'They wouldn't let me lead from the front, but I still had to shoot them dead, and I did. I don't know why they had to leave their planet, or come to steal ours, or why the worlds aren't all united like the oldest stories say. But I'll kill them. Wherever the All-Father leads me, that's the only place I can go.'

'That explains a lot.' Dropping down beside Sophia, Roza took a swig from her flask. 'And don't worry about the other thing; the Mil-Net broadcast will say you charged out in front of the enemy and killed fifty at least. They'll have videos to prove it too.'

'I see. That kind of thing might make someone unsure who they were.' Sophia stared out 'I know who I am though. I'm a servant of the All-Father. I'm the Sophia Susanin my parents remember. I'm me. It's you that I'm afraid for, Roza.' Her dark eyes pleaded. 'You should trust in the All-Father, and find something to give you peace. I don't ever want to lose another sister.'

'So chose a better sister than me...?'

'Nobody choses family. By blood or fate, they are the ones we are tied to forever by power above our own.' Sofia gazed across the battlefield, 'If you ever meet my parents, after this is all over... tell them I never changed. Tell them I was always a hope-bringing hero, with faith that was never shaken.'

'Is that the truth?'

'If it is the All-Father who has spoken to me, it must be. Wherever I must go, to serve him, I will go.'

'And most of the nation is going to follow you.'

'I know.' Sophia looked so suddenly weary it was almost pitiful. 'That's why we need to win, because I want to help the people of Muskovia more than anything on earth. That why you have to protect them, Roza. Roza, can I have some of that, just this once?'

'If it were the last in the world.' Roza passed the flask to Sophia, laughing as she sipped and made a face. 'I won't tell your parents.'

'It wasn't long after that. Someone fouled up, reinforcements were delayed; she was captured by the Celestials... and they killed her. Afterwards, we broke their main force at Valmy, and we've been pushing them steadily out the country. The Tzar said that we'll be building a better country from the ruins; better for him than it was, at least.'

Her story finally finished, Roza stared at the table. She wondered if she should've told the Susanins any more. The Celestials hadn't tried to tease out Sophia's motives, force a recantation, or put her on trial.

They'd just strung her limbs up on the nearest tree, and spent the time before she asphyxiated in breaking her arms with shock mauls. Maybe the Susanins could bear to hear how their last daughter had died, but she couldn't bear to tell it. She hadn't been at that battle of course; after she'd heard, a week-long drunken stupor had even flushed every trace of Sophia's speeches from her brain.

The Celestial had been taking ground back for weeks before Sophia died. The nobles' squabbling over tactics and responsibility had become impossible to work through; maybe Sophia's legendary vision had even flagged. After the battle when Sophia died (when no records seemed to exist about how the reinforcements had been permanently delayed) the Tzar had a martyr. And once cyborg commandoes had recovered Sophia's body, they had her mind, for dissection and reconstruction by Imperial scientists. Maybe it was only their story that the data-packet of pure devotion to the Tzar and Motherland, bright and certain as the dome of heaven, was reconstructed from Sophia's brain. But every soldier with a Mil-Net implant had received it. Roza had welcomed it like a drug, compelling her to kill and march for the Tzar with the old joy in her heart.

In the name of Sophia Susanin, the army had burst out in a flood of righteous rage. At Valmy, endless human waves had charged to their melted deaths willingly, with the courage of Sophia Susanin filling every breast with superhuman self-devotion. The Celestials were finally being pushed out for good, and a new Motherland was rising up. From now on the Tzar's cyborg soldiers would follow his every order with holy joy, whether against the Celestials or traitors to the Motherland. It was like having a spirit on your shoulder, a man-made conscience, beyond any human weakness. Having restored the Tzar to his throne, Sophia would preserve him there forever. Whether his acts were conventional or cruel, she could no longer protest at anything, like a good dead Muscovian. Maybe she could never have expected anything better.

'Madam Susanin?' Roza finally got out, 'I'm sorry for your loss.' Sophia's mother stared at her in confusion, then simple dignity.

'We haven't lost Sophia. She saved our country and the Tzar. That's all we've got, so that we can go on... and I know she'd want to keep the farm going, together. She wouldn't want us to change.' She placed a hand on her husband's shoulder, as Roza stood up.

'You know, not everyone could live the life you do. I couldn't –

Sophia couldn't. I mean... the best of health to you. That's all. Thank you.'

'You should stay for the night.' Madame Susanin spoke hesitantly. 'You could come with us to church, next Sixthday—?'

'Your daughter did her best to change me. She was a sister, not a saint to me, that made it harder... but I wouldn't trade being her sister for the cleanest soul in the world. We all have a place set by in heaven, right? Just take this, if someone else comes asking about the real Sophia Susanin.'

Roza produced a plasma pistol from her coat, placed it on the table, and walked out. The Susanins sat in silence for five minutes, before they saw she'd left her empty hipflask on the table as well.

Outside, Roza Vronsky struggled through the snow, back to the road towards town, and the mag-lev train. And towards the sleek black skimmer hovering beside the road. The five men in thick green greatcoats marching towards her.

'Major Vronsky. Captain Karenin. PSG.'

'What brings you out here, Captain?'

'We simply wanted to ask the parents of the martyr and national heroine, Sophia Susanin, a few questions, and acquaint them with her official biography. Yourself?'

'Just an old soldier, come to lie a lot about how wonderful their girl was.'

'Don't be reckless, friend. I don't like the way you talk about the heroine who restored the Tzar to power.'

'You're saying I could still be a traitor, with Sophia Susanin branded in my head, like everyone else?' Roza grinned. 'You people have Mind Probes don't you? Why don't you have a look?'

No one had ever volunteered to the PSG captain for a brain implant scan; even inviting the interest of the secret security service could be suicidal. Slowly, all five officers turned the dials on their own implants, staring at Roza as she whistled and smiled. A hum of data transfer for some minutes was interrupted by all the PSG men pointing their plasma pistols straight at the soldier with a gasp of alarm.

'Something scare you, penpushers?'

'This is preposterous!' Captain Karenin spluttered. 'How can you believe that Sophia Susanin doubted the goodness of the blessed Tzar – that she would have the monarchy and church overturned *to benefit the common people* – that she was betrayed to her death by the Tzar!'

'I know that last one; at least I'm sure. The others are just what I believe. I knew Sophia, as much as anyone. I heard how she was with her family, her real self. And you put her dying psyche in my head. So now I want to bring down the Tzar, the nobles and the church – folk can build them again if they want it, but they're rotten. And I want justice with all the passion she had – because they programmed my head with it, just like yours. Well?'

'Blasphemy! You're insane. The real Sophia Susanin died for the Tzar, you cannot prove she was a populist!'

'Don't need to. Real or not, she's my Sophia; a million of you can fight for the Tzar but I'm the one fighting for her.'

'Sir?' A younger PSG man spoke up. 'If the Tzar betrayed the Blessed Sophia to her martyrdom, it changes a great deal—'

As Captain Karenin turned to the dissident, his weapon lowered slightly. Roza smiled, dived forward, wrenching the gun away while driving an elbow through his face.

Two more guns were thrust at her waist; there was a flash, and one man fell back, melting. Roza spun to sweep two more aside, kicked another guard down, and threw the last one headlong into the ground, with a fatal crack.

Then she laughed and laughed, slapping the surviving PSG man on the back and embracing him. He looked like he wasn't even sure which way was up, as Roza fished a bottle from a dead man's pack, and finished about half of it, without visible effect.

'… I… I shot him. I had to, for the blessed Sophia…but they saw your mind like I did, why didn't they see the truth I saw? She fought for the people, not the Tzar… they've corrupted her memory…'

'Maybe. Believe what you want, like she did. And don't ever change, because she didn't. I only just saw that, now.' Roza stuck her hand out. 'Every cyborg in Muskovia has Sophia's spirit loaded into their skull. Let's tell them what she really cared about, justice and peace, and see how many of them believe her. And then we'll change this rotten Motherland, for justice, peace and revenge on the Tzar and his stinking minions. Everything they let my sister suffer – I'm going to brand it on their minds the old fashioned way.'

The ex-PSG stared at the blaze of belief in Roza's eyes; he could almost imagine the same in his own. Then they both walked through the snow to the black van, and started back to the capital.

SILVY'S STORM

Christopher Cavill

Christopher Cavill, when not seen astride his scooter, draws illustrations for various literature, listens to the heaviest rockabilly and occasionally blogs.

See his stuff at www.cloudpine451.blogspot.co.uk.

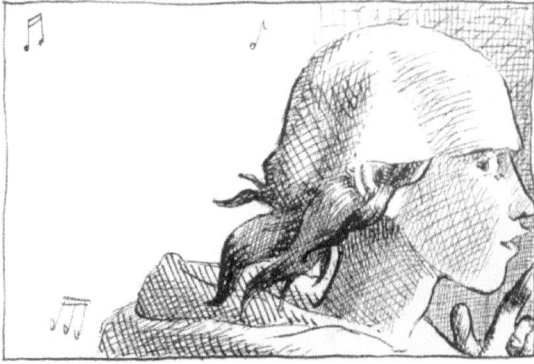

 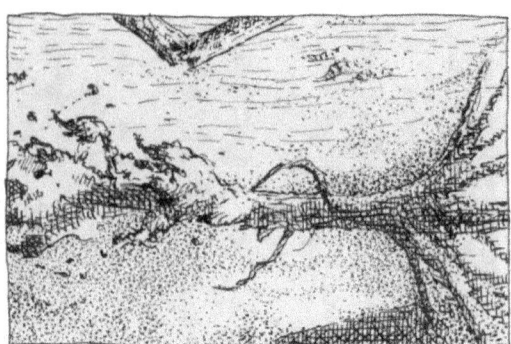

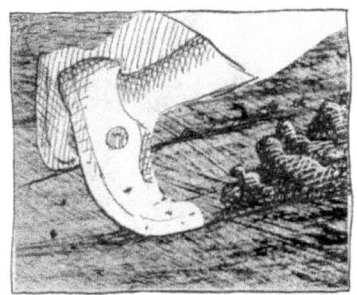

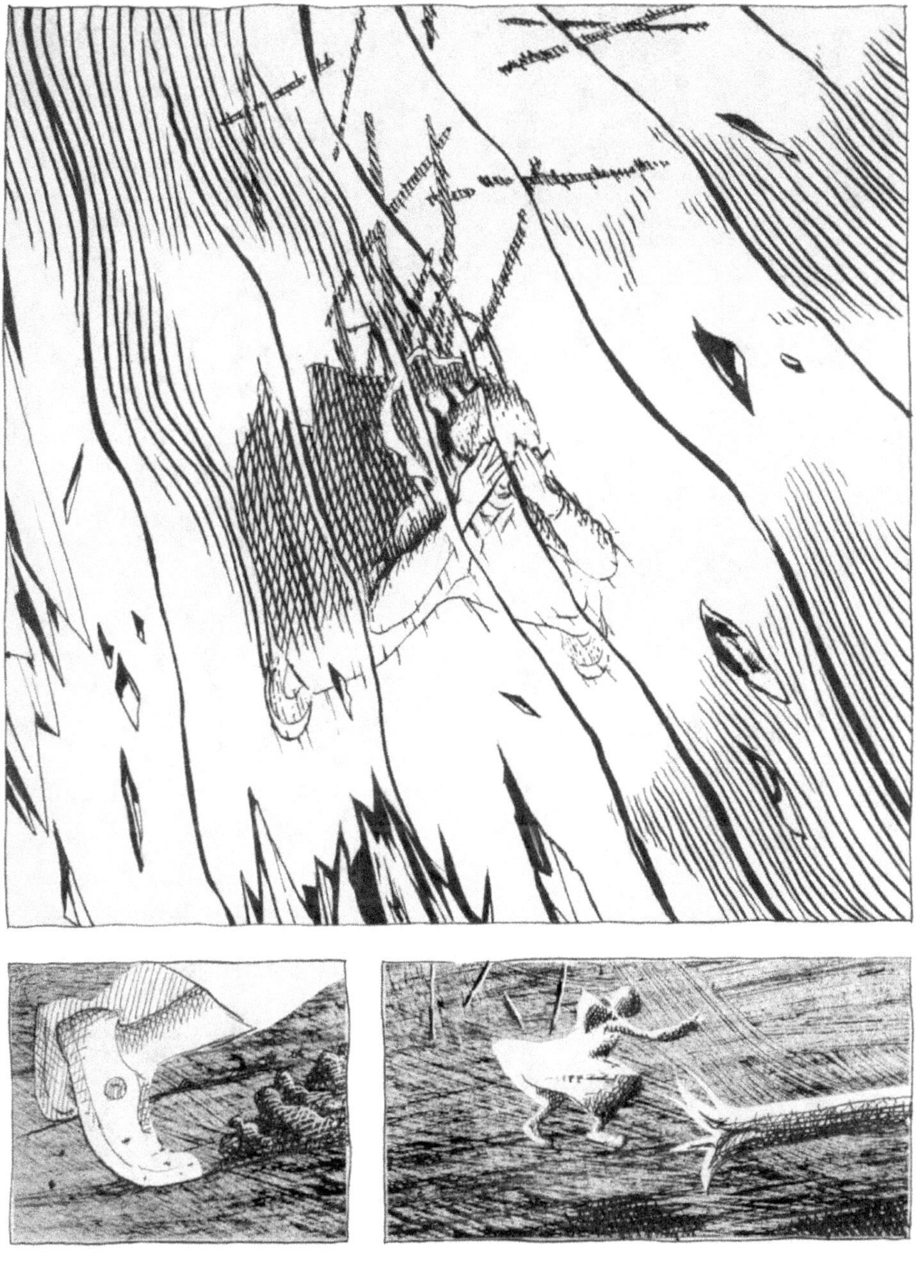

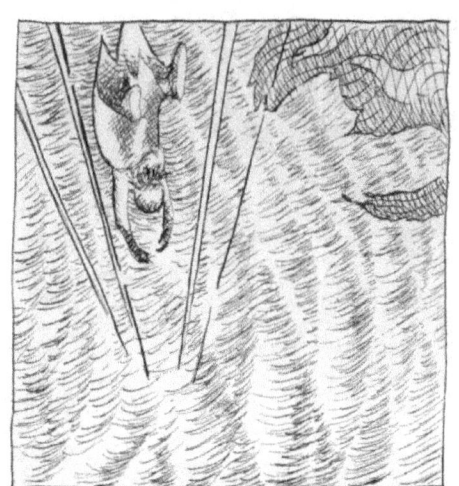

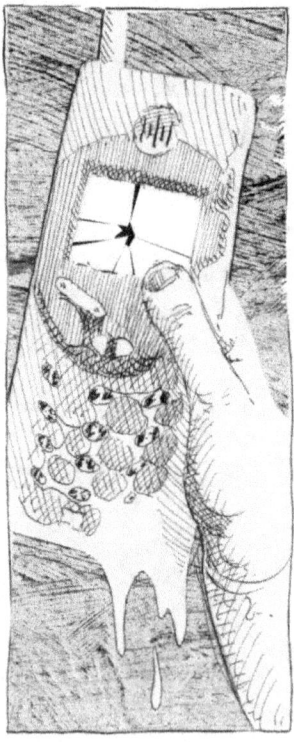

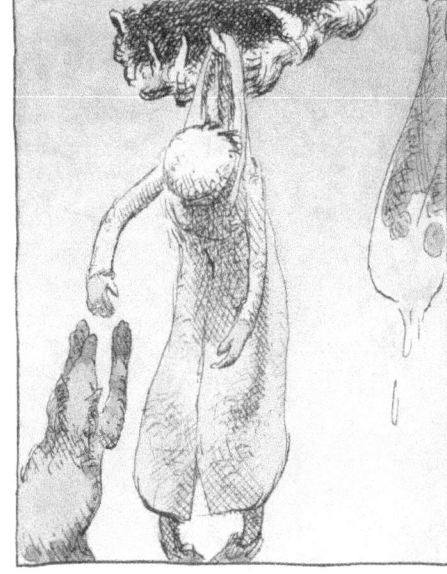

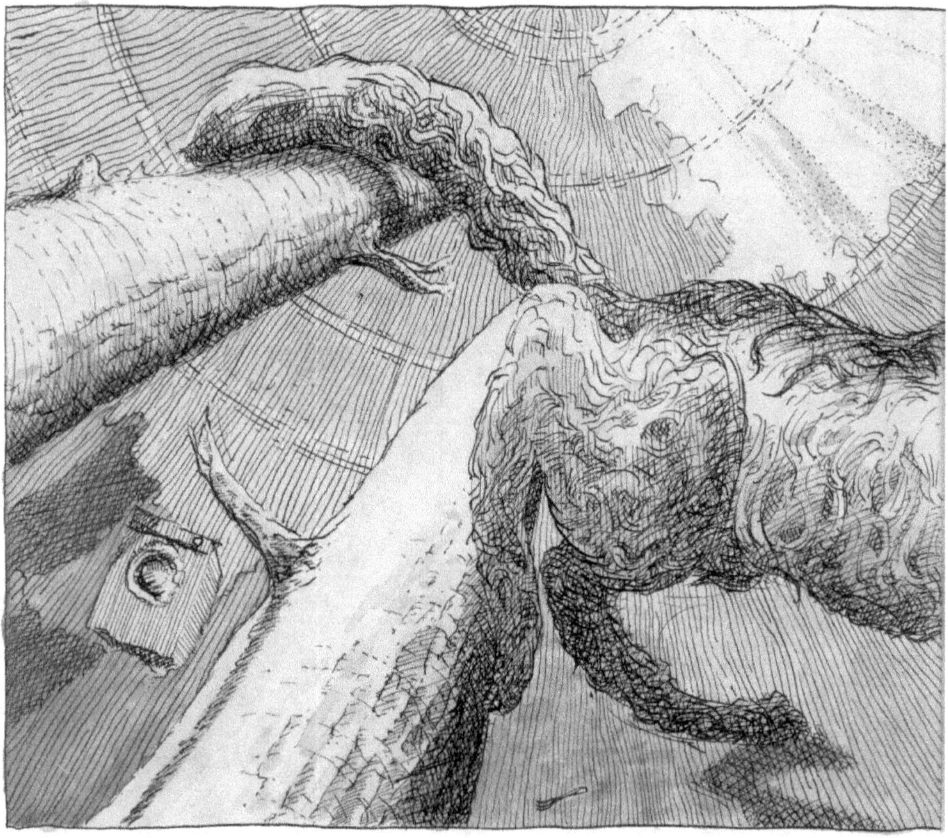

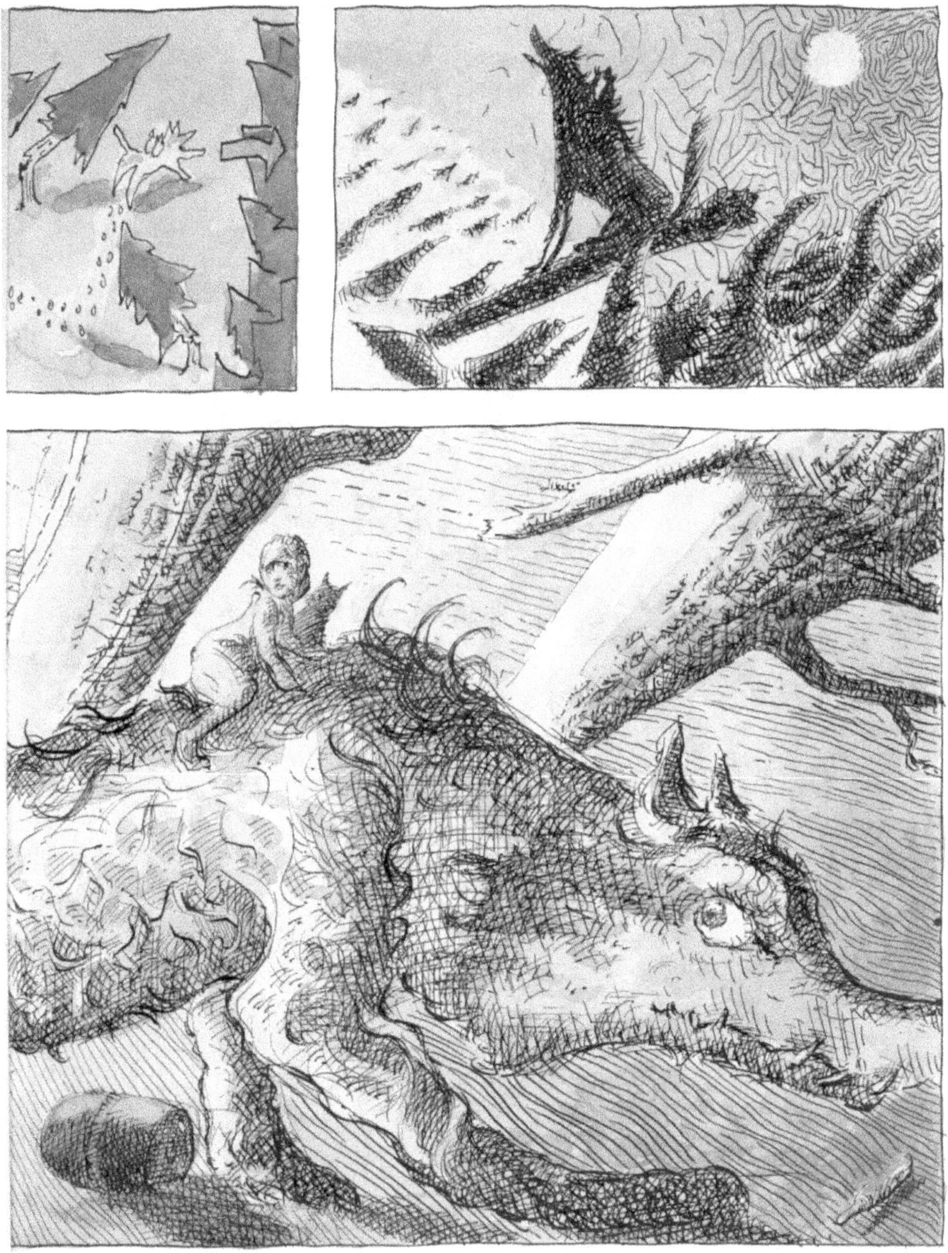

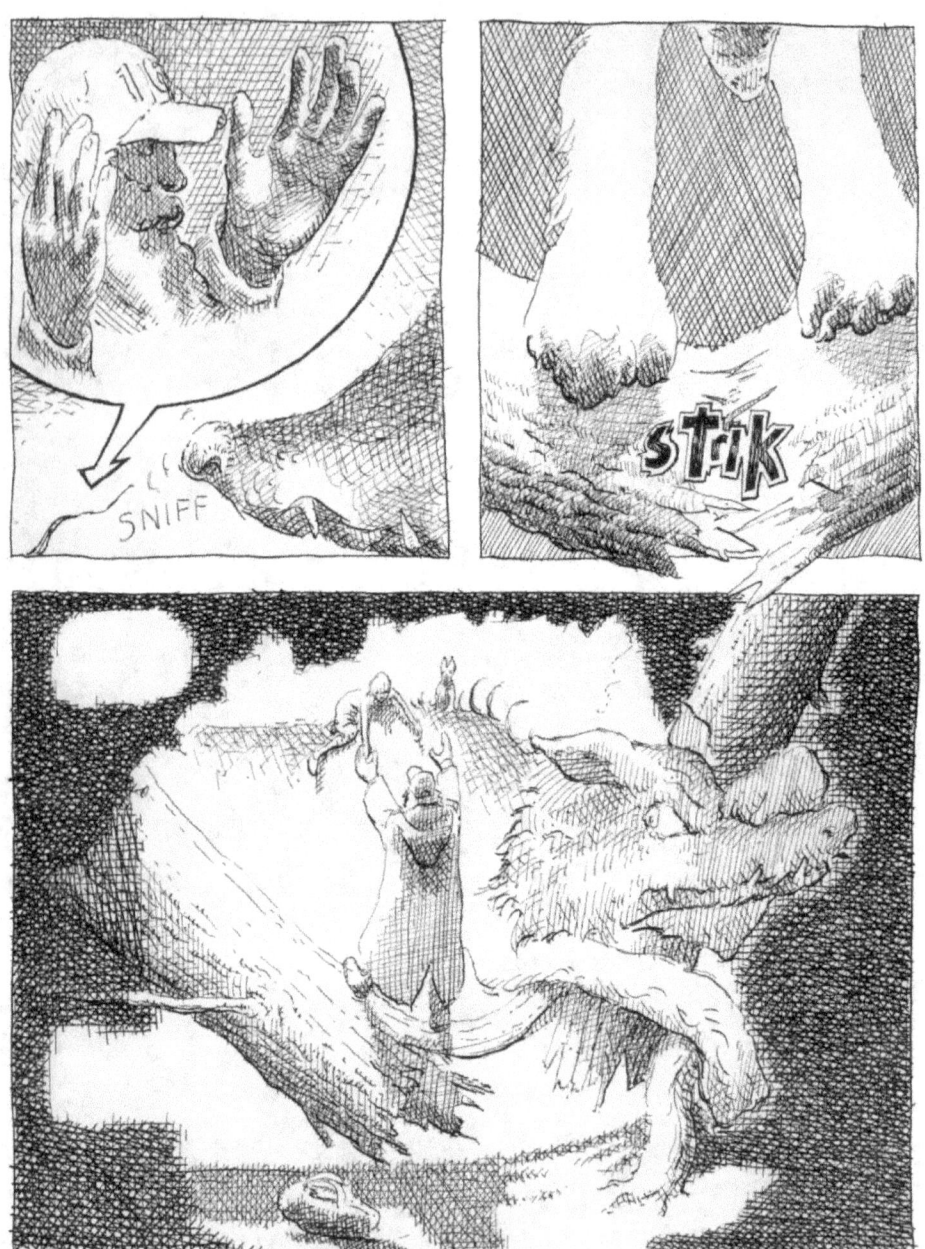

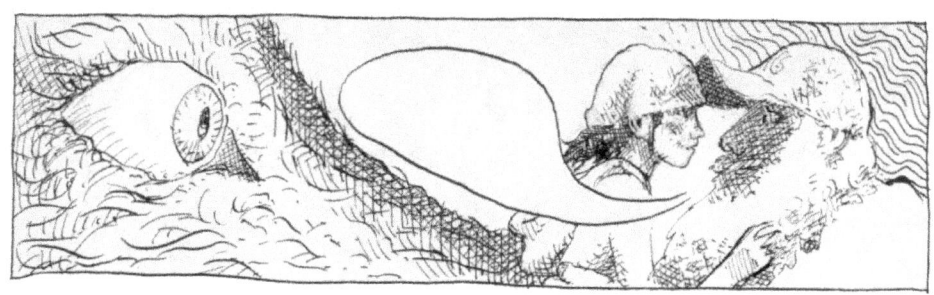

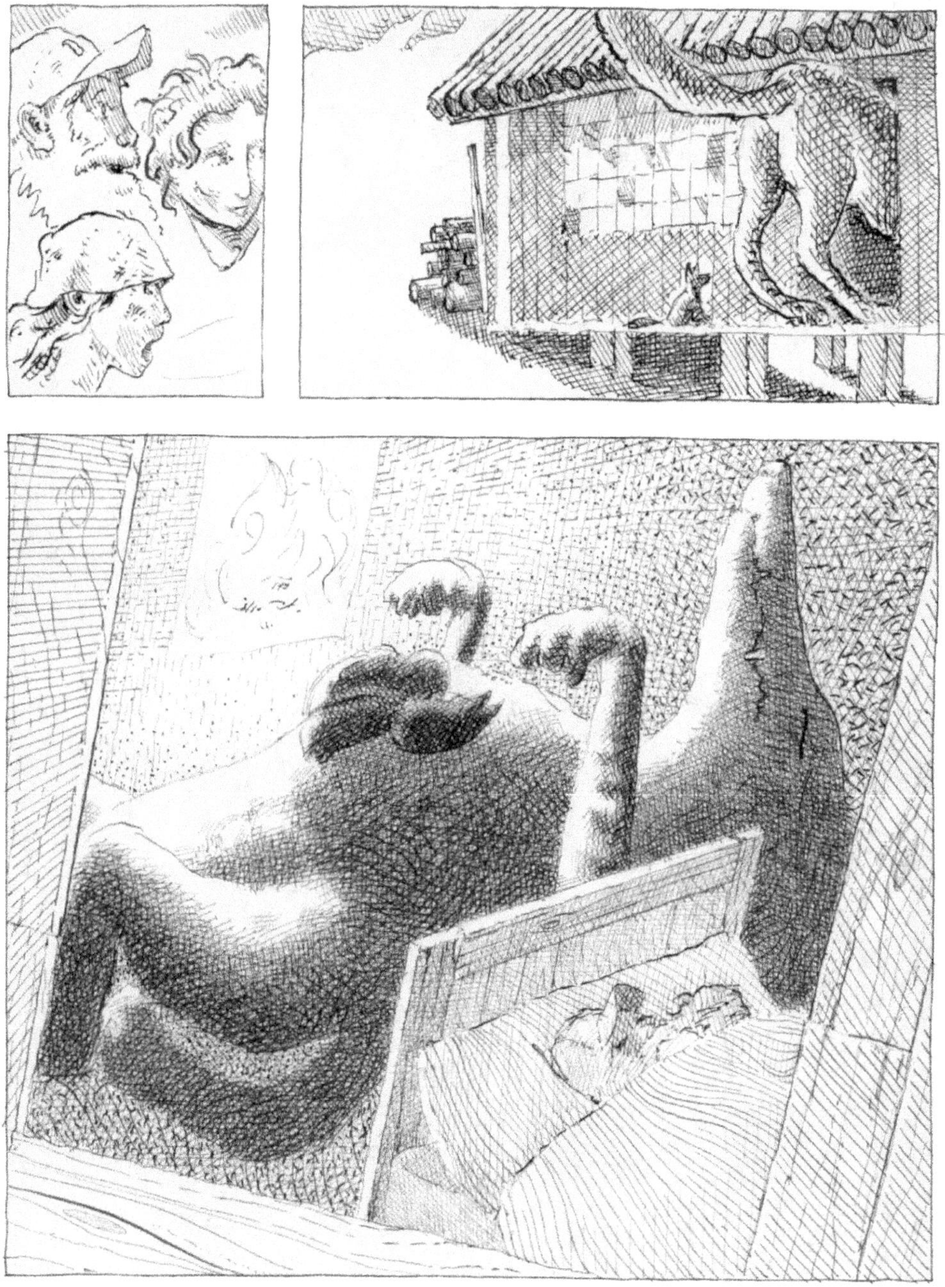

ENDANGERED SPECIES

Peter Kendell

ENDANGERED SPECIES

THERE WAS NO MILK IN THE FRIDGE. IN FACT, THERE WASN'T VERY much of anything in the fridge, but it was milk that George needed just at that moment and it was milk that wasn't there.

'We're out of milk, love,' he called into the sitting room, hoping he'd be heard through the closed and draught-proofed door. 'I'll have to go out and get some.'

No reply. George returned to the sitting room. 'Rosy?' His wife looked up. She'd been snoozing again.

'I'm just popping out to the shops. We need some milk. I'll pick up some bread too. Anything else?'

'I can't think of anything.'

'All right. Won't be long.' George checked that the fire was set to low and that Rosy's Zimmer was in the right place next to her chair in case she needed to get up. He bent over, kissed his wife gently on the cheek and pulled up her blanket. He was sure he could see her breath floating on the air. 'Back soon. Shall I turn the telly on for you?'

'No. I'll look at the paper.' That meant she'd be searching for coupons to cut out and special offers to apply for.

'Bye then.' George closed the door carefully and, pulling a bobble hat over his head and a scarf round his neck and zipping up his fleece, left the house. He let the garden gate spring back into place with its familiar click and squeak and turned right down Park Street. Once,

George had tried oiling and greasing the gate but both of them had missed the welcome-home sound it made. Also, as Rosy had said, it was like a burglar alarm. Their bedroom was at the front of the house, and if an intruder tried to get in George would be sure to hear the gate squeak and that would be a useful warning. They'd be able to ring 999 and call the police. Nobody had ever tried to break into their house by the front door, but you couldn't be too careful, as Irene Bagot, who lived two doors down and often came round for coffee and a chat, always said.

Pepper's, the corner shop where George and Rosy, before she was confined to quarters, used to buy their groceries, had closed several years earlier. Nobody could make any money out of it now, not even that nice Mr Patel and his wife and their three daughters. They'd kept it open eighteen hours a day and paid themselves nothing at all, as Mr Patel had often told George, but in the end they'd had to sell up. There hadn't been any unpleasantness of the kind you heard about on the news, just high rents and not enough people who could afford the kind of prices a small shop was obliged to ask, even though it was paying its staff nothing at all. So now George had to go to the petrol station on Royal Road, which was three-quarters of a mile away and where the prices were even higher than Mr Pepper and Mr Patel had charged.

George tutted as he passed the shop. What use was a nail bar to the likes of Rosy and him?

Three-quarters of a mile to get bread and milk. Three-quarters of a mile back. No joke; not when you wouldn't see seventy-five again and an icy wind was blowing off the hills and the scent of impending snow was breathing in the air. George told himself that the exercise was good for him. He had to keep in good shape, for who would look after his Rosy-Rue if he wasn't around? He took the blood pressure and cholesterol pills the doctor gave him, and he made sure they both got their flu jabs every October, even though that meant making phone calls and organising a lift down to the surgery from the local volunteer group. And even though he kept himself as fit as he could, it was for the ten-thousandth time that George regretted buying a house halfway up a hill. A house that was too big, and too draughty, and cost much more than they could afford to keep warm. It had all seemed so perfect fifty years ago, when he'd had a well-paid job and gas bills were low and they'd known they'd be needing lots of space one day. Now, it was a millstone round both their necks.

Every so often, a young man in a suit would come to the door and try to sell them things. Not the same young man every time, of course, although it was hard to be sure. They all had the same slicked hair, the same Burton's rig-out, the same leaflets and the same ready patter. But George very wisely distrusted all young men with laptops and financial illustrations. He had read some shocking stories in the *Daily Express*. So he ignored the estate agents' letters which said they'd make hundreds of thousands of pounds by selling their house, or using it as equity release and moving into so-called sheltered accommodation. He'd seen the new retirement homes next to the Lidl by the new roundabout. They'd looked like prison blocks to him, and even though he knew they'd be warm and there'd always be someone to come and help them at the press of a bell, George held fast to his distrust of offers from keen young men with shiny suits and gelled-back hair. He thought that maybe he'd been put on a blacklist, or that one of the reps had scratched a secret mark on the gatepost, such as tramps used to leave, because they received very few unexpected knocks on the door these days. Phone calls – now that was a different matter. It was a constant surprise to him that the Microsoft support team had not yet worked out that he had neither a computer nor a virus to put on it. Rosy liked the calls, despite being rather hard of hearing, and she loved to chat with Maureen, Barry and Jim from Bangalore.

George bought bread, milk and two apples at the petrol station, dodged a hasty Ford Focus on the forecourt, and started back home. He preferred to keep his head down when he walked up Park Street. It helped divert the gusts of wind that would otherwise have sneaked past his scarf and into his clothes. So it wasn't until he reached the front gate, and tried to open it, and found that it was already open, that he realised that he and his wife had a caller.

The caller was standing on the front door step, ringing the bell. George knew that wouldn't do any good. Rosy couldn't hear the doorbell these days and probably wouldn't have answered it even if she could.

'Hello,' said George. 'What can I do for you?'

'Do you live here?' said the caller.

'Yes, I do. Now, can I help you? You've seen the sign, haven't you?'

They had got a little self-adhesive notice from the library a few years previously and stuck it to the door. It said:

**WE DO NOT BUY AND SELL AT THIS DOOR, NOR
DO WE REQUIRE ANY FREE ADVICE.**

THANK-YOU

and it had a picture of a policeman printed on it, to make it look official.

'Yes, I've seen it. But I'm not here to buy or sell anything and I'm sure you don't need my advice.'

'Then what do you want?'

The visitor handed George a buff envelope. Inside it was a sheet of paper. George read the paper, shook his head, and read it again. He looked at the caller.

'Is this real?'

'It certainly is. Look, it's signed by Lord Battenberg.'

So it was.

'Well,' said George. 'You'd better come in, then.'

'If you'd like to pop into the kitchen,' said George. 'I'll be with you in just a minute. It's straight ahead.' The visitor shambled down the hall, while George ducked his head round the sitting-room door and told his wife he was back. She smiled up at him. It was the same smile she'd given George outside the Gaumont cinema one fine June evening in black-and-white 1958, when he was a junior draughtsman at Mason's and she a clerk at the council offices, out for the evening with her friends from the typing pool. George kissed her, as he had that very same evening, under the canopy of the Grange Street bus shelter.

'I hope you don't mind,' said the visitor when George joined him in the kitchen, 'but I've filled the kettle and put it on. I mean, under the circumstances, and all.'

'No,' said George. 'That's perfectly all right.' He was, to tell the truth, rather dazed, what with the effort of climbing up Park Street and the shock of finding this completely unexpected individual waiting at the front door. He wasn't sure he was making sense. It was all somewhat dream-like. For a moment, he thought he must have had an accident and was now lying in hospital, hallucinating under the influence of powerful pain-killers.

The kettle boiled, and the teapot was filled and three cups and saucers, a sugar basin and a little jug of milk were put on Rosy's favourite Alpine view tray – arranged properly, the way she liked it.

Daintily, she might have said. George and the visitor went into the sitting room. The visitor sat in the best chair, just as George asked him to, making it creak and groan, and Rosy poured the tea and hardly spilled any.

'Sugar, Mr...?'

'Bliss,' said the visitor. 'Two teaspoons, please. No milk.' George handed the cup over. There were no biscuits. They never had biscuits with their morning tea.

'You're not from the Social, are you?' Rosy said. She had often sent bright-eyed young social workers packing and told them (politely, of course) what they could do with their assessments and their carers and their day centres and their offers of home help. 'We can look after ourselves, thank you very much,' she'd said to them, and 'What a blooming cheek!' to George.

'Mr Bliss is coming to stay with us for a while,' said George. 'Until everything is sorted out.'

'Stay?' said Rosy. 'Oh, that is good news!' George smiled at his wife. He'd been wondering how well she would handle the situation.

'I'm George, and this is my wife Rosy.' George held out his hand. The visitor took it in his paw and shook it vigorously. 'Shall we call you Mr Bliss? Only I can't read your name on the letter. I don't know any Chinese.'

'My full name translates as Forest of Incandescent Bliss,' said the visitor. 'You can call me, er...' He put his head in both paws for a moment. 'Paul! Yes, Paul sounds right. Paul Bliss.'

'Nice to meet you, Paul,' said Rosy. 'George! Get the spare room ready!'

'Yes, dear,' said George. He looked across the room at their guest. Would the bed be strong enough for him?

'Top of the stairs and first right,' said George. Paul led the way. 'Bathroom's on the left. Have you got any luggage? Will they be sending it on?'

'No, no luggage.'

'Well, get yourself settled in. Come down when you're ready.'

'Righty-ho.'

George re-joined Rosy in the sitting room. They could hear the floorboards creak as Paul moved around upstairs. 'Let's have a look at that letter,' said Rosy. George got it out of the envelope and handed it to her. It read:

WILDLIFE CONSERVATION TRUST

Dear Mrs Tompkinson,

Thank you so much for kindly offering to help with our Adopt-A-Panda scheme. As you probably know, these beautiful animals have been suffering from the effects of the destruction of their native habitats, to the extent that they are now officially classified as an endangered species.

Without the freely-offered assistance of such generous patrons as yourself, the decline of this precious species must inevitably continue and, I'm sorry to say, end in extinction. I find it quite impossible to overstate the tragedy that such a loss would represent, not only to the Wildlife Conservation Trust, but also to the well-being of the entire planet. It is a great comfort to know that at least one individual is safe.

Your panda's personal details:

Name:	林白樂.
Age:	15 years. (Note: one panda year is approximately equivalent to three human years.)
Place of Birth:	Wolong National Nature Reserve, PRC. (Note: destroyed in 2008 earthquake.)
Family:	None. (Note: records lost in 2008 earthquake.)
Preferred diet:	Fresh bamboo. Also fond of sausages.

Once again, thank you for your help.

Yours sincerely,

David Battenberg (Lord)

P.S. Please see attached slip regarding remuneration, expenses, etc.

George shook the envelope and looked at the flimsy that fell out.
    'Bloody 'ell!'
    'George! Language!'

'No, look! They're going to give us five hundred and fifty pounds a week to look after Paul!'

'Let me see. Ooh, yes. But what about his bamboo? They don't sell bamboo down at Pepper's. You'll have to go to a Chinese supermarket for that. It'll cost a fortune.'

George read the flimsy again. 'It's all right. They say there'll be regular deliveries of bamboo, already paid for. It's coming all the way from Holland. In fact—'

A van pulled up at the front of the house. A uniformed man knocked at the door. 'Mr Tompkinson?'

'That's me.'

'Consignment of bamboo for Mr Bliss.'

'Kitchen's straight ahead.'

'I never thought,' said Rosy as two burly men hauled sacks of bamboo into the larder, 'they meant a *whole* panda.'

Paul proved to be remarkably easy to live with. At first, Rosy and George thought he might become rather a burden, and they couldn't help suspecting they would well and truly earn their five hundred and fifty pounds a week. But actually, they soon learned that what Paul most liked to do was eat.

'I have to spend about fourteen hours a day eating,' he said between mouthfuls of bamboo. 'In the wild, anyway. By the way, this scran is absolutely top-notch. Crammed full of vitamins, I shouldn't wonder. I expect the Conservation Trust has it reinforced with mineral supplements.'

'Like at the health-food shop?' asked Rosy.

'Oh no! Much better than that rubbish! Let me tell you, I can feel strength and vitality flooding through my veins right now!'

The other thing they learned – and that in pretty short order – was that Paul liked to watch television. When he found out they only had Freeview, he immediately demanded they order cable so he could watch natural history programmes on the Discovery Channel. 'You never know,' he said, with his head set at a piteous angle and his huge black eyes brimming with tears, 'but there might be a programme about China, and I might see my Mum and Dad in it.'

They couldn't refuse him, and the subscription didn't make too much of a hole in their new and improved monthly budget. Nor did the payments on a sixty-inch Sony television (pandas have only average eyesight and an aging nineteen-inch Philips wasn't going to cut the mustard) or a futon for his room – the guest bed didn't survive the first night – or even turning on the radiators upstairs and in the hall and the (previously disused) dining room. Rosy was able to get around the house much more easily now it was a bit warmer. They would have gone the whole hog and had a stair-lift installed, only the staircase was quite steep and narrow and they could see – because Paul pointed it out to them – that a fully-grown male panda would have a difficult time of it, squeezing past the rails and knocking against the controls. So George still had to help Rosy up and down the stairs and, as pandas are liable to shed fur and aren't all that handy with a vacuum cleaner, do quite a lot of brushing and sweeping and general tidying up. It just went to show that you couldn't have everything, not in this life.

They had to have the plumbing seen to. It seemed that what came out of a panda wasn't all that different to what went in, and as what went in was quite bulky, what came out tended to clog the pipes. In a mad moment, George suggested a bucket on a chain, but Rosy quickly pooh-poohed the idea. Instead, they found there was a company called Throne Room that made and installed extra-large facilities for extra-large people. George arranged a grant with the Wildlife Conservation Trust for that. Rosy was afraid she would fall into the Throne through the Emperor-sized seat, so George made her a special one out of plywood and foam rubber.

Now that Rosy had a companion (she and Paul had started watching daytime television together, especially the shopping channels), George was able to go out more. He looked up some of his old friends – Cyril, Harry, Eric and Gerald – from Mason's and met up with them in the public bar of the Idle Cog, where he told them all about his new lodger.

'Are you sure it's all kosher?' Cyril asked. 'Isn't he an illegal?'

'Oh no,' said George. 'He's got papers. Signed by a Lord, you know.'

'That must be nice for you,' said Gerald. 'Having no kids, and that.'

It had been a long sorrow for Rosy that they'd had no children. No grandchildren either, of course, nobody to send presents to, nobody to look in now and then to make sure they were well. Rosy's sister Grace had moved to Cornwall in the 1980s and they hardly ever saw her, or even heard from her. Never mind, Rosy-Rue, George had said. We've got each other. But they had minded, all the same.

'How did you find him?' asked Eric. 'Did you go on the Internet?'

'Oh no, nothing like that. It was Rosy. She likes to fill in forms and coupons and send them in. From the paper, you know. I don't think she looks at half of them. We've had some funny stuff in our time.' And he went on to describe the foreign stamps on approval, and the chair covers, and the Velcro slippers and the pleated skirts that turned up unexpectedly at the front door, not to mention the junk mail that blocked it from time to time.

'You should bring him down here,' said Harry. 'Does he drink bitter?'

Paul's tipple turned out to be Australian lager, which lowered him considerably in the lads' estimation, but when he joined them the following Wednesday he proved to be excellent company; full of entertaining anecdotes, but a good listener too. It was fortunate indeed that smoking was no longer permitted in pubs because, as Paul said, it would have stained his fur quite badly. Colour pictures of pandas from the library (Paul had joined straight away so he could access the Internet and keep his Facebook up to date) showed a certain build-up of matter in the tail area, but Paul was fastidiously clean and hardly smelled at all. Certainly no worse than Cyril, who had lived by himself for most of his adult life.

They swapped stories of what were once called the smoking-room variety. The humans were astonished to learn that female pandas only came on heat for three days each year. 'Yes,' said Paul, 'you primates have all the fun.' In turn, Paul learned more than he needed to know about the lads' adventures as young men – of dance-halls and juke-boxes and scooters and coffee-bars and girls with names like Susan, Julie and Stephanie.

'No wonder you lot are dying out,' said Gerald to Paul. 'Never getting your end away, like.'

Three months after Paul's arrival the postman knocked on the door with a special delivery for him. It wasn't yet another order from www.pricechop.com, but a signed-for letter. Paul took hold of the postman's pen with his claws and opposed thumb and wrote his name. He carried the letter upstairs to read in privacy. George looked at Rosy. She had been feeling ever so much better these past few weeks. They'd even been able to afford to take a taxi into town and get around the shops and buy some clothes, instead of getting them out of a catalogue. It was amazing how much difference a bit of company (not to mention the extra money) had made to their lives.

'What's that about?'

'I hope it's not bad news.'

'Suppose he's leaving?'

'What we will do?'

They waited anxiously.

But not for long. With a crashing and a banging and a splintering of the banisters Paul came catapulting down the stairs and burst into the sitting room. 'They've found her! They've found her!'

'Who?'

'Your mum?'

'Your auntie?'

'Your sister?'

'Your Nan?'

'Nah! Not that! No, they've found my mate!'

'What – someone you knew in China?'

'An old friend?'

'An electrician's mate?'

'No, silly! My mate! The panda I'm going to mate with! She'll be here in a day's time!'

'What?' Rosy and George sat back in astonishment. 'Another panda? We're getting another panda?'

Paul's face fell, an odd sight in a panda whose physiognomy, though expressive, is not particularly mobile.

'Oh! Do say she can come!'

Her English name was Sharon. They never learned what it was in Chinese. Paul was completely besotted with her and so, once they discovered that the Wildlife Conservation Trust was paying them a further four hundred and fifty pounds a week, tax-free, were Rosy and George. Panda-sexing is a difficult science – it's more of an art really – but as Sharon weighed a few stone less than Paul and had a lilting voice with none of Paul's gruffness, there was never any confusion between them. Just as Rosy had quickly become fast friends with Paul, George found himself drawn to Sharon. They found they were well matched at draughts, chess and Go.

Now that they had two paying house-guests – though they quickly became like family to George and Rosy – it seemed only fair to rearrange the house to accommodate them. George took out a loan and had a conservatory built on to the back of the dining-room, reserved as daytime accommodation for the pandas. There was a handy shower fitted in one corner and George constructed an enclosed area for the cubs, when they came. And come they surely would. Whatever the formal mathematics of panda breeding may state, it seemed that Paul and Sharon were going to do all they could to make sure that when the three-day fertility window came, they would be well and truly in it. As the best way to manage this was to do the cub-making thing as often as possible, that is what they did. Day and night, the house trembled with the rhythmic thump of panda against panda; in the bedroom, the kitchen, the bathroom and, most scandalously but less noisily, the front garden. Rosy and George looked on and beamed with joy. If only they had been a decade or two younger themselves!

A happy year passed. To Rosy and George's surprise, the neighbours made remarkably little fuss about their new housemates. No muttering about foreigners moving in or complaints about the bamboo delivery vans blocking the road. Not even jealousy at their good fortune. Meanwhile, the pandas made every effort to assimilate into the area and it was not at all uncommon to find one or the other of them leaning against the bus-shelter, chatting to people and telling them stories about life among the conical mountains and forest groves of upland Schezwan. There were some scurrilous rumours to begin with that Paul had been teaching some of the local kids to swear in Cantonese, but it soon turned out that he was showing them how to pronounce the names of the dishes offered at the Jasmine Garden Rice Bowl and Takeaway. Mr Chong was most impressed to be asked for 馄饨汤 instead of "Number 25, mate."

One day Irene Bagot knocked on the door in a state of high excitement.

'What is it, Rene?' asked Rosy, who had got up and answered the door all on her own.

'Where's George?' asked Irene.

'He's in the shed, making cub-beds out of chipboard. Only a few weeks to go now!'

Irene knew that. She'd been told it several times a week for the past year.

'Anyway, look. There's someone I want you to meet. Say hello to Rosy, Cecil.'

Cecil extended a paw. 'Pleased to meet you,' he said in a soft furry voice.

'What is he, Rene dear?' Rosy whispered.

'"He" has a name! I'm a three-toed sloth. I'm at risk of dying out, but Miss Bagot has agreed to look after me.'

'Isn't that nice! Are you enjoying life in England? You must come in. I'm sure Paul and Sharon will be back soon. We can have some tea and biscuits.'

Everything became quite hectic once the cubs finally arrived. A team of panda experts from Edinburgh Zoo turned up and set up shop in the conservatory. They were very kind about George's home-made shelter, but they removed it all the same and erected something complicated and high-tech, full of sensors, cameras and computers. Paul felt rather left out of things, so he and George spent quite a lot of time in the Idle Cog where, after a few pints, Paul would reminisce about the Long Lost Days Of Wolong and tell George he was his Best Friend Forever and he didn't mind that George had been rather chummier with his Sharon than was strictly called for. George stroked Paul's ears in a perfectly comradely manner and bought him another drink.

The cubs, when they came, were a disappointment. They looked like tiny pink pigs, with none of the distinctive markings that made, as Paul often said, the giant panda one of the world's most handsome and best-loved creatures.

'Don't worry,' said Eileen McIntosh, PhD (Edin). 'They'll be cute as buttons in a month or two. Right now, we've got to stop Sharon rolling over on the puir wee mites and crushing the daylights out of them.' Eileen had a cot in the conservatory which she hot-bedded with her colleagues. They were on cub-watch, 24/7.

The house had never been so busy and full, and Rosy and George soon came to realise that this was the way it would have been if they had had children of their own. Odd people coming and going at all times of the day and night, loud discordant music playing, strange herbal smells, long telephone calls. Yes, Rosy said, it was just like living with teenagers.

'Just think what we missed,' George said.

'All that crying and wailing into the small hours.'

'When they were babies, too.' George laughed.

Sharon and Paul came over rather moody and aggressive in their defence of the cubs. There were three of them, all girls, and they were called Milly, Molly and Mandy. As Doctor Eileen had promised, they became quite indecently cuddly and adorable as they grew older but, to their dismay, Rosy and George weren't allowed to touch them unless they were wearing special blue plastic aprons and had been thoroughly disinfected. This extended to the camera crews who made weekly visits to the house and left webcams scattered everywhere, connected to what a goateed young man called a "mofo fat pipe" which expression fortunately meant nothing whatsoever to the couple. Meanwhile, an architect came round with plans for a full-scale panda enclosure, which would take over the whole of the back garden. There were telephone calls at all hours enquiring about the cubs' progress and the postman brought two sacks of fan mail every morning and afternoon. All this attention was most entertaining, of course, but it was also becoming increasingly irksome. In fact, as George often remarked, it was rapidly turning into a blooming nuisance. Their house was being overrun to the extent that it hardly felt like home any more. George thought it was time he made a few enquiries. Nothing serious, though, not yet.

The last straw was a letter telling Rosy and George that Lord David Battenberg was going to come round in a week's time to interview them for a television documentary.

'I'm not doing that!' said Rosy. 'Telly's for watching, not for being on.'

'Quite right,' said George. 'But don't fret, love. I've got a plan. Let's get a taxi into town, and I'll tell you all about it over lunch.'

They could afford to eat in better restaurants now, modern places with famous chefs' names on the menu. The waitresses were ever so nice and friendly and explained very clearly what went into all the funny-named dishes and actually – as Rosy said while digging into her *tarte aux poivres avec crème parfait de cerises* – it was an education and proved that even older people like themselves could take on new things and enjoy them.

'I'm glad you said that,' said George. 'I've got a little proposition for you.' He explained the little proposition, and Rosy's eyes grew wide with disbelief.

'No!' she said, shaking her head vehemently, 'Not ever! I'm not going to listen to another word. You must think I'm mad!'

But George went on talking, and when he pulled a paper from his jacket pocket and showed his wife a certain number printed at the bottom – a number with more zeroes on the end of it than she had ever seen before – she began to waver. And after they paid and took a short taxi ride and he showed her what the zeroes could buy she became more than half convinced.

And finally, as they fought their way home past the sightseers and the paparazzi and the satellite ground stations and the food delivery vans (the Carrs opposite had taken on a couple of white tigers, Irene Bagot was run off her feet looking after her sloth colony and there were rumours that the Brightman family down the road were building a multi-storey wolf habitat), Rosy turned to George and said, 'You know...'

Rosy and George have never been so happy. They have a lovely bungalow in the grounds of the old hospital that was converted into flats in the 1990s. There are no stairs, it's always cosy and warm and, at the press of a button, a nice girl comes and asks what she can do for them. They've got plenty of space – George has his own little workshop out at the back – and there's a large television fixed to the wall of the sitting room, next to the log fire that George so enjoys keeping going. Most importantly, it's only a short ride by scooter to the shops. And, even more importantly than that, they have a big spare room, fully equipped with an en-suite Throne, where Paul, Sharon and the girls can stay when they come to visit.

The pandas negotiated a fabulous lifetime contract with the television companies. Paul hosts his own chat show on Channel Four and Sharon has played a number of minor roles in *EastEnders*, *Doctors* and *Emmerdale*. Next year, they're going to have a stab at writing their autobiographies.

And in the end, as Rosy liked to say to George, it was families that mattered the most, and their family in particular. And George very sensibly agreed, while at the same time closely watching his wife for any further signs of form-filling and coupon-collecting. 'Let's not push our luck, eh, Rosy-Rue,' he said.

'No, love. Only—'

'Yes, dear?'

'Have you heard about the poor red pandas? The firefoxes?'

'No!'

'They're only little, you know. They're so sweet, and they'd take up hardly any room…'

STRAYING FROM THE WAY

Darren Everett

As a child, Darren Everett was often berated for telling tales out of school. Now he's a systems administrator for his local council. He hasn't been accused of telling tales out of work yet, but that's only because he writes them down when no-one's looking.

He lives in the south of England with a wife, a son, a dog, and lots and lots of Doctor Who *toys.*

STRAYING FROM THE WAY

*C*HRISTMAS, *AND YOU'RE IN HOSPITAL. YOU'RE ON YOUR BACK, LEGS akimbo, hollering yourself hoarse. The ceiling is yellow. Not soothing pastel yellow, but hazy toxic nicotine yellow. You crave a ciggie, more than anything. Timothy is by your side, telling you to breathe, stroking your shoulder.* Deep breath, *says Timothy,* deep breath, *says the midwife, and Timothy strokes your shoulder, strokes your shoulder, strokes your shoulder.*

Deep breath. But there is no Timothy. And on your shoulder there is only the scar.

March 1963, and it's snowing again.

You're clutching your purse through thick wool gloves as you wade through the fresh snow on Mersey Road. There's been nowt *but* snow. It was a white Christmas, which was nice, especially as it was your first Christmas with Timothy at the flat, but it's been a white new year too, and now you've had it up to here with it all. The sky had been clear when you left home and the reflection of the sun on snow was blinding. You put on your large glasses and wrapped your scarf over your head and under your chin, just like the First Lady in those pictures at the yacht race last year.

Ericka's up, says the voice. I was there.

You look around, but there's no one about. The snow is undisturbed save for your footprints. No one goes out in this weather if they can help it. It was a small voice, just on the edge of your hearing, as though it was coming from behind a closed door. However indistinct it was, it's enough to remind you of the yacht race: America's Cup. That was it.

You like your scarf. It's made of silk and it does bugger all to keep you warm, but it's soft against the skin and it reminds you of the day Timothy showed you round the flat. He pulled the scarf over your eyes and tied it at the back like a blindfold, and he slowly guided you up the narrow steps at the front of the building. It's a surprise, he said, and when you tried to peek he slapped your wrist, playfully. Only inside had he allowed you to remove the blindfold. He was down on one knee with an engagement ring in one hand and the keys to the flat in the other. And he was stark naked, too, the randy so-and-so.

You smile at the recollection and a snowflake settles on your lip. He's in west London, filming a BBC drama about a spaceship. *Rose Snowball* or *Magenta Snowdrift* or some such. It won't be popular, you're sure: everyone's sick of the snow. You think about giving him a bell this evening, see how the filming is going, but you called him only the night before and he'll get bolshie about the phone bill. You wonder if he misses you as much as you miss him.

Two ticks, I'm almost you, says the faraway voice.

You? Or was it *through*? It's louder than before, but still difficult to make out. Like Timothy's voice down the telephone line last night, you think, full of cracks and pops and static. So far away.

I'll be with you soon.

You're nearly back at the flat. It's been a wasted journey: you hadn't made it half-way to the corner shop before the sky darkened and enormous white flakes started to settle around you. You pulled your scarf up over your mouth and chin and struggled on for a few yards until the wind picked up and the flakes began to spiral about you; then you swore and stamped a wellington-clad foot in surrender, and turned around and stomped back towards your flat.

All for a pack of smokes. It's about time you gave up, anyway.

It's snowing again, you huff into your scarf. It's snowing again and it's sodding *March*!

The Ides of March, says the voice, muffled, maybe by the snow. It sounds more like *eyes of March*. You ignore it. You just want to get inside, out of the cold. You struggle with the gate, dragging it open through half a foot of snow, and you carefully make your way along the path to the steps. Mr Marksby from the floor above cleared them this morning, but they're already icy again. You fumble inside your purse for the key, brandish it before you, reaching for a lock that's a dozen treacherous steps away, and slowly, very slowly, make your way to the door.

Wait, I'm nearly there; and you can hear the voice more clearly now, almost as though it's right behind you. You turn to look, misjudge your step and—

You slip.

Mam!

Your right foot slides outward and your whole body lurches sideways. Your left foot can't take the weight and your leg buckles beneath you, and you fall backwards, turning as you tumble, so you hit the frosty ground face first.

For the rest of your life you'll recall what happens next: your forehead crashes into the paving stones, sending a shockwave through your skull and through your eyes and through your brain; your nose crunches flush against your face with a sickening tear of flesh as your cheeks are thrust back towards your ears; your front teeth are crushed inward, splintering, slicing into your tongue.

You'll never forget it. Which is strange, really, since none of this actually happens.

I shouldn't have done that, comes the muffled voice. But you shouldn't have fallen, either.

You're cradled in his arms.

It'll scar pretty bad, he tells you. Could've been worse, though. Could've been your face.

The world jolts.

You're reminded of the year before last, on Timothy's twenty-second birthday, when he drove into a ditch. It was your fault, perhaps, since you were giving him a blowjob at the time. He wasn't concentrating on the road. You were both drunk, you'd been out in town with his friends from drama class, and he shouldn't have been driving.

There was a moment of glorious weightlessness as the car left the road, followed by the sudden slam into the ditch.

That's what the jolt feels like, except it's not the car, it's the entire world, and it lasts only a heartbeat.

You're sitting on the bottom step, ice cold on your arse, and you don't know how you got there. You can feel a dull ache in your shoulder. It brings tears to your eyes.

I don't have an awful lot of time, says the man who caught you. Just gimme a mo, then we'll skip inside.

He's squatting in front of you in the snow, his warm hands resting on your knees. His voice is still muffled, and when you look up you see it's because of the mask. It covers the whole of his face, with no holes for his eyes or mouth. It's the colour of sour milk, like old bone. Tousled black and grey hair frames the mask like a lion's mane. He's wearing a knee-length black jacket, a grey cravat, scuffed charcoal denim pants. His feet are bare.

That's what strikes you as the weirdest thing about him. Not the bone mask, not the crazy wig, not the wooden crutch he's just rescued from the snow as he stands up. It's that he's not wearing any shoes. His feet must be freezing.

You have questions, lots of questions, crowding your mind, and they're all clamouring to be asked at once, quickly, before they fade, but all you can manage is: Ouch. Fucking ouch, that fucking hurts.

We've strayed from the way, he says without sympathy. Can't explain. Take my hand. Let's get you indoors.

No! What the hell's happened to my shoulder?

The man tilts his head to one side. Indoors, he says.

He snatches your hand in his and you're sitting on the settee. There was barely a jolt this time.

Gets easier the more you do it, he says, glancing about your flat. Let's get those clothes off you, get you into something dry. He limps slowly out of the den, towards your bedroom, leaning heavily on his crutch.

Who are you? you call after him. Then you add: How did we get here? And then: I'm not taking my clothes off, you fucking pervert. Get out of my flat.

The masked man is already making his way back. Under his spare arm is a bundle of your clothes. He drops them on the settee beside you.

You look him up and down. He's probably no taller than you. His clothes are old, crumpled, like he's spent a lot of time in them, with the reek of cigarette smoke and sweat. Even his mask is dirty. Three rusted rings are pierced through it where his left eyebrow might be.

Fancy a cuppa? he asks. I'll pop the kettle on whilst you get changed.

The mask is beginning to annoy you. It's difficult to make out his words. You stare at him sullenly and it's only then you notice that there are tiny black letters etched into it. You laugh. Despite everything that has happened, you actually laugh. It's old newsprint! The mask isn't made of bone at all, but papier-mâché. You're surprised and slightly embarrassed that you ever thought otherwise.

He starts his slow limp to the kitchen.

You call out after him: Did you hear what I said? Who are you?

He doesn't turn to face you, doesn't even raise his voice, so his response is more muffled than before. It sounds for all the world like *needy poof.*

You raise an eyebrow. Come again?

He turns this time, from the kitchen doorway, and speaks slowly, as if to a child.

Easy. Puss.

You're convinced you haven't heard right, but you don't ask him again. He's already shuffled into the kitchen and is filling the kettle. Easy Puss? What the hell? That doesn't explain who he is. Or how he appeared from nowhere to catch you, or how he brought you inside, or why he wears a mask and no shoes.

Or why your shoulder is so sore.

Wincing, you stand up, pull off your gloves, shrug off your coat, and let them fall to the floor. The pain in your shoulder is less than it was but it's still a persistent ache. You unbutton your cardigan and drop it beside your coat and gloves. You undo the top couple of buttons on your blouse and pull it open so you can look at your shoulder properly.

Sorry it's a mess.

Easy Puss is standing behind you. You didn't hear him come in. Tea's brewing, he says. It won't be long.

He unwinds your scarf slowly, careful not to touch your shoulder, and then he gently pulls your hair back. Your shoulder is pale yellow, like his mask, and bumpy with scar tissue.

What have you done to me? you gasp. What have you…?

Easy Puss shrugs. Like I said, it weren't meant to happen. I had to improvise. You were gonna fuck up your face, falling like that.

But… my shoulder! What have you done to my bloody shoulder?

Puss looks away, and when he speaks he sounds irritated. I can't just take stuff away. It don't work like that. Be grateful I hid it in your history, gave it time to heal.

You pull your blouse back into place and start to do up the buttons, but Puss's clammy fingers reach from behind you and brush your hands away. He doesn't bother with the buttons – he lifts the blouse up and over your head, and it joins your other clothes on the floor.

He's suddenly standing in front of you, close, touching. You're in your bra and knickers, though you don't remember unzipping your skirt. There are two mugs of tea on the side table.

Your dry clothes are on the settee, Puss reminds you.

You're sitting on the settee, taking careful sips of your tea. You didn't want Puss watching you dress, though you weren't keen on him seeing you in just your underwear either, so you took a blanket off the bed and wrapped it around yourself. Easy Puss collapsed gratefully into Timothy's armchair, and is now leaning forward and massaging his left ankle.

The tea is exactly how you like it. Strong, the smallest dash of milk, half a spoonful of sugar.

You clearly found everything okay, you tell Puss icily.

Yeah, he replies, sitting back in the armchair. You'll live in this flat for *ages*. Won't be long until you and I get to know each other really well, and I'll live with you for a few years.

You frown, confused. I don't catch your drift.

He shrugs. You don't need to. But it's already happened for me, and I remember where you keep your tea and sugar.

You can't help but make a face at him. So, you're saying you come from the future? Freak.

The snow'll be gone within a week, says Puss. In some places, it'll last until April. But not here.

Okay. But that means I have to wait a week to see whether you're right or not. Tell me something that's going to happen *now*.

He lets out a sigh. Look, I don't care if you believe me or no. I'm not explaining myself.

You clutch your blanket tightly, trying not to shiver and show him how weak you are. I want you to leave my flat now, please, you say in a small voice.

Easy Puss nods his head. Soon. Soon, I'll go, and you won't see me again until... Well, not for a few months. And you'll be pleased to see me then, I promise.

You take another sip of your tea. You don't know what to say, don't know what to do. Should you phone Timothy, tell him to come? But London is a long drive away.

Finally, you look at Puss. If you're right, you say slowly, it's good about the snow. I'm sick of the damn stuff.

I like it, he says, sniffing. It's cleansing. I've just come from a city, a tarnished city. Felt like it left stuff on me, every time I touched something. A patina. Verdigris on my spectacles.

What?

Oh, nothing.

Your and Timothy's bedroom. There's been another jump. You're getting used to them.

You are standing by the foot of the bed. Easy Puss is unwrapping your blanket. It falls to the floor. He kneels down, tugs on the waistband of your knickers, lowers them. You step out of them, then help Puss to his feet. He stands clumsily, trying not to lean too heavily on his left foot. You think he may have left his crutch in the den.

He reaches around you and fumbles at your bra strap, but you push him away. Take off your mask, you tell him, and you raise your hands, stroke the papier-mâché cheeks with the tips of your fingers. And how do you see through that thing, anyway? There're no eye holes.

He shakes his head, but your fingers are already prising it from his face. It's fastened with a frayed ribbon, which unravels. You drop the mask to the floor, where it joins the blanket and underwear and, spiritually, the rest of your clothes in the den.

The first thing that strikes you is his glasses. The frame is made of thin copper, tarnished green-blue with – what did he call it? – verdigris. The circular lenses are made of red smoked glass, impenetrable to your gaze. You wonder what colour his eyes are.

The second thing that strikes you is the agelessness of his face. He could be twenty years old or he could be forty. He could be your age or your father's. His skin is pale, not a dissimilar colour to his mask, as though his face has never seen sunlight, and there are slight wrinkles around his mouth and, from what little you can see, beneath his spectacles.

The third thing that strikes you is his hair. It isn't a wig after all.

You run your fingers through it, following the grey streaks, trying to tame the unruly curls.

His fingers shadow yours, caressing your hair.

You lower your right hand, place it against his chest, over his heart.

He lowers his hand, cups your breast.

You free your other hand from his tangled hair, run your fingers down his temple and—

Before you can pluck the glasses from his face, his hand is there, tight around your wrist.

Nope, he says.

So take off your clothes, you tell him.

You're astride him on the bed. He's removed his jacket but is otherwise still dressed. You tug at his cravat, pulling it loose. You unbutton his shirt, dark blue, with sweat stains beneath his arms. He pulls one arm free, and then the other, but because he's lying on his back you can't get the shirt out from under him. You leave it there, spread out beneath him like wings.

His chest is pale, like his face, save for his nipples: two beads of blood upon the snow.

He reaches up, caresses your breasts. You're still wearing your bra.

You lean forward then and kiss him on the lips, just for a moment. Stubble scratches your chin. Then you reach down and unbutton his jeans.

Mind my foot, he says quickly.

His left ankle is twisted, swollen. You can't believe you hadn't noticed it sooner.

What happened to it? you ask.

My feet were bound together, he says, and I was hung upside-down from a tree for three nights. Ain't been right since.

You lay the jeans on the bed next to him. Somehow, you don't like the thought of them on the floor with your clothes. Why would anyone do that to you? you ask quietly.

Puss looks away. I did it to meself, he says. I was looking for *chalice*.

You lean back, staring at him, naked, in your bed. I don't understand... you begin.

Puss interrupts you. It's a state of being, he says. But it's a real place, too. It's just not always where I left it. Or when, for that matter.

Freak, you say. You're a fucking, fucking freak.

That's the second time you've called me that, he replies drily. Listen: you won't know anything about *chalice*, so there's no point me trying to explain. Not everyone can use it, not everyone can go there. Not everyone can keep to the way. They call it different names, too. Kairos, mistletoe, the slowfox… It's just – it's how I got here.

You lean forward and slap his chest hard. Freak! Leave my flat. Leave now.

But you're astride him and he isn't going anywhere.

At first, you fuck slowly – not gently, just slowly, mechanically – and his voice is slow and calm:

There's a danger with *chalice* that you might stray from the path. You gotta choose your way and keep to it. I chose my way, my history. Got it set out, in diaries and film and photographs. In blood and snot, in spunk and shit. I know where I'm going. And I strayed.

The pace quickens: it becomes a rough arrhythmic thrusting, and his words become louder between breaths:

Twenty years ago, a French journalist writ a book about time-travel. About the grandfather paradox. It goes like this. A man goes back in time, back before he's born, to meet his grandfather. He kills the guy, but that means his grandfather never gets married or has children, and that means the time-traveller's dad was never born. *He* is never born, either, so he can't go back in time to kill his grandfather… If his grandfather doesn't die, though, he'll get married and have children and the time-traveller *will* be born and *can* go back in time and kill him… and on… and on…

And you fuck faster and harder, you caught in that moment and he caught in his story, and he shudders beneath you as he comes, and then you come, and the whole world jolts again.

In the calm, just before sleep takes him, he whispers, slow and proud:

I strayed from the family way, and I solved the grandfather paradox.

It's like a dream, you think as you lie beside him, staring at the face on the Artex ceiling.

There's a bit near the window that was chipped by the stepladder when Timothy was wallpapering last year. When the bedside lamp is on, it throws peculiar shadows over that patch of ceiling, and you think it looks like one of those Greek tragedy masks.

You draw your gaze from the shadow face and glance at Puss. He's laid on his side, snoring gently. His mask is still on the floor. Carefully, you reach down with one arm and feel for it, but all you can find is his jacket. It's heavier than you expect.

Gingerly, you climb out of bed. Puss rolls over into the hollow left by your body, but he doesn't wake. You stare at him for a long time, studying his face. You wonder if you should take off his glasses, but you stop yourself. You think you now know his name, and you're scared at what you might find beneath those smoked red lenses.

You walk quietly into the bathroom, taking his jacket with you. Inside, you shut and lock the door, and sit on the loo. Inside his coat is a parcel, brown paper bound with string. You try to untie it, but it's tight, and strong too. You stand up, open the cabinet above the sink, and take down the nail scissors.

Snip, snip, the string is free. A hardback book slips from the paper to the floor.

You hold your breath for a minute, maybe longer. It feels longer. It's probably just seconds.

You know you won't find all the answers in here. You think you know some of the answers already, anyway.

Another deep breath. Then you open the book.

A strand of hair, red like yours, sellotaped to the first page.

A rust-coloured stain on the next page.

On the third, a photograph. It's you, in a wedding dress, standing beside Timothy.

You flick to another page at random. Another photo. You, in a hospital bed, bleary-eyed, holding a baby.

Another page, another photo. You, your hair cut short, on the beach, paddling your toes in the sea.

The wedding dress is low-cut; you're naked in the hospital bed with only a blanket to cover you; you're in a yellow bikini on the beach. Your shoulders are visible in all the pictures, and there's no hint of a scar.

You touch your stomach. You can feel his seed inside you.

Now you know that he's only just started his journey, following the family way, back through his bloodline. He'd always planned to stray. He's creating his own way, off to kill his father and his grandfather, down through the generations, a paradox, an impossibility, determined to ensure his own survival whatever the cost.

It's simple when you think about it. If his father ceases to exist, all he has to do is make sure the woman who will one day become his mother still falls pregnant.

And you know where he's headed next.

He's already dressed when you return to the bedroom. You watch him put on his mask. You even fetch his crutch from the den for him. You just want him out of your flat. It's not like you can change anything.

You can't change anything, he tells you.

You're coming back, you say matter-of-factly. Emotionlessly.

What?

You said earlier, you said I'd see you again in a few months.

He looks away. Well, he says, kind of.

I won't answer the door to you, you tell him firmly. I won't let you in.

You already have, he replies. Look, I've gotta go. I've an appointment at a film studio in London.

Then, just before the world jolts, the masked man bows low and says: Merry Christmas, Mam.

You're in hospital. There's no Timothy, only the scar.

And your new-born son.

You lean close, kiss his forehead, whisper: Hello again, Oedipus. Know what? You look just like your dad, you little freak, you.

EARL

Laurie Blauner

Laurie Blauner is the author of six books of poetry, three novels, and a novella. She received an M.F.A. from the University of Montana. She has also been the recipient of several grants and awards including an N.E.A., Seattle Arts Commission, King County Arts Commission, 4Culture, and a Gap Grant. Her work has appeared in The Nation, The New Republic, The Georgia Review, *and many other magazines. A poetry chapbook was recently published by dancing girl press and a new novel called* THE BOHEMIANS *was recently published by Black Heron Press.*

Her web site is www.laurieblauner.com.

EARL

WHEN I WAS YOUNG

EARL WAS EYE TO EYE WITH ME. WE WERE THE SAME SHORT HEIGHT. We were different ages then, a teenager and an adult. But we were the same person. I believed Earl was just some extension of me. Sex had happened again a few more times. I had knocked at his house. If he was alone he let me in and he was silent afterwards as though he were busy, speaking without words to someone else, someone invisible. I had my suspicions. But now it was Sunday, we were outside the church and not allowed to touch in public. It was cold, even in my parka, it felt like a metal knife against my heart, my arms. Surfaces of the ponds were all white and powdery and hard. Clouds looked down on us and shivered. Winter seemed to stand still with its ice and snow, quiet as death. Water was frozen into long teeth hanging from tree sleeves and roofs. Part of Earl's church with a window, houses with a chimney, a bit of gravel from the road peeked out from the thick whiteness, the surrounding hardness and cold. As though we were partially blind, seeing only some of what was in front of us. My breath hissed a white vapour that almost touched Earl's nose like some veil spread out between us. I swallowed hard and rubbed my gloved hands together. My mama was in the car with the engine running, long tails of warm smoke fuming from the tailpipe.

I held one black glove tucked in the other hand, feeling the bones accordioned together under the thickly padded plastic. 'I love you.' It came out small, childish. I cleared my throat.

'You want too much from me.' His words were frozen into a pale fog in the air, then faded. The ragged wind pulled down the sky, a curtain it would shred.

'I need you.' And I wanted to run scraps of his hair through my fingers, feel the blizzard of his body, his stunned muscles under his taut skin. I couldn't touch him. He touched me instead, with the tip of his brown suede glove, under my eye where tears were collecting before they could reach my mouth.

'And what about them?' He nodded over his shoulder.

'Who?' Now I was sniffling. I could see blurred white trees, hurried faces like snapshots taken while the person was moving too quickly.

'My congregation. The Korrys, the Jacksons, the Chapmans. Poor Mrs Chapman with her husband recently gone.' He blew into his hands balled up in front of his chin. He looked into the cool, hard, infinitely white landscape.

'And pretty Evelyn Cornwall?'

'Yes. Even Evelyn Cornwall.'

I told him the truth. 'I don't care about them.'

A small laugh. 'Yes, but I'm supposed to.'

'Don't you love me?' And I thought that he must. Somewhere I believed he already did. His familiar handsome face was smudged.

'We'll talk about that another time.' And he turned. I could see the hair standing up along his neck, the top of his jacket jewelled with snow, the back of his hat steaming as though his head was too hot. The white ribbons curling and then fading.

I stopped breathing. Then I knew I was crying, the tears trembling, jerking, cold down my cheeks. I was a pencil of ice that fell, glinting, fractured into a thousand pieces against the ground. I wondered what it would be like to die. Nothing was worse than this. Sick of Earl not letting me love him. As if it was a choice. Like my father. Just last month. After Earl and I had met three months before. Papa was going out the door wearing plaid pants, a brown tee shirt with a beer bottle printed on the back, his hair thinning into a triangle at the top of his head.

'Where are you going?' I was sitting on the sofa with a schoolbook open but not reading or writing. Thinking about other things.

'To the grocery store for cigarettes, orange juice. Why?' He was half out the door.

'Can I come with you?'

'No, I'll just be a minute. Do your homework, Chloe, and you'll be the smartest one in this family.'

'Take your coat. It's starting to get cold.'

'Naw. I'm not cold.'

'I love you, Papa.' As if I knew.

'Yeah. Okay. Bye.' And he went out the door. The triangle of his hair pulsed, growing smaller, swallowed down the street. Then the distant gun shots like a car's flat tyre, in someone else's life. I didn't even think about them, not until later.

'It wasn't you,' Mama said later. 'Don't take it personally.' Her hair, empty blonde stalks, a collapsed garden nearing winter, her tight red sweater snaked with blue thread around her breasts, down her arms, another skeletal body thinly engraved against hers. 'Some marriages are hard to explain.' The slight southern accent sewn through her words made them seem thick and lovely.

At that time I'd thought of myself as the by-product of an unhappy marriage. But now there was Earl. There was history. I watched snow unmoored from the trees, dropping heavy, still wet, exhausted in a human gesture. My gloves were damp. Water stung my eyes. I could hear snow and ice crunching under my boots like fresh, crispy vegetables. The cold seared through my coat, pants, and socks, keeping me alert, awake to my pain, yet stumbling across the expanse of white resembling the exposed sheets on Earl's bed, covers folded down, waiting for our happy bodies. Mama's old car was laboriously breathing, chugging tendrils of smoke. I thought it would be warm, comforting inside. And I thought about death, how easy it would be to slip into, just a step into the wrong neighbourhood: strangled trees; a lost toupee; falling through ice and arriving at yourself; after a sunny day night coming, eclipsing the world.

I didn't know what death was. Or God. I was sixteen and alive then. I wanted Earl's boiling body against mine again. I wanted all of him. I wanted him to have all of me. The rest was meaningless.

Water puddled on the tips of my boots. Even the church seemed to shiver. I held the car door open, the rusted metal handle cold and stiff through my glove. The air was chill and sharp at my back and warm and blowing at my face. I could feel the complicity of the vast, white landscape behind me as though it was whispering advice, so accustomed to hiding everything. It was as though it wanted to concur, to help. I listened. I sneezed over the top of the car into the infinite snow and ice. I realised that they couldn't stop me from loving them, Earl or my father, dead or alive. I wasn't even sure I could stop myself.

'Get in the car, hon.' My mama, Daphne, with her too red lipstick, her tight sweater with martini glasses knitted into the design, the olives, green balls of wool, nestled in the creases.

Inside the air blowing was dull and warm with the delicate scent of a fruity perfume. Rivulets of water trickled down my boots into the mat. The cold slowly leaving, slinking into the back seat like another body. The new heat hugged me. See, it's easy enough to switch, I told myself. And then I noticed my gloves over my eyes, my eyes unravelling, squeezing into them.

'Now, now, honey.' Mama was patting my thigh, my pants, the deep green balls were bouncing along her arm.

I looked up through the frozen windshield, took my gloves off. An ocean of snow spread out before us. Inclining into high areas and gradually falling like a white scarf carelessly draped over trees, hills, houses. I felt lost, no visible road, no way to leave, each direction looked almost the same. As though every street would lead to one identical place. The side windows were icy, melting, distorting the white landscape into twisting waves. The sky smeared like a watercolour with too much water. The clouds ran smack into the ground. The world was blurring. I couldn't separate myself from it. It felt unnatural, hot in the car.

'Did you tell him?'

The question hung over the blower, tittering, about to tumble into my lap. I hated her then, her careless make-up, her red fingernails poised, impatient on the steering wheel. As though she had someplace to go, as if she wasn't suffocating on all the whiteness. A widow. The martini glasses empty, silly and cartoonish, drained except for the bouncing olives. I couldn't take her seriously.

'No.' I watched the last bark of a tree vanish. Mama put the car into gear and I wondered where we would go. All the roads seemed to lead to snow and more snow. I was waiting for the earth to heave, to upturn the snow and ice, for it to gather into piles, revealing the structures, the trees and animals, the men again.

Earl

* * *

Mama was going out now, late and not coming home until early morning. I didn't leave the house, not even for school. She said, 'Education hasn't done me much good either,' as she made her way out. I would peek at her through a crack on my bedroom door when she came home. She looked smeared, messy, as though she'd been through a rainstorm before coming back to our front door. Her sweaters were limp and pulled, her skirts hung on barely attached to her hips, or as if someone very distracted had zipped them. Her make-up from tubes and compacts, bottles, and brushes appeared spilled across her features. Her high heels dangled from her feet wearily. Before she left she would spend over an hour getting ready. She would make herself perfect in order to be disassembled. When I finally asked her about it she claimed, 'I'm a hostess. Somebody needs to make money now.' I didn't really want to know.

In the mornings I'd leave her toast that I heard her pushing around her plate, orange juice that she sipped once or twice and then allowed to get warm and sticky. Neither of us was hungry.

A week went by and then another. The snow glimpsed our lives and left. Wind rummaged in the trees, then twitched the clouds into hurried shapes, and moved on. I never knew what to wear. Each morning I draped my clothes side by side, spread out on every surface in my bedroom. My invisible earlier selves lay flat and empty all around me. Like some child's tea party without the tea. I wasn't sure they would fit me anymore. I was unfit. I ended up wearing the same long, rustling, spacious skirt every day anyway. Jade-coloured, entreating Spring to begin. I alternated shirts, a lemon one with the sun embroidered in red stitching on the back, and a black one with Brother's Wine stencilled in white. All the days seemed the same, helplessly running into one another like beginners at a dance class. Lurching and comically familiar. I'd eat cereal early. Then quietly return to my bedroom and read until Mama woke up. I reread *Green Mansions* by W.H. Hudson with Rima, the mysterious bird girl, and Abel, a man of the world, unable to be together. A few Nurse Ames and Nancy Drew books. The only books in the house. School no longer interested me. Sherry called, 'I thought of you today while I was smoking a cigarette with Carrie. She's really nice, you know. Not all stuck up like we thought. So when are you coming back to school?'

'I can't. I have mono.' It's what Mama had told anyone who asked. I complied. Erasure was the centre of my life. I thought about making myself over, reinventing myself in another town or city one night while watching Mama rub a rich emollient into her skin, dabbing some fruity perfume on her wrists, the back of her knees. I thought: I can look different, be different, smell like someone new – then will he love me? Later when Mama pushed the door open, needing mending as usual, I realised I didn't have to be so desperate, that I would always have Earl.

I kept the schedule of the lovelorn, sulking after lunch, writing letters I would never mail even though they became more resigned. I kept them in my underwear drawer. They were beginning to say things like 'I can wait. You can't disappear in me.' and 'I understand the push and pull of the ocean.' I wasn't sure if they were for Earl or just reminders to me.

I made dinner for the two of us, spaghetti or a frozen dinner, and I sat in front of the television, the flickering light lively against my clothes and the couch. Images swirled against my shoulders, moving up to my face, embracing me. Words rushed over me like a river. On television they could argue all night, stun one another, be comical until the end of time. I missed the talk when I slept. And I would turn it off when Mama left, swaying in her new high heels, staining the air with a fresh application of perfume. Upstairs, in my bedroom, Earl's scent lingered on my unwashed shirts and my one skirt hidden behind my closet. I lay on my bed, the chintz bedspread with flowers, the doll I pushed to the floor. I blindfolded myself with Earl's smell. The wrinkled clothes bundled against my own clothes, across my breasts, my stomach, my lips, an empty body on top of my own, a phantom, an intimacy I created for myself. The bundles of clothes reminding me of the time he lay over me, pulling both my lips into his mouth at the same time. He held my lips between his teeth until I couldn't breathe anymore. The teeth marks were swollen, little ridges that faded before I went home, that told me how much I'd learned.

Then the phone rang. I ran into the hallway, spilling my clothes onto the floor. 'Hi.' I expected Sherry.

'You can come over at any time.'

'How about soon, tonight?'

'Do you know who this is?'

'Of course, Earl.' As if I couldn't recognise his voice.

'You haven't been to church in weeks. The Jacksons were asking about you.'

'What about you?'

'I've heard rumours.'

'We can talk about them. We can make some up of our own.'

'Very funny, Monkey.' And I heard a click. He didn't like talking on the phone.

I scissored the air with a terrible urgency. My joy echoed in the hall as though the house was completely empty. My little screams, came back to me, rang again in my ears. The furniture flared against the sound, trying to absorb it. I held my skirt in my hands in fistfuls and danced. My socks nibbled the wooden floor in quick steps. He called me "Monkey" after I climbed to his roof one night in the Fall to cover a leak into the bedroom. Lying in his bed, his back glistening with sweat, Earl was poking my navel when I had felt the voiceless tap of water along my hipbone. The kisses skimmed across me, rolling onto his white sheets, plaiting into a long dark stain. We tried to ignore the dripping.

'So, Earl, have you done this much before?' Not that I really cared about the others. It just sounded so adult.

'Really only a few times. Sometimes someone unmarried threw herself at me, but then she would regret it the next day.' He was sliding up toward a pillow on his stomach. 'I always knew that by the next Sunday it would be over.'

I tried to think who he was talking about from the congregation. Evelyn Cornwall came to mind, rich and beautiful. Widowed, with long, red hair. 'And lately?'

'Before you, there wasn't anyone for a long time.' He rolled over onto his back, his burly chest with its tangled hair, his penis curled, soft and delicate, nesting along his inner thigh, something loose and pink like the unoccupied sleeve of a sweater. 'Now there's you.'

Sex to me was a metal staircase I climbed slowly, learning all the steps without thinking, savouring the ringing my soles made against the metal.

The damp, steady leak detonating against my skin, gathered into a puddle between us. 'I'll go out and put some plastic over that hole.'

'It's too bad I can't just fly up there, fix it with a wing and a prayer.'

'No, I'm serious. I'll fix it.' I was getting dressed, pulling my skirt over my wet hip, scrambling into the kitchen for a plastic bag, a stapler. Outside the horizon was whitened, tired, translucent, a colour between

moths and pale birds. Drained. I pulled my skirt above my knees, my heart fluttering then clanging against my ribcage, ready for flight. I hoisted myself up a trellis, covered the leak, balanced on the shingles in my collapsed, beige socks. Afterward I let myself down, swinging by my arms, hanging onto the gutter, the wooden slats of the trellis. Back in Earl's bedroom he didn't seem to have moved. I removed my clothes, lay in the damp bed. There were no more leaks. I smiled.

'My little monkey,' he said.

I sat at Mama's dressing table. The scalloped, wooden edges were painted avocado green and rimmed in gold. A rounded mirror loomed over it etched with vines and flowers. There were three drawers on each side and the surface was littered with coloured bottles and tubes and powders, some spilled in trails across the top. Corners resembled small abstract paintings. A set of light bulbs lined up in half a circle underneath the mirror's edge. I pleaded with my reflection. *This is where Mama transforms herself.* I waited for the make-up to reveal what to do. I knew how to apply make-up deftly but tonight I wanted to make the same old moles and pockmarks disappear, bury the stray hairs, make my face perfect. An incantation. I could see Earl's hands stroking the soft part of flesh at my cheeks. Everything would be wonderful again. I swirled the dropped powder and oozed gel into whorls, trying to divine my future, and then I began. I switched on the extra lights and applied mascara, eye liner, foundation and then a powder that smelled sweetly of honey. A streak of blusher that was almost used up, a thin pumpkin coloured layer stuck to the bottom of the compact. I opened and unfurled ten lipsticks before I settled on "Burgundy Rose". I stared and stared. It was Mama's face, younger, no creases or lines, no hints of a furrow between my eyebrows like Mama or her hair like a sudden blonde hurricane when she returned home. I couldn't ignore the face in the mirror. I widened my eyes, downturned my reddened mouth, filled my cheeks with pockets of air without ruining my new make-up. Mama still looked at me. Night soaked the room, collapsing in large chunks under the furniture in Mama's bedroom, except for the intense light at the table. I wondered if she would notice or if she would care, exhausted and turned inside out when she came home. Preened, I thought, slick and sophisticated. I viewed my new face from forty five degree angles. I smiled, bursting to see Earl.

I slipped into one of Mama's parkas, figuring she wouldn't mind. I disappeared into her. The stars formed a collar at the back of my neck as I left the cold, empty house. I thought the body changed so easily that we needed to pin it down to one version at a time. I was what I believed Earl wanted, beautiful, desirable, sexy in Mama's low cut blouse, my tight black pants. I had never tried so hard before except when I'd briefly thought about death, the electric radio in an extravagantly long bath, or the plain and simple razor blade across a wrist like lightning cutting night into two halves. I'd seen the thin, spidery lines across Mama's wrist that she refused to discuss. Since then I've learned about the body, the frail way we sleep against pillows, our dreams pouring into the pillowcases and bed sheets. Shaking them out in the morning. I couldn't breathe in the old junk car that we still kept around. Underneath the peeling, grey paint was rust, the engine frothing black smoke, my breath whitening against my cheekbones in the cold still contained in the car, the seats thickening then thinning, losing their springs. I was afraid of losing Earl, again. I felt like I'd aged ten years since I last saw him. I watched the white spine of the road, the night sky churning up stars. I couldn't have been happier, my future unrolling in the distance, heaped into the small house I turned toward, the light inside broken into little square windows that rested outside, on the ground. I clicked off the motor and car lights, parking in a hidden clearing surrounded by trees near his alley. I could see Earl's shadow pass through his kitchen window toward his back door. Then the door flung open and Earl stood on his steps with the light flooding behind him, pushing him out the door, toward me. I couldn't help myself and I ran toward him. I hoped none of the neighbours would see. My arms ribboned behind his shoulders and he removed them, placing them at my sides like something he'd never seen before or wanted. I looked at his too-serious face.

'Come inside,' he said.

And I thought: this must be a dream. I'm really at home waiting for Mama, smelling Earl. His garment of flesh, his smile escaping at the sight of me. He couldn't help it in that other life. Then I felt my feet on the solid stone steps into his house. The beginning of rain, no, it was my heart against my ribcage, thumping. My ears were full of confetti and my arms were going in different directions. I walked into the house and part of me, my arms, wanted to return to the car. I was confused. The shape of his voice seemed wrong. I wished I was dreaming at my own house. But I was in Earl's house. I could feel his kitchen table nudging me as I passed by. The dusk thick behind me, outside the door, enveloping my old car. Inside, I had memorised each piece of furniture, every space, wanting to come back, remembering. Everything was blazing with light, every detail, every nick and scar too visible on a chair or table. As though it was a too real dream. My stomach was spinning.

'I need to sit down.' I fell into his torn, tired chair. I felt like crying but I didn't want to ruin my make-up, diminish the effect it took me hours to achieve. I was locked out even when he allowed me into his house. I was as weary as a child stuck in the back seat of a moving car with her sobbing face plastered to a window, the world going by and I couldn't stop it.

'Would you like something to eat or drink?' He was occupying another chair, his legs spread, his serious face framed by black suspenders, his hair lifted, a dark stain.

My own hair seemed full of itself, a froth of trees. My small, wilting face nestled between my half-exposed breasts. The stars were outside, circling, trying to find a good place to rest in the charcoal sky. I was a bouquet of flowers I wanted to give to Earl. I exhaled. 'No thanks. It's like 9 or 9:30 at night.'

'I'd heard rumours that you're not eating or drinking.'

'That's not true at all.' I patted my stomach with both hands without thinking. He looked at my too tight black denim pants, the zipper taut, exposed, grinning with its square metal teeth.

'I'd also heard other rumours.'

I wanted to dare him to say them out loud so I would feel exposed, ashamed. I could see the brown mole at the top of my left breast heaving itself at my neck. I could see my cuticles stained with blue ink and traces of pink blusher. My legs were crossed and I could detect every hard curve of my right kneecap beneath my pants in the too bright light. It all seemed so clear and uncovered. 'And?'

'I wanted to talk to you about them.'

'Why?'

'I need to know what's true and what's not. My congregation is talking.'

'So.' I had my own problems. Earl was one of them. Things never seemed to turn out as I hoped.

He smiled slightly. 'Don't you know, Chloe, that the wages of sin is death.' His suspenders seemed to lift with his grin.

I couldn't help laughing, too hard. Great guffaws that didn't seem to stop. Rolling waves of laughter that would calm down and then I would look at Earl's quiet, concerned features and begin again. A roller coaster. I was almost to a rest, then a suppressed giggle would work its way to explosion. I thought my pants would burst and I would become weightless. But to me death seemed more of an escape than a punishment at that time. Now I would say death was more of a transparent thing, clarifying my past, not hiding it. But that night I was uncomfortable that Earl had named it. I said it like a secret that had no power over him.

I started hiccupping and Earl finally held me in his arms. We sat in his chair, both of us. I was on his legs with my arms around his neck. He held me so that my breasts ballooned against his forearms, fleshy globes tucked beneath my chin. We were threaded into one another and then I began to cry. He rocked me. I stared at the small hairs at his neck, at the way his ear swirled like milk dropped into coffee and stirred slowly with a spoon, the circles reaching the edges of a cup. That was my world. I could lose myself in Earl's side. I could see every cut hair, every scratch and pore enlarged in the unremitting light. I was sniffling. I liked it when he called me "Monkey".

'Better, Monkey?' He stroked the back of my head the way I absentmindedly brushed away an insect on a chair arm, inadvertently killing it.

I nodded, nuzzling the intersection of bone that comes down from his ear and becomes his chin along the jawbone. I didn't want to return to my life with Mama, TV dinners, see-through dresses, wobbling high heels, sad dreams, pity thick and returning like memories. I lightly touched the elastic stream of his black suspenders tumbling down his shoulder. He held my hand.

'And about the other rumour?' He exhaled into my hair while still combing it with his palm.

I was gauzy. 'Yes, it's true,' I whispered, 'I'm pregnant.' I ran my hand through my tousled blonde hair, unburdened.

Earl leapt off the chair and I almost fell, steadying myself in mid-air and sitting again in the other chair. 'I should have been careful sooner.' He began pacing. 'I was distracted.'

I watched him gliding back and forth, caught up in the calamity of his thoughts. I looked down at the corners of the chair. I noticed pen marks etched into the varnish, someone's initials, EC, carved along the edge, the top of the letters peeking over, reminding me of naughty children. I was glad he'd forgotten me. I didn't want to make him angry. I glanced around the room. The shabby living room, the dented sofa, old wooden television, worn blue-grey rug, the thrum of too much light and still it was better than Mama's. His hands danced, his clothes flew by, barely missing me. I was thrilled to be near him, even if he was a jack-knife cutting the air in zigzags. He lit up the room, ferocious, crazy over the way things were, the way they just happened.

'How far along are you?' His eyes flashed, remembering I was there against the back of the chair.

'Not very. I'm not really showing.' I held my stomach as though it would be alive soon, walk away from me, grow up and become famous.

'You're sure you're pregnant?'

'Yeah, I saw the doctor.'

'So you don't have mono?'

'No way.' I thought I knew what he wanted to believe. I sank into the rigid chair. I knew my make-up was all cried out, washed and streaked. There were stripes of foundation and blue eyeliner splattered across the back of my hands. Mascara, lipstick and bits of eyeliner were at my wrists, dappling my chest, spots on the right side of Earl's neck. Parts of my skin resembled the surface of Mama's dressing table with its abstract paintings made of make-up. I must have looked a mess in my crushed sexy clothes, huddled into a chair. And after all that time getting ready. I was glad he wasn't looking at me, only at the walls. How could I ask him to care about me?

'How old are you now?' He almost spit out the words. He was a radio turned on too high, too shrill, the words cascading. He was excitedly rubbing his hands together, his pallid cheeks mottled with red spots.

'Seventeen.' I looked at his shoes, thick-soled, black, laces tied up neatly like lattice waiting for something to grow there, to be used. They took brisk steps back and forth, back and forth. They reminded me that he was older.

'I'll have to ask Daphne's permission.'

'For what?' I was alarmed that Mama would be involved with our relationship. She had slipped into that night life, erasing herself, dishevelled by darkness, by drinking, by men. I didn't see any of it happening, just the results.

'To marry you.' He stepped over to me and ruffled my hair as though it wasn't wild already. 'Silly Monkey.' And he smiled.

'Are you kidding?' And I smiled.

'No.'

I wondered if I really existed I was so happy. The bright light wrapped itself around me. I wanted to dance but I felt funny around Earl. My feet skimmed across the floor and I hugged him and he remained stationary and hugged me back. Fragments of shadows rested in our intertwined bodies, on his back, along the length of my arm. We leaned into each other, the light and dark, Earl and I, our bodies and thoughts all tossed together, a big stew. According to the doctor, the baby was the size of a twig. I had tried not to think about it but now, finally, I wanted all three of us together. I stared at the mascara-soaked skin stretched across my knuckles and for the first time wondered what the child would look like, surprised that it would actually come out of me. I turned to the fleshy part of Earl's ear, the short, cut hair leading down to the nape of his neck. 'No one will ever love you as much as I do.'

He looked at me and smiled. 'God works in mysterious ways.'

HIS OTHER SELF

The first time Earl was punished, he liked it. He knew he deserved the spanking from his adoptive parents for biting his father's leg when he was asked to finish his spinach at dinner one night. He was proud of the elaborate green circle of teeth marks on his father's beige pants, an odd frog coming to life on his father's calf. Mostly, he felt he deserved it for all the other things he'd done and had not been caught at. He learned to punish himself. He killed ants, by digging a small pit with a stick across, crushing the ones who didn't make it over into a brown tinged paste at the bottom. Then he would let the surviving ants crawl over him, their frenetic searching over his body, rushing anxiously on his skin, under his clothes. He hoped they would bite him. In his youth, if he said something wrong he wouldn't speak to anyone for days. He would sit placidly in front of his powder blue wall, on the corner of his neatly made bed, and look past his parents if they attempted to speak to him. They were invisible. Sometimes he would put stones and dirt in his underpants for transgressions. The invention of punishments became studied, more interesting than the crimes. If he didn't raise his hand fast enough for a math problem at school Earl would go home, wet his hand and hold it on the ice tray for several minutes. It reminded him to feel. They were such small punishments that no one noticed.

Earl believed sacrificing a piece of himself for a wrong was religious. "An eye for an eye". Just a variation. He thought of Chloe and her youth and he began to cross himself. He hadn't been thinking. He was in a trance, unaware of his hiccupping body. His mind was darting, chattering vividly about people from the congregation, money, what he needed to do the next day. He didn't need his mind at all when he was near her. Perhaps it had all been her fault.

Everyone in the congregation knew by now and didn't think it was a bad idea to get married, with the mistake of a child on the way, a soul leaning over and then entering the world. Mrs Myrtle said, 'People all over the world do it every day.'

'What?' Earl inquired, afraid married life held more sexual obligations than he'd heard from his parishioners. Afraid that white-haired Mrs Myrtle would describe some sex act in detail. But at least she hadn't gotten angry over Chloe and left the congregation as some others had done.

'Get married and have children.' She mumbled. He was a silly goose. And that, unfortunately, events didn't always occur in that order.

Evelyn Cornwall had gone up to Earl and held his hand a little too long and looked into his eyes. 'Even though I've never been married, if there's anything I can do to help, just let me know.' She flipped her long, red hair.

'A husband,' Earl said to himself and he conjured images from his counselling. The body transparent under a knowledgeable wife's hand. The consequences. Even "a father" with the constant vigilance, the protection, the branchless tree still trying to make leaves. The soft little person with their voice. Surrounding them with Earl.

Daphne, the mother, came, hips sheathed in brown, earthy polyester, her sweatshirt autumn leaves in velvet reds, yellows, and oranges stitched with gold. Her dangling earrings were lemony circles with a large round pumpkin coloured disk in the centre. 'It's about time you had me over.' She glanced at the shabby house and thought: *I'd hoped for something better.*

'Would you like some coffee or tea, Daphne? Would you like to sit down?' He offered her the chair he and Chloe first used to swallow each other up.

Her hair crackled like wheat in the sunlight. It slapped the back of the chair when she sat down. The hothouse colours bloomed against her ample chest, somehow amplifying it, making it seem larger. 'Actually I'll be glad to get her out of the house.' Her earrings twirled to the rhythm of her words, her heel tapped at her ankle repeatedly.

When Earl looked at her, he thought of a beetle, a hard iridescent shell reflecting all the sunset colours, armour with waving antennae at the head testing the air. The vulnerable, lacy wings tucked underneath and uncovered periodically like sexy underwear during a seduction. He found her beautiful, generous, colourful and too difficult. He thought of the young, hatched and wriggling from the jewelled parts, made from water, leaves, earth, and light. That they eventually metamorphosed into replicas of their parents. 'Why?'

'Because she spies on me. I come home from work feeling… exposed, you know, and everything and all I want to do is lie on my bed and get a little privacy.' She sat up straight and looked at him. 'But I can feel her eyes on me from the moment I enter the house, following me. Waiting for me to do something wrong or strange or something. I just want a little rest.' She sighed.

'So I take it this means you approve.' He was pouring some tea into a cup before the kettle had a chance to whistle. He sat down opposite her.

'She's carrying your baby, Earl,' she said seriously, 'and that means a lot.' She fidgeted with her red fingernails, anxiously tapping the table, the sound imitating the hearts of large birds. Petulant that the conversation didn't involve her numerous problems. 'I'm glad she finally told you.' She was glad that Chloe wasn't mooning around the house in her drab petticoat anymore.

He smiled to himself. 'Actually I had heard some rumours.' He sipped some tea. 'How are you doing, Daphne?'

'I'm tired.' She touched the teacup to her lips briefly and then put it down. 'I'm looking for something I lost a long time ago. But I'm in love again.' She thought of all the men who had shivered between her legs, apparitions who zipped up their pants and left. They had stared at her intently while she was serving drinks or dancing, but afterwards, after the money and her body that they could reach through, they couldn't look her in the eyes. She had become suddenly invisible to them. 'He works at the club too. He's younger, he's fun. His name's Dan.' It was easy to confess to Earl with his quiet, compact face.

'Does Chloe know?' His hair an upright field stretching around his head.

'No. Unless she knows from spying.'

There was silence. No sound at all except Earl occasionally stirring his cup with a shiny spoon, distilling his features onto the surface, blending into the tea again. Daphne could actually hear Earl breathing after a few minutes. It sounded like the wind doing strange things to leaves, small sighs. Daphne began kicking the leg of the table, jostling it, as the faraway light waltzed along the window sill, stopping, looking at the two people with curiosity.

Earl stood up. 'So Chloe and I will be married next week and I can count on your blessing.'

'Done,' said Daphne, standing, the sunset coloured clothes matching the parasol of evening thinly spread over the horizon at the window. The fiery earrings knocking her jawline. 'My new son-in-law.' She kissed his cheek leaving a bloody smear of lipstick, a small cut. Her palm was warm against his forearm for a moment. She teetered out the front door into the near darkness, her high heels rhythmically clattering along the walk.

Earl wondered what purpose anyone had for him. He asked again and again. 'I am listening,' he said at the Eucharist, a blue opalescence scattered in red light from the stained glass windows. The chalky taste of a wafer descending the back of his throat, coating his tongue. The crimson wine ebbing and flowing like some stained sea, accustoming itself by darkening in the melancholy light. The religion didn't matter, for once. Only the response. 'I want to know,' he said during hymns at another church, the wooden pew bouncing along its length because of the restless child half way down. He didn't mind being a supplicant, a part of the audience, on the receiving end of the sermon. Things change, he thought, but I just can't stand His silence, His turning away.

God had spoken to Earl a few times in his lifetime. Never when Earl wanted it or expected it but often when he was gathering Fall leaves with their rustling, dry, brown skins or walking along a river with its noisy current or watching a crackling fire to determine what would disappear next into the panic-stricken flames. Earl could barely hear the soft voice. He had to listen closely. He didn't understand the words completely. It was 'Eat an apple and you'll be left with the seeds,' or 'What is a ghost story?' or 'On a hot day the shade is tempting.' That was what he thought he'd heard. One day it was 'become a preacher' and he did. That was a calling loud and clear. But often the sentences seemed like translations that he couldn't decide how to apply to his life. Now he wanted a sign, no matter how esoteric. And this time perhaps he would get a chance to talk back.

He remembered his new parents' dog when he was a child. He'd sat on his bed quietly for days, not speaking, the old poodle would curl at his feet snoring. Earl watched the coiled, whitish fur around the dog's ribs rising and falling, her head tucked under a darker paw. The sound like water dripping, raspy sometimes, then growing softer. Somehow soothing. He would listen intently for other voices hidden there as though the snoring was simply a pretext for a deeper meaning. But in the five more years the dog lived, he never heard whatever it was he hoped to hear.

Chloe showed up with Daphne at his church one Sunday and she'd been insistent after that, always wanting to talk to him, but not having enough to say. Earl tried not to think about sex when he was young, but something sensitive and urgent simmered in his muscles, knocking his knees, pounding out a surprise. He would daydream about a classmate's curved lower lip, a girl's moist palm against her thigh that left a wet imprint, a red haired girl's shirt whose button slipped out of place showing a pale clot of breast. Everything was stolen. Without thought or intention. Then there was the whore. A bully at school said that he had already paid for her. 'Go to her house after school or else you're a big Homo.' Earl reluctantly went and her bleached blonde hair waltzed around her head like a halo, her watery blue eyes were tired, stagnant when she opened the door. Inside, she put down her cigarette near a torn, flowered couch and opened her terrycloth robe to Earl. A bony, saddened body leaked out that he immediately scrambled over. She exhaled smoke. He was done in time for her to take another puff from her cigarette.

'Where's the money?' she said, stretching out a scrawny hand.

'I don't have any, but I'll get you some tomorrow.'

'Get out of here, you little shit. Jumping on me like that.'

She chased him out the door. The boy from school was laughing outside. Earl swallowed, turned beet red. At home he slipped $20 from his father's wallet. The next day he knocked on her door after school.

'The little shit,' she said, wings of blonde hair at her head, smoke confusing her face, a thin dress with faded roses.

'Thank you,' he said politely to her hips nibbling the seams of her dress but he knew he was afraid of her.

Earl tried gravel in his shoes, small burrs in his hair, then no sex until after he became a preacher. Yet then he began to wonder if a lot of money could bring him happiness. He wondered if attractive Evelyn Cornwall was happy. Feeling his heart beat quickly, parts of him growing redder, anxious, someone else always disguised as himself.

Before Chloe was supposed to arrive, Earl scoured his cupboards, searched his dresser drawer, spilling clothes over the sides, found the bottle tethered to the serpentine, metal pipe slithering underneath the sink. Just a small one, Earl thought. He poured the colourless liquid halfway in the Goofy the Dog glass. Goofy's black lined caricature was submerged, imperceptibly drowning in the glimmering liquor. Earl picked at the bottle's colourful label until a woman's miniature head was partially peeled off. The glass sweated under his fingers like hard skin, a continuous round surface, never-ending. There was no scent, no heavy liquor smell, so Earl thought of lilacs, a sweet, thick odour to go with the drink. He tilted his head and poured all the glass's contents down his throat. Goofy looked empty, alone, bored on the table. One more, he thought, to placate Goofy, and he filled the glass again to the top and the dog floated there looking above Earl with his big, sad eyes. Don't worry, Earl wanted to say, and emptied the glass. He cleaned it and returned Goofy to his rightful place. He pulled the tattered label off and underneath was rough, damp paper still stuck to the unknown bottle, a shore holding the sea, a container holding the contained. A lovely ocean he contemplated as he turned the bottle sideways, thinking of waves. He wedged it back under the sink.

His body extended itself vertically, the kitchen incongruous with its distant drawers and corner. The room recoiled. It made him think of the soul losing the body. Thinking: *Is that all I was?* A frayed washcloth hanging from a sink faucet, a lopsided kitchen cupboard, a lampshade when touched that orbited a light bulb. He felt the puddle of warmth in his stomach. He glowed. His fingers were delicate, fragile, useless. The room didn't want to stay still. Always one step away. The way he would remember someone looking just a little different. He stepped outside, scouring the cold ground outside the house, sitting for a moment and watching light spill from his kitchen window, the bare-chested trees. A doughy-faced neighbour pulled the shade over her window. Earl plucked a scraggly weed and brought it into the bright kitchen and put it into Goofy and filled it with water. The water swirled with silt and Goofy looked overwhelmed. A small purple flower at the top, leaves the size of confetti. The water sloshed back and forth. Even when he placed it on the kitchen table, it seemed to be galloping across the room. He breathed in too much air. His hands collided nervously. His feet became tangled in his chair. He was tired, tired of everyone's problems, tired of hearing them all. His life seemed composed of bits and pieces of everyone else's lives. It was time for him to finally live his own.

Chloe knocked. It echoed loudly. Earl felt the few minutes it took for him to respond. He was jellied into slow motion, every gesture took on the importance of ballet. Chloe was already smiling. Her clothes were too large, as though she planned to grow into them or lose herself within them. Earl wanted to guess where the different parts of her body were hidden, an arm tucked near her waist or a knee closer to the floor than he might imagine. Her long flowered skirt draped against a calf, an abstract sketch of her body's outline. Her blonde hair folded against her skull like paper. She was so young it seemed that she took up just a small corner of the room. Earl would have to hold her to keep her from slipping away.

She went and sat on his lap. 'They're not sure who to blame. You or me.'

'Maybe we can keep them guessing.' He stroked her hair as he tried to calculate all the income he would lose. It was lifeless, inanimate between his fingers, unlike Chloe, who was quick to run toward anything that interested her. His hand insisted on the length of her skirt.

She placed his palm just below her waist. 'This isn't just about us anymore.'

The roundness of another body growing there, hard, smooth, circular like newly formed bone. It was protected. He wanted to reach through her and pick up the tiny child, hold it to the light and appraise it. See who the child would grow up to become. 'It's just that there's more of "us".'

'I want promises.'

And Earl kissed along her hairline, drowning out most of her words. 'Never happens...' the bulging veins at her neck, 'whatever,' and her hair surrounded him, buried him, 'mad and frail,' he was along a tense shoulder, his lips blistered, 'leave.'

Then she laughed, bouncing his head on her collarbone. 'Thanks for the poor, pathetic flower.'

'I knew you would like it.' He extended his arm in the weed's direction. He lost his balance for a moment, embraced her more tightly. He raised her arm as if it was his arm, surveying the savaged fingernails. 'These are more real than we are,' he said.

She kissed him back, his lips trembling. 'You are a little off today.' She clasped her wrists behind his head.

A hand was in his hair. He thought about the woman's dark hair and large dark eyes on the label of the bottle, the long nose, how she peeled off into nothing. There was no dark hair on the woman he was kissing.

'You are really strange tonight.'

'There are worse things to be.' It was then that he lost himself along her neck, below her ear. He didn't want to think. His hand trembled as it slid between her legs, over the small white scar from a childhood cut along her left thigh. *Too many people are there*, he thought when he reached the end of skin, the beginning of bone and soft hair. *Am I really doing this?* he wondered as though he was under the sink with the bottle, not really with Chloe. The hunt for her body under the clothes. He pulled each piece out, discovering her changing limbs, yet thinking about his neighbour's doughy face, the woman with the dark hair. Her mouth nibbling along his stomach, his chest, then what was left of his mouth. And then it was too late.

Chloe, flushed, touched each one of his fingers. She was naked and dishevelled on the floor as if God had suddenly made her and dropped her there. He could see the slow curve of her belly, how her belly button was being pushed skyward, a whirlwind beneath it. The puckered hole where she had begun, a lake in the centre of her distending body. It reminded him of the wind, gathering disparate twigs, leaves, dirt, cellophane wrappers, petals, and dropping them in a pile at his feet.

'Us,' she said, her hands crossed on her belly.

What has been done? he wondered. *And who should be punished for it?*

The Family Way

* * *

The day of the wedding the weather was volatile, clouds convened over birdless trees and the earth was damp from rain. The sun felt flung across the sky. Now you see it, now you don't. It made its appearance. Earl thought of the tiny extra bones in Chloe suddenly snapping into place. Certain organs developing at certain times. And the sun, in its usual spot for 1 p.m., visible and warming and then receding behind the tedious clouds, trees, houses. Like a bride turning a corner, behind a building, realising her mistake.

Daphne was there in an elaborately beaded pink dress with a low neckline, her earrings pink and blue mobiles in baby shapes. Matching pink satin shoes. Earl's remaining congregation. Neighbours and families and more. Earl's adoptive parents weren't there. He hadn't spoken to them in years. Both were absences, one of silence and the other of a useless closeness. When Earl's mother kissed him goodnight as a child she seemed startled to feel his soft, warm skin against her lips. He could see her face in the vanishing light from the moon the few times she strayed into his bedroom. She was anxious to escape the confining, dark room. And he had felt sorry for her, for her uncomfortable attempt. And he could see Chloe, although it was considered bad luck, in the storm of her white dress, the lace crawling over her arms and neck, the chiffon tumbling down her back. The white satin pooling at her feet, lovely. Earl watched her flattened belly rise and fall with her breath. He could feel his heart buried in his body but bulging and hitting his bones, thumping out its own song, growing loud and large. Ticking. He never believed it would happen to him: marriage. Blood raining through his veins, pounding in his head, his suspenders bouncing against his jacket, his white shirt peeking out at him, across the landscape of his chest. It made him think of snow and whether that could happen today.

The older pastor who married them was an acquaintance, a colleague of his. The man's face at fifty was perforated with blemishes, his hair beginning to whiten as though it was tiring. Earl had let Chloe choose the man. Earl stood beside the tables draped in white tablecloths. Like God he was a stranger in another man's house, polite, uncomfortable near the dishes and casseroles. Clouds and a greyness shellacked all the white turning it a dull pearly colour. Then the sun would appear in fragments highlighting pieces of things, a collar, a corner of the tablecloth, a strip along Chloe's gown. Earl wondered about this man's experience of God but something in him stopped him from asking.

The two men shook hands.

'It's like a bowl,' the older man said, 'you pour a little bad weather in one side and it spills toward the other side then falls back again.' He reached into his pocket. 'A cigar?'

'No thanks.'

He lit the end of the cigar, smoke blending into the sky. 'Do you believe in superstition?'

'No, not really.'

'That's too bad because the Japanese believe a rainy day brings good luck in a marriage.' He inhaled and exhaled. 'Of course in Portugal the couple are supposed to hit one another on the head during the ceremony for luck. In the Philippines if there's a full moon you'll be blessed with children.'

Earl was smelling lemon in a nearby dish, listening to a guitar and morsels of conversation. His heart was slowing down, he was beginning to think that belief was locked in one room with the same furniture for years. And it couldn't be rearranged.

The pastor put out his cigar. He patted Earl on the back. 'I remember you as a young man, angry at your real mother for giving you up even though she was just a child. I suppose you still haven't gone to look for her.' Earl shook his head. 'Good luck, dear fellow.'

Earl wanted to crawl into a box and vanish. Earl bent over a hot casserole and dipped two fingers into the food and ate some. It felt good to not do what people expected you to do. He tried to remember the scar on Chloe's thigh, the angle of her cheekbones, the way she gasped before she laughed. He glimpsed her talking to Daphne a few yards away.

The trees bent down, thinking. Grass flattened. Earl wished it was over. And that's when he felt the bolt of grief for the self he had punished. He was as dizzy as the wind. Rows of champagne drinks lined the billowing tables and he drank several, leaving the glasses empty, out of order. The air seemed foggy and smudged, full of music and chatter. The low notes revealing a too human voice. A little bit of sun. Then the ceremony began. Chloe clasped her dress as the whiteness fluttered away from her. He repeated the already spoken words. Chloe's mouth moved.

'Your turn,' she whispered to him but the vowels unravelled, blew away.

Earl watched the red marks on the older man's cheeks rise and jump as he spoke, shifting. His collar tight and black, hiding his neck.

The inlaid pink beads of Daphne's dress rattled at Chloe's side. Earl's feet shuffled. Not now, he thought. I've just been introduced to my other self. He could taste cold metal in the air. Chloe nudged him with her bouquet. Earl closed his eyes. Leap, he thought, go ahead, let go. His heart circling itself. Daphne's nest of blonde hair nodded. He wanted to cry out, why me? But he turned to the older man and he said, 'yes.' Twice. The black necked man smiled in agreement and Earl heard the booming 'no.' It sounded familiar, distant. The wedding party was stung with a brief light.

TWISTER

I was thrilled to be in my own house, watching clouds peel back, light searching our cupboards and kitchen table for hours. At first I walked around the house, touching all the furniture, whispering 'mine' over every doily, fork, and lamp. Then I thought of them as friends filling up the long hours of the day, hungry for details I could maybe fix, a dent or a scrape, a scratch in a wooden table showing the wood's true, paler colour. History. I thought, yes, each body has a memory. I was growing bigger by the minute. My new orange dress was too tight, the elastic pushing the fabric to fullness like the rind of an orange. I could feel Little Earl kicking at night. Little Earl inside me, squirming sea-sick in the strange, fishy water, measuring the furnishings to see if they could hold us. When the lights went out at night, he would remind me that he was captive.

I didn't have to go to school right now. Earl said so. I waited for Earl to come home on those soft evenings when stars seemed to melt across the window. I came to understand Earl's presence by the things he left behind, his watch with its hands sweeping around its face, a leather belt, his shoes reconciled to his feet, notes to himself about sermons, his wedding ring with its gold hoop of light reflected on the bedroom wall. Earl was returning home later and later, involved with other people's lives. He cried out 'Evelyn' once in his sleep as if he was still working on her problems. No matter, I told the little one, absence makes the heart grow fonder. I missed Sherry, and our cigarettes with their orbits of smoke blending together, the mystery of boys and how to love. But I knew I was beyond that. I'd lay out Earl's black suspenders, his underwear, socks, pants, shirts alongside my outfits on the bed each day. Two empty people lying across the bedspread. An invisible family of cutouts waiting for one more, the little one. I still believed my love would make things perfect. But at night, when Earl turned his back to me, the covers burying him to his neck, his steady breathing on the verge of snoring, I lay still and awake and waiting for the familiar sounds I'd known all my life. The creak of a step, the blinds rattling, Mama in the middle of the night. It was just the little things that took getting used to. Like the morning after our marriage Earl said, 'You're supposed to make me coffee and get my slippers, I think.'

'I don't know but I'll do it.'

'I don't know either.'

It was a Friday night. A baked fish stripped to its skeleton lay weakly on a dish. Stars in a carousel of darkness outside. The overhead kitchen light looked at us upside down. I scraped the fish bones into the garbage, pulled at my special, expanding underwear, gripping my rear end. 'What is it in me that keeps little Earl alive?' I asked, grateful that Earl was doing the cooking, wanting a little conversation.

'We've looked at the books, Chloe. Many times.' Earl thought suddenly of a dark bar with writhing bodies and a warm, beery smell. 'There's the fluid and that he's attached to you.'

'He eats what I eat, right?' But I was really talking about other things too.

'Yes.' He was tired of being the teacher. He stood up, went into the living room.

I could hear his shoes on the old beige carpet, a muffled walk, an old man shuffling. I would have been talking to my friends, smoking cigarettes on a Friday night. We were aging and going backwards in different ways.

'Do you think he'd mind vanilla ice cream and watermelon?' I yelled to him in the other room, my voice loud and ringing, a bark.

'Don't worry about it.' And then more quietly. 'Can you come in here?'

'Do you think I could find watermelon ice cream?' My hipbones, collarbones, the tree of my chest and rib bones fattening, my knee and wrist bones all sinking into my thickening flesh. Soon I would have to dig myself out from my own body. But by then there would be two of us. I peeked around the door, my stomach bumping the frame then the wall in its unending expansion. The doughy smell of bread came from me. Recently the odours began: powdery, musky, sometimes sharp. The baby was a concept. I had showered a few hours ago, the water slippery on my limbs until the bulge of my stomach, then it shivered, rained down, and dripped slowly into the drain. I noticed my legs disappearing. I couldn't see the tops of my thighs. It was subtle like the regression of sunlight across a square of yard until it was gone and suddenly there was night. I didn't know that I would miss my body someday, unwieldy and pasty as it was, no longer completely mine.

Earl was leaning forward from the couch, the oblong antimacassar along the back, delicately sewn threads, made by a church member. I wanted to pick it up and hold it together. It seemed half there. 'How do I clean this?' I said, dangling it in the air like a large, dead insect.

'You don't.' He snatched it away, spreading it, a white ropy map, across the brown cotton sofa.

I hated it. His hair a dark wool cap tight on his head, the cooperative black suspenders bending, adapting to his every move, a short sleeved purple shirt. The light from a lamp, in the shape of an ice cream cone, flooded him. Watermelon ice cream. The rest of the room was still in darkness, the furnishings hidden.

'Come here, come in.' He waved at me.

His invitation reminded me I couldn't wait. It was like having Earl from the beginning of his life and watching him grow older.

Once I was ten years old and waiting for my papa at a train station. Mama was in the bathroom. A boy about eight got off the train and walked up to me. 'Can I ask you a question?'

'Yes,' I said, staring at a white scar zigzagging down his right cheek, a deep, white river with serrated edges that puckered the flesh around it.

He turned his perfect left side to me, 'Do you think I'm cute?' And then he turned his profile to show the damaged cheek.

'Yes,' I cried, but ran to my mama coming out of the bathroom. Her silver sweater looked like rain. I could spot her from far away, the silver threads sparkling, small, thin mirrors making light panic in splatters against the walls. I put my arms around her waist, feeling the frantic electricity pass into my plain yellow sweater, the static making the wool stand on end.

The body doesn't lie.

It was then that I spotted it. In the light, Earl, the sofa, a wooden coffee table and the game spread out next to it, on the floor. *Twister*, with its green, yellow, blue, red dots in rows. Earl was bent over the circles, smoothing the edges, the spinner was furiously swimming over the bright colours, a hand, then a foot and around again. It slowly came to rest limply between a hand and a foot. I could feel the little one paddle the flimsy membrane of my stomach, clamouring for a better position. Light doused my shoulders, warming sweat, a cold fever.

'That looks like fun.' I slipped off my flat shoes. The carpet underneath my bare feet was scratching my skin into clenched fists I could feel up to my knees. Like Earl's stubble in the morning. I shifted the weight of the baby from leg to leg, rowing, finally settling in the middle.

'Let's play naked *Twister*,' Earl said removing his white socks, his black shoes. He wiggled his toes in the carpet like animals. He kneeled down onto the white plastic. The spinner flew.

'Blue right foot,' he called out, as if ordering an alien body part.

Light fixed me in its gaze. I fitted my foot in the blue dot, noticing the scraps of red polish on my toenails. The *Twister* sheet was cool and slick under my foot. Earl and I had not touched each other in months. I didn't know whether it was the baby or not. I brushed my teeth and turned toward Earl in bed every night. I left minty kisses along his back, but he moved away from me and I woke up tired in the morning, sunlight washing over me and startling me awake in an empty bed.

'Green right hand.'

The dot leered at me as I bent against it. My hand splayed out over the blue circle. Earl spun twice for himself, the needle skipping before it stopped. In a sidelong glance I could see the purple smear of his shirt. I could feel our legs crossing at our knees. As I stooped, my check shirt bulged with my overripe breasts. I was happy to remove the shirt. Earl hit the arrow, which he moved between us on the plastic, with one finger. The purple shirt flew across the room, a banner in a swan dive, and landed draping itself across a tin waste can unsure whether to go in or out. I giggled. And off came the swelling skirt, dropped and kicked aside like a bedspread after a difficult night's sleep, and my heart lifted toward Earl. I laughed as he leaned into me, our cheeks brushing for a moment. The spinner jerked with the flip of his finger and then my breast rested on his warm back, our legs dancing, one arm flared out over another. My stomach was in the way, a planet without an orbit, without any place to go but down. Then I understood the moon.

Every slight change left us more naked and toppling over one another. My tiny mouth tried to find his nose near his knees. I was down to my blue cotton underwear. My legs were crossed and my hands spread far apart. Earl had on his suspenders and pants, one arm paralysed under me, the back of his thigh against me. I remembered his hipbones and pelvis, his fibula and ribs, a fence. His cropped hair tickled my lips. I missed his body, the surface of it unchanging, unlike mine. I felt his blood coursing down the back of his leg. I wanted to be seduced. We were scrambled against each other. I lay down with the smooth plastic on my side. I held out my arms, hovering over the multi-coloured, perfect circles, but Earl stood up. He looked at me, my thick thighs, erupting breasts, big stomach, big feet, big arms, big, big, big… He raised his hand as if he had just remembered something, wanted to make a point, and then he laid it on my shoulder a little too hard.

'Okay, that's enough now.' He walked away, into the kitchen's far square of light.

No one called. Not my friends. Some of the people from the church had left because of us and Earl's congregation was cut in half. Few of them called. It was September, six months after our marriage, I was due in two weeks. I lay in bed, alone, arms akimbo, my middle too heavy to lift by myself, a paperweight against the swerving sheets. My friends were back at school for a last year, after a summer of baby-sitting and cigarettes and boys. At the window above the metal ridges of the radiator I could hear warbling in the long, thin, dying arms of the trees. Paw prints of light were scattered, fading on the walls. The wings of birds motioned like waves through the glass. My flimsy nightgown barely covered my waist, melted along my breasts. It was a Saturday. Earl knocked and I pulled the sheets to my neck. He came into our bedroom. He sat along the side of the bed, the mattress indenting, remembering him. One of my legs slid toward him.

'After the baby I want to paint my nails and toenails matching colours.' I was thinking about all the things, afterwards.

'What colour?'

'The colour of a dark ravine.'

'How about plum-coloured?'

'Too fat and juicy and purple.'

'I know what will cheer you up. I'll get you dressed. Let's go for a drive.'

'Where?'

'How about Two Lakes?'

I nodded. He knew I'd go. Where else do I get to go now? I needed help just getting in and out of the bathtub. I almost looked forward to church on Sundays because he would dress me up, I'd waddle into church, try to get comfortable in a wooden pew with two pillows for help, listen to Earl attentively, say hello briefly to a few people and shuffle away. Some people were still uncomfortable about the situation, some offered help, but I always said no and sent them on their way. They gave up. I was glad, solitary. All I needed was Earl, yet Earl always sought God. Sometimes I'd walk into the living room and find Earl having a dialogue. Earl mostly seemed to be complaining or asking questions. I really didn't think about it much. I was more concerned about all the living I was just starting to do and the creature inside me, a little god.

Earl stuffed my legs into pants, pulling them toward my waist. He shook the candy-striped polyester from side to side as he lifted it. I picked out a baggy mauve sweater that draped over my abundant breasts, the slope of my stomach. I thought of how difficult oranges were to hold onto, always rolling someplace else. Earl had to put on my socks and shoes, looking tiny and insignificant when I glimpsed them. I remembered myself a few months ago, small and fallen. Suddenly I felt so much larger than Earl.

He levered me into the passenger seat of the car. I had to be angled to fit. The old Impala, a once white interior, sky-blue outside, covered with scratches and pockmarks. It even limped a little. But it got us to the lake in about an hour and a half.

We sat inside the car and looked at one of the lakes. Again he hadn't thought about what to do when we got there. But it was lovely. Sunlight was laughing in the bald trees, a patch of green grass lined the shore. The sky stared at itself in the placid murky water. A duck paddled across the distant surface. There was a thin, rocky beach with foam between the stones, all bubbly, then disappearing. It looked slippery and quiet.

'You can go out and walk around,' I said, unrolling the taped window. I was closer to the smell of decaying leaves, the damp earth warming from afternoon sunlight. It reminded me of a panting dog.

I watched Earl as he slowly strolled around the lake, picking up stones and throwing them into the water, the sinking making little ripples that faded below the surface finally. I wanted to go out, be with him, but I didn't want to hold him back. He was having one of his conversations. The two lakes joined in the distance behind some trees and some jagged land. I wanted to float between the two, let the water lift me.

Earl walked up to my car window, crunching gravel, like some beast chewing bones. He brought a pocket of warm air with him, a hand-shaped splotch of sunlight resting on his back.

'Hey, Monkey, have you ever been baptised?'

I thought for a minute. 'No,' I said. 'No, I never have been.'

'We'll have to do it tomorrow, after services. Here.' Before the child is born.

'Won't it be cold?' I glanced at the glittering lake.

'Yes.' The insect light flitted across the limbs of trees, sparkling in the air. 'But you can make it into what you want.' He got back into the car. 'We'll dress you warmly. Do you want to invite people?'

'No. Animals and their gods.'

Sunday, September 21st I didn't feel well. I skipped church, instead watching leaves raked off from thin trees by the wind humming against my window, pushing clouds around the sky. It looked lonely outside as though I could break through a layer of icy clouds and keep on falling with no one to catch me. I would fall through air.

I was curled up on the bed, my stomach eclipsing the flowered chintz bedspread, the sheets sinking underneath the climbing roses. I didn't bother to try to dress yet. Something hissed through me, a bird fluttering its wings. The wind was under my skin. I held on to my body.

I thought about loving someone so much who didn't love me. He cared for me as if I was a child. Dressing me, feeding me, careful. Concern reshaped his face, his features burrowing. I guess we shouldn't have done what we did out of love.

I closed my eyes, saw myself hurt, a warm red blanket of blood over the hill of my stomach from the kitchen knife I held to my own throat. The shock of Earl's face. Maybe the hint of love. I could give my body away. His hair bristling, it seemed lonelier, farther away. It seemed silly.

Earl knocked and entered, tiptoeing to the bed. 'Time to get dressed, sleepy head. How are you feeling?'

'Okay,' I said opening my eyes. I sat up. Let him dress me, my wool skirt that barely fit, the white sweater that was stubborn around my waist, inching higher, knee socks for warmth. It was piecemeal but nice enough. He took another print frock with a V-neck for later. I couldn't wait for fashionable clothes with zippers, form-fitting, with pockets that worked and hems that stayed straight. I was lopsided. I held onto his black suspenders with one hand as he pulled the wayward beige socks up to my knees. I was finally ready.

The phone rang downstairs and Earl scrambled to get it. I couldn't hear much, just the worried tone in Earl's voice on his end, but I couldn't decipher any words. It was about fifteen minutes and then Earl came back and his face didn't know what to do with itself. His mouth twisted into a new shape, his eyes darting nervously over everything, his forehead distorted into the lake's rippling movement. It convulsed.

'What's the matter? Someone from the church?' I could feel my hipbone making room, something nudging the surface of my belly like a school of fish, the butterfly wings of my pelvis spreading out.

'Yes, yes. Someone from the church. It's a big problem.' He spat out the words. He put his head in his hands. 'It's Evelyn.'

'What?'

He looked up at me. 'She thinks she's going to have a baby.'

'I don't think we should go today. I can get baptised another time.'

'No, no.' He wiped his eyes. 'It's important. Let's go.'

'Did she say who the father is?'

When we reached the bottom of the stairs he turned away, said, 'Go on out to the car. I'll be there in a minute. I need to go to the bathroom.'

I leaned against the car. It was a crisp, sunny day. My ribs rising and falling with my deeper, harder breath. I was engraved against the cold, metal door handle as I felt a wave inside me washing through. I held on for dear life. When it was gone, the top of my forehead was slick and I wiped it on my sleeve. Earl came out, his teeth clenched. I didn't want to say anything. I thought he might burst.

The drive out to the lake was silent. Empty trees studded the roads, small umbrellas of late weeds edged the white-lined highway. I was camouflaged in the deep blue car, a piece of sky moving through sky. A damaged piece of sky. Earl stared straight ahead. I tried to pat his hand but he removed mine. His hands melded to the steering wheel, one circular plastic object. His face distorted. Then the trees ended. There was a big ship of sky floating above the lake, bright blue, caught behind the sleeveless trees. My belly pulsed. Pain took apart the landscape. I'd focus on a branch, a bush, a distant house. I didn't say anything. I probably grimaced or shook or tensed up into a ball sometimes but Earl didn't seem to notice.

Earl got out of the car, walked along the ridge around the lake. He was talking to God. This time he was gesturing with his hands which I'd never seen him do before. First his palms up, extorting, then shaking, and then he covered his face. He went on and on for some time, walking and conversing and signalling, as if to the lake. At first I was interested and then water gushed from between my legs, perhaps in sympathy. I took my extra printed dress and wiped the seat underneath and the darkened white carpet under my feet. Warm liquid still dripped from my legs and I imagined the baby, a small piece of flesh with a sadsack tuft of my hair, tiny fists and feet whorling in the air, milky skin throbbing with blue rivers of blood. And I realised someday I would die and not be with little Earl. Not be able to pat his head, look into his eyes, little Earl's and mine. Could I miss him before I knew him? I realised I'd missed him for the past eight months. I hoisted myself out of the car with some effort, leaving behind a wet outline, a damp shadow of my bottom half. White becoming a stained darker grey, the interior messy, smudged, and peeling. There was a slight wind like breath inhaling. I cleared my throat but felt it was the baby clearing his throat. I could feel him working my skin, my limbs, just below, surfacing, getting ready and getting what he wanted. A nervous squirrel looked at Earl and hurried by.

'Are we ready?' I massaged my stomach with one hand, shutting the car door with the other.

Earl awoke from his reverie, came over and held my face between his hands. He started to speak, the words tangling, 'car accident,' 'truth is relative,' 'dead,' 'God,' 'marriage.' I thought that the birth nearing reminded him of our sins. Again. I wondered if we could get beyond it, a city's stutter muffling our conversation. I tried to explain that. The way the world forgot things. But it didn't seem to apply to us. Although I tried. I thought that I would wear lipstick and make-up again. It was darkening. A thin blue line was exhausting itself over the lake. The tree branches started disappearing into the purple shadows, a pale blackness. Our car turned into another colour, a deep, tender grey. I wanted to hurry. I wanted to run into the arms of the trees. I went to the water and hesitated. I could feel Earl behind me mumbling. We both went into the waist high water at the same time. But I still felt the cold of it, pulling at my skirt and socks, making my shoes sodden. It eased the pain in my stomach, freezing it, for a moment. Then I screamed even though I didn't mean to. Earl began reciting something fast, rambling. He jumped through the heavy water. The top half of my body shivered, the bottom half was sheathed in ice, numb, painful. I thought I could feel silt between my chilly toes, rocks bumping the soles of my shoes. I imagined fish mistaking my legs, nuzzling. I was crying and saying things that faded above the lake. My stomach contracted and something was slipping out. I was pushing.

'And the way of the world...'

I could smell liquor on his breath. I could see Earl's contorted face, his arms raised into the air. He didn't seem cold. Then his hand at the back of my head, my face under the water. I couldn't bend for a moment and then I doubled over, the splash of water wetting all my hair.

'Help me to make it right...'

I gasped for air. My face chilled, my hair plastered to my skin along my shoulders. Water dripped down, smoothing and staining my sweater. Then warmth between my legs and something dropping out of me, limb by small limb. I was pulled apart. I didn't want to be separated. I wished we could remain in one body. I would have happily just given him mine and he could have done what he wanted through my limbs. I looked at Earl and said, 'We need to hurry.'

For a second I saw the corrugated grey surface of the lake ruffled by wind, heard a rustling. Then he pushed my head underneath again, hard. I heard nothing but trees swaying. I opened my eyes and saw layers of dirt papering the water, darkening it, long, thin water plants waving. A school of tiny fish, seeing my hair floating out around me, turned and darted away. I saw my skirt rising, my socks falling, a tiny head and neck swimming out of my body, a thick liquid dispersing, clouding the water even more. I wanted to help the baby, wanted to reach down and touch his warm, compact body. But I could feel Earl's strong hand at my neck. I struggled. My arms thrashed above the water, reaching for a god or Earl's black suspenders, finding nothing, flapping like two fish out of water. My eyes widened. For a moment I thought I saw God and he looked so familiar. Bubbles tore away from me, wet Os of air. They surfaced. I tired. I could taste the water all around me. It was dirt and metal and cold emptiness filling me. Silt settled on my head and shoes and shoulders, in the creases in my floating clothes. I saw the baby boy, detached from a cord that still led to my body. I saw Him rise to the surface.

THE LOST GIRLS

Rosalind Mitchell

Rosalind Mitchell lives on an island in South Cumbria with a white-and-black cat called Tosca. When she's not writing she makes jewellery, plays crown-green bowls, watches classic films and walks for hours along the beach.

She thrives on Sibelius and gin.

THE LOST GIRLS

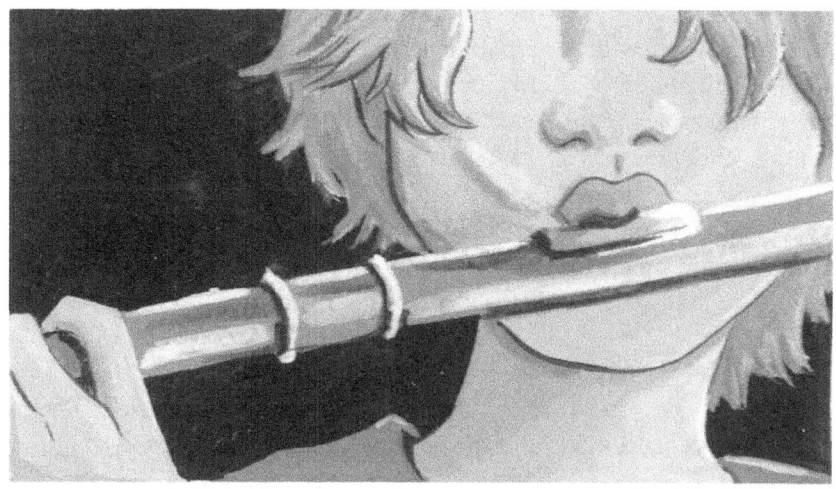

I

THE MUSIC SPOKE TO ME FIRST, A FLUTE FANTASIA OF JOHANN Joachim Quantz shimmering like quicksilver in the November drizzle, a sound so unexpected and so familiar that it lightened the gloom of a Monday morning and tied my entrails in knots at the same time. Quantz isn't a name on many lips. Why here? Why now?

I was late. The Tube was fucked up again so I was short and irritable with everybody around me, jostling to get down the steps and out into the street. As in a nightmare the faster I tried to hurry myself the more my feet refused to respond. They were out of my control, perhaps enchanted by the baroque tapestry that demanded my attention. I tripped over myself and stumbled into the man in front of me, who said sorry so I cursed him for being so stupidly English and then returned his apology. I had to stop anyway because the air had drained from my lungs, and then the music called ever more sharply.

A young woman sat on the pavement across the road, using the railway bridge as shelter. That's nothing special, round here it happens all the time. I read somewhere that in the middle of the Pacific Ocean there's a place where all the plastic bags and other detritus of our disposable culture come together to make a floating island. This neglected part of west London seems to work like that; the disposable people of the world are drawn here and cling together for warmth and some semblance of security. I know a lot of them, you do if you pass them nearly every day, and quite often I'll stop for a chat or offer them a sandwich but on a day like this one when I'm late and it's raining I'll usually hurry on by because I have other things to worry about. Pass by on the other side, if you like. This young woman, as I say, was on the other side and she wasn't even in the direction I was headed, but this clearly wasn't going to be just any old day and my instinct to hurry was overpowered by the music of Johann Joaquin Quantz being played with such oblivious serenity. I let the stream of humanity pass either side of me and scurry on up St Mark's Road, then I crossed to the other side knowing even as I did so that it was a bad idea.

She was younger than I'd thought; fourteen I guessed, fifteen at the most, and so slight that I felt the wind from a passing bus might lift her up and send her spiralling in the air with the fallen leaves and scraps of paper. She sat cross-legged on a red anorak with her back propped up by a matching daysack, crushed as if used as a pillow which it probably had. Her jeans hadn't come from any discount warehouse and her flute, a modern silver one not a baroque instrument, looked more expensive than any that I could ever have afforded. The only thing that spoilt the image was her tawny hair, clumsily cropped short to frame her face like a mass of ruffled feathers. She didn't look as though she cared. She barely noticed me until I stood in front of her and cleared my throat.

'We need to talk,' I said.

'How's your egg, Melanie?' I asked. I'd taken her to a greasy spoon I was fond of, being careful to seat myself to obscure her face as best I could from prying eyes. Her self-inflicted barbering had been effective enough in distancing herself from the sweet-and-innocent school portrait released to the media, but I didn't see any point in taking any unnecessary risks.

Her head whipped upright when she heard her name. 'Don't call me that,' she scolded. Her eyes, I saw, were vivid green, the green of new spring shoots, and for an instant they flashed with venom. I found myself liking her more and more.

'What would you like me to call you?' I offered. 'That is your name, isn't it?'

She lowered her eyes. The anger subsided into sullenness. I could read in her face the battle raging within her. Should she trust me or not? She didn't have to, but if my hunch was right she needed to find somebody to trust. She just needed some convincing. 'How do you know?' she asked, her eyes once again flickering into mine and then away again.

'Does it matter?' I said. She knew perfectly well how I knew and I wasn't going to dwell on it.

'My name's Mel,' she said. 'I hate Melanie, it's what...' Her voice trailed away.

'It's what your parents call you?' I suggested. 'Who introduced you to Johann Quantz, Mel?'

'I hate him,' she said.

'You play his music pretty well, considering.'

'I don't hate him. I love the music.' She was probing for the words again. 'They made me... You know.'

I did know. She knew that I knew.

'They – your mum and dad – they make you play?'

The green eyes flashed again. 'Like a fucking performing seal,' she said. 'Every time they have friends round. They say they want the best for me. But they don't care about me or what I want. It's all about making themselves look good.'

I could only nod, slowly. Something had cracked. I saw Mel's eyes glaze over with tears. I knew exactly what she was thinking.

'You don't have to decide anything just now,' I said. 'But would you like to come with me, before somebody decides for you? I want to tell you a story. And I think you might recognise it.'

It was too late to go to work now anyway.

II

Another life. Another time. Neil Armstrong and Buzz Aldrin are walking on the moon, there's not much else in the news. Thunderclap Newman is top of the pops and I'm in mourning for Brian Jones but then I don't know better. And I'm in Ostend, Belgium, although I shouldn't be because I'm on the run and I don't know which way to turn. There's a man with me. The man is my English teacher, or used to be because both of us know he can't go back. Don't worry, he's taking good care of me and not doing anything to make things worse for himself, although I don't think anything can help him now. He's in deeper shit than I am and it's me that dropped him in it.

It's early in the morning. We checked out early from our rooms above a backstreet bar and left our bags in a back room to collect later. My eyes are heavy and my legs feel leaden; even though last night's was the first proper bed I'd been in for a week the burbling of eccentric plumbing kept me awake for much of the night. There've been chilly railway platforms long after dark, me wrapped in a blanket as overnight goods trains rattle by. But right now the sun is shining and for some reason I feel ecstatically happy. We wander, hand in surreptitious hand, along the *Visserskai*, the Fisherman's Quay, inspecting the offerings of the stalls lining the harbour; flayed wind-dried fish, trays of shrimps and mussels, steaming cauldrons of *wollekjes*, hot whelks that misted and perfumed the morning. We debate the merits of the different delicacies. We walk on past the fishing boats and out onto the beach, and then back again, drinking in the sharp scents of salt and seaweed and diesel. I watch gulls circling lazily above the harbour waiting for the night boats to return, and I envy them their freedom to float over the seas. For so long I'd felt like a caged bird, yearning to stretch my wings, and today I was free.

When we'd wandered enough and I'd worked up an appetite I pointed to a dish of shrimps on one of the stalls and he asked for a bowl of *wollekjes* for himself, and we sat laughing together on a bench with the warmth of a new sun and the chill of the North Sea massaging my skin. That's the moment I remember best. It felt as near to bliss as I've ever been. If it was in my power to freeze time forever, this is the moment I would choose.

The streets of Ostend were coming alive. From the *Visserskai* we strolled to the railway station where he bought tickets for Brussels, and from there we walked back to the bar to collect our bags. In the street outside a few locals were standing around smoking cigarettes and gossiping. There was a car with English plates. It lodged in my mind without seeming significant. A cherry-red Austin Cambridge; I can see it perfectly, I could probably tell you where it was splashed with gullshit. There was something in the air, something that wasn't the breeze from the sea but which made my skin creep just the same. A hand fell on my shoulder. I was being pushed, no, pulled away and something like a blanket or a coat was flung over my shoulders and I was being bent double and pushed, hustled into the back seat of the

Austin. A woman's voice clucked behind my ear, saying it was all right, it was all over, I'd soon be home. And it bloody wasn't all right. Then came the blinding blue camera flashes like a summer thunderstorm. I screwed up my eyes, opened my mouth and screamed.

It was dark when we got back. Nearly midnight I think, or maybe after. I'd lost all sense of time. I was exhausted and empty of emotion, drained by screaming and crying, all I could do was stare with eyes that saw nothing but dancing shapes that seemed an ocean away. They took me on a morning ferry to Dover. Three of them, keeping me very close so there was no chance of escape, watching every breath, monitoring every step. They bought me doughnuts and Coca-Cola and I wouldn't touch them. I wouldn't speak to them. At Dover they hustled me through customs and passport checks, I think there must have been a special arrangement to clear the way in advance. Then they bundled me into another car. I didn't see much. Part of the time I had something over my head, it wasn't a hood, more like a coat, mostly at the times we weren't moving very much. The rest of the time I just switched off my mind. I couldn't move; I was wedged into the middle of the back seat with a uniformed policewoman on one side of me and another woman in a tweed skirt who smelled of lavender on the other.

What I find so strange when I look back on that long shivery night is that, cold and miserable as I was, I didn't want it to end. I knew that the real torments would begin when I was delivered into the stodgy world of my parents. And so it was that, when the steady whine of tyres on the motorway gave way to gear changes and stops and starts that a fresh chill seized my body and my liver began dancing a jig inside me. Too soon, everything was still. My mother was pulling me into her bosom, unlovely and smelling of fabulous pink Camay. Far away, my father's prim tones said 'Let's get you to bed, young lady.'

III

'What was his name?' Mel said.

'What was whose name?'

'His. Your teacher's. You just said 'he' and 'him', as if you were trying to rub him out.'

I couldn't fault Mel's perceptiveness. 'Andrew,' I said, 'his name was Andrew.' I knew there was a quiver in my voice.

'What happened to him?' She seemed genuinely concerned.

'He went to prison. I think. I was ill for ages after I got back. I never went back to my old school. They – mum and dad – they sent me away to boarding school. I'd let them down, you see. I'd made them look bad. I was supposed to reflect well on them, whatever I might have wanted. They had my life planned for me. Somebody must have told me about him – Andrew – but I can't remember. I believed I'd killed him.'

I fell into silence, fighting back the tears that welled into my eyes, aware that Mel's eyes were fixed intently on my face.

'What will happen to me, do you think?' Mel asked at last.

'You'll have to go back,' I said, 'whether that's under your control or not is up to you. The hardest thing you'll ever have to do is something you don't want to do under your own control. But you won't like the alternative.'

She was silent for what seemed an age, wrestling with her options. Then she looked directly into my eyes. 'Will you come with me?' she asked.

'I'll drive you back and talk to your parents if you like. The sooner the better. But let me show you something first.'

I still had my old flute, the wooden baroque flute. I hadn't played it in years but something had made me hang on to it. I found it in the back of a cupboard, took it out of its case and tried a scale or two. It took a few tries to get the embouchure right but my fingers fell readily on the keys. I played a few bars of a sonata for two flutes. Mel smiled in recognition.

'Quantz?' she asked.

'Telemann,' I said. 'Want to try it together?'

I drove her up north, the slow way. There was less risk of being trailed, and besides although she said nothing I had a hunch she'd want to spin it out for as long as possible. I'd packed a bag for myself, just in case, and for no particularly good reason I threw my old flute in with all my other things.

'Will you be my sister?' Mel asked, after we'd been silent for a long time. 'I always wanted a sister. It would have been easier I think.'

'I'm older than your mum!' I said. But I wasn't convinced. I liked this girl a lot; in so many ways she seemed so much more mature than I ever was. 'If that's what you want. Let's see how things go, hey!'

She said nothing, but seemed happy enough with that.

'I know I made a mess of things. But it's not too late for you, you know.'

'Yeah,' she said. 'I know. And it's not too late for you, you know.'

My turn to be silent.

We drove on, into the growing dusk. She slept. She was very relaxed, considering. I was tired myself and the drone of the engine was soporific. It was bringing back uncomfortable memories of that other journey years earlier.

Mel opened her eyes. 'I need a wee,' she said. I pulled into a filling station and watched her go inside the shop, ask at the counter, and go through to the back, still wearing the red daysack from which she seemed inseparable. I lay back in my seat and waited for her.

Twenty minutes went by. Nausea washed over me. I got out of the car and went over to the shop. No, the attendant didn't think he'd seen the girl come out. I went into the toilet. There was nobody there. A window was open. I remembered how slight Mel has seemed when I first saw her.

I sat still in the car for an hour, thinking and waiting for the nausea to pass. There was nothing I could do. I felt sure Mel would survive whatever she did. Maybe it was for the best.

I fired up the engine and headed for the motorway. At the roundabout I swung right for the London-bound slip road, and at the last moment skipped it, completed the full circuit and headed northwards.

BEN

Peter Kendell

BEN

SAMANTHA HAS A NEW BOYFRIEND AND BEN COULDN'T BE MORE delighted. Of course she's had boyfriends before, lots of them. She's not ugly – not butt-ugly, that's certain. But this guy is seriously cute. Way out of her league, in fact.

His name is Ryan.

Is he fucking her? That is the question. If Ben were the kind of man to stop off at a bar on the way home from the office that is the question he would ask of his beer buddies after the third or fourth. Of course he is, would be the reply. Wouldn't you?

But she's my daughter!

It is always a pleasure to receive Ryan when he calls round to take Sam out on a date or down to the mall for some shopping and hanging out. 'Good morning, ma'am,' he says when Iris answers the bell and invites him in for coffee and home-made cookies.

'Ryan's here,' she calls up the stairs.

'Coming,' Samantha replies from the shower.

Ryan sits patiently in the kitchen and allows Iris to fuss around him.

'He's always so polite,' Iris says to Ben later, after the young folks have driven off in Ryan's VW. 'I noticed he always calls you "sir."'

'He's not like the others. Not like them at all,' Ben agrees. 'He's sensible. Steady. Reliable.'

'He'd make a fine husband for Sam.'

'Let's not get ahead of ourselves.'

Ben worries about Iris. She is not good at dealing with disappointments.

Sam is on a nine o'clock curfew, not because she is irresponsible but because her parents have heard such terrible stories of what teenagers get up to in the late hours. Wild driving, illegal drinking, even illicit drugtaking.

Not to mention sex.

Ben does not mention sex – that is Iris's job. It is up to her to remind her daughter that no boy worth knowing will take liberties with her. She has bought Sam a purity ring – a good one, it could have come from Tiffany's – and she makes sure her daughter wears it. It says, look! This is a nice girl. Treat her with respect.

Ryan is nothing if not respectful.

Ben, Iris and Samantha live in a decent neighbourhood. People here work hard. They have kept their jobs – mostly – despite the downturn. Their houses are neat and well-maintained, with tidy lawns and paths, and sidings regularly painted or constructed of low-upkeep vinyl. Occasionally the postman passes a house whose front yard is defaced by a foreclosure sign, but they are fortunately rare. People here are nice. They are God-fearing – and if they do not actually tremble in fear of God they behave as if they would if it were required of them which is, as Iris says, all that really matters. They bake cakes, and go to church, and arrange flowers, and meet for coffee, and nobody speaks of whited sepulchres or concealed sin. That would be bad manners, like slackening your belt and showing your underwear or slouching around in a baseball cap. Ryan – neatly pressed khakis, check shirt, good quality sports shoes – does none of those things.

Ben is becoming just a little jealous of Ryan, who seems to be enjoying all of life's advantages with no apparent effort. It is a relief to discover that he paid for his apparel from a combination of his monthly allowance and some after-school hours working in Home Depot. Sam assures her father that Ryan get straight As ('But once he got a B+ and was grounded for a whole week,' she says, eyes wide) despite having to spend study time standing behind a counter or walking the aisles looking for customers to help.

Ben is not stupid, nor does he lack a proper measure of self-awareness. He has heard all the jokes about middle-aged men and their pathetic last grasps at youth – the sports cars, the motorcycles, the gym clubs and the running shoes. And the affairs, of course. And it's all true – although he'd rather the car in front of the house carried Shelby stripes than a hybrid badge, he genuinely prefers women his age to the shorts-wearing nymphets who crowd the shopping malls and school yards he passes on the way to the office. What would he say to them? What would they talk about?

In other words, he is faithful to Iris.

One day, Ryan comes up with a proposition. He's leaning against the breakfast bar, practicing that slow, lazy smile he's read about. 'Say,' he says, like a cowpoke might say it, 'what say you and I – your good lady allowing, that is – take off to the woods and do ourselves a little hunting?'

'Hunting?' says Ben, taken aback.

'Yeah – with guns. Let's load for bear.'

Iris enters the kitchen. 'You boys going hunting? That's nice. Sam and I can do some shopping while you're away. I can catch up with my baking.'

'I don't have a gun,' says Ben.

Ben has rented a truck for the expedition. He feels that a Prius does not have quite the right outdoors image for a huntsman. The truck has a gun rack mounted behind the seats and Ben clamps both rifles to it, his and Ben's. He keeps the tele sights in his backpack for fear of damaging them. They take turns to drive and stop off at diners and motels on their way to the woods. Ryan's driving is fast and confident. Ben likes to take things a little easier. It wouldn't do to roll the truck over. He'd lose his deposit, even with the collision damage waiver he signed up for at the rental counter.

This is turning out to be an expensive trip, what with the camo gear and the boots, the stop-offs and the gas for the truck; not to mention the brand-new hunting rifle that sits clamped in the rack behind Ben's head. Ryan has his father's gun. Ben has never owned a firearm before and if he had it would have been his father's as well. It is clear that Ryan knows far more about surviving in the wilderness than he does. He never thought he'd be looking up to a younger man like this.

They drive deeper into the mountains, up forest slopes and unpaved rutted roads. Ben both relishes and dreads abandoning civilisation. And as the roads narrow and the trees eat the sky, he feels a change taking place. Something ancient is rising in him. At last, he is beginning to understand. To see. To believe.

They camp in the woods. There are lodges for hire, and bars where, when it comes to beer time, well-padded men boast of their achievements. Ben is not a boaster and he has spent enough money already. So they pitch a tent in a forest glade and sit on the ground and cook over the open fire that Ryan, with his training in the Eagle Scouts, has shown Ben how to build. They find a nearby stream in which to wash. Afterwards, they unroll their sleeping bags as the sun blazes behind the western mountains and lie side by side in the darkness, sharing each other's exhalations. Only Ben is surprised at his reaction to their closeness.

On the first day, Ben blunders and crashes through the trees and bushes and every creature for miles around senses humans on the prowl and makes for cover. Neither Ben nor Ryan sees any game, let alone a chance to make a kill. This, despite Ryan's attempts at showing Ben how to walk silently through the forest and his setting up a rail with tin cans on it for target practice. He does his best to teach Ben to pull the rifle properly into his shoulder and carry it safely when he is not firing it. You raise the gun, you gotta fire it, he says. Otherwise, point it at the ground even though you know for sure it's not loaded and the safety's on. Ben listens and nods and does as he is told. Again, he is the younger man's pupil. He willingly lets himself be led. That way he can watch Ryan, without the boy knowing exactly how he watches him.

Day two, and Ben is beginning to learn about the wilderness. He is slightly less clumsy today, he keeps his elbows in and watches where he puts his feet. He's taking more in. They catch sight of deer and bear, but Ryan says no, wait. Don't fire unless you are sure you will kill. That is the humane way. The true huntsman's way. Ben nods, and remembers the light and shade on Ryan's body the previous evening, as they bathed in the creek. That day they make no kills.

His gun... Ben has rarely handled a gun before, but today he has held it in his hands. He has seen movies and read magazine articles about infantrymen and their guns, and he is beginning to gain an inkling of the relationship that builds up between a man and a precious personal possession, like a weapon or a musical instrument. He has seen the way hands move up and down the barrel of a gun or the neck of a guitar, and it reminds him – he cannot help himself – it reminds him of sex. *Hold a gun like you would hold a woman.* Is that it? Is that the line he remembers? Did it come from *Platoon*, or *Full Metal Jacket*? Or *The Deer Hunter*?

What does it mean; to hold a gun when the safety is on? What does it mean; to take the safety off?

Day three, afternoon. The two men have been up since early morning, packing up the camp and stowing their gear away in the truck. Only the third day, and already their trip is nearly over. Others may come – perhaps Ryan will want to go hunting again, or Ben may find some men in the office who would like to get away for a few days of living it Iron John style. But for now, they are on their last hunt.

Just before noon, Ryan caught the scent of bear. His senses are younger and more acute than Ben's and it has taken the older man a while to catch it himself. Now it is strong and – as if the bear's energy were being passed to him as through its spoor – it fills him with a new animal strength. He is keeping up with Ryan much more easily than he did on their first day in the woods.

Not far to go; and Ryan is ahead of Ben, moving silently through the undergrowth, hiding in the shadows between the trees or pressing his body against their trunks. He has become part of the forest, part of its life, absorbed into its world. He is the hunter, but Ben is close behind. He feels the blood surging in his veins, buzzing in his head. It engorges him. It fills him with power. It makes him strong and erect.

Ben cannot help the way he is reacting now, despite its shamefulness. He holds the store-bought rifle – his gun – close by his side, or raises it in front of himself to hide his growing excitement. Ahead, Ryan ducks down to a kneeling position. He turns and holds a palm to the ground to indicate to Ben that he should do the same, while putting a finger to his lips. Quiet now. The bear must be very close by –

doubtless Ryan has seen it. Its scent is clear and sharp on the air, heavy with musk and excrement. Ben's feelings grow ever more intense. He knows what he wants to do now, what he must do.

Fuck him in the ass. Yes. He wants to grab hold of the younger man as he is now, kneeling, presenting himself to him. He wants to force himself into him, use him, violate him. Show him who's boss. The pressure, the demand, the need – they are growing uncontrollably in him (he tells himself this.) Ben; insurance agent, hybrid-owning suburbanite – he believes that he has become his true self, a real man at last. Rejoicing in this truth, Ben lifts the rifle, slips a round into the breech and points it at Ryan. And takes the safety off. And fucks him in the ass. He pulls back the bolt and reloads, and fucks him again. Blam. And again, blam, blam, while both men jerk and spasm uncontrollably. 'Hallelujah!' they cry.

The last shot spangs away through the trees. A splintering sound in the middle distance, and the bear is lumbering off, aware in its vague animal mind that this is not the day it will die and that safety lies anywhere but here.

Ben rises to his feet. He shakes his head and then, remembering the cop shows he has seen, gathers up the empty cartridge shells. He will dispose of them later. For now, he must leave the scene of the crime. That, and wash his pants.

'That was a good trip,' says Ryan as they drive back to the city. 'A real good trip, don't you think, sir?'

ELIZABETH

Nicholas Goodrick

After graduating with a degree in Scottish History, Nicholas has settled in Edinburgh, where he now spends most of his time setting himself ridiculous challenges.

Check out his progress and suggest new challenges at http://nicktroptopolis.wordpress.com.

ELIZABETH

THE WARD WAS EERILY QUIET. THE ONLY SOUNDS IAIN COULD HEAR were the rasping breaths of the man by the door, the occasional sound of someone walking past outside, and the boy to his left murmuring faintly in his sleep. Sighing, Iain lay back and closed his eyes, trying to fall back asleep. The man who had been in the bed to his right had screamed through the night, until he finally passed on less than an hour previously. The nurses had insisted that there was nowhere else they could move him, so the remaining six men had been forced to suffer through their compatriot's agony.

Just as he was beginning to doze off, Iain was disturbed by the door opening and footsteps walking into the ward. Iain kept his eyes closed. There was only one set of footsteps, which meant they weren't bringing in another injured soul.

'Wakey wakey, rise and shine,' the nurse said, pulling the window open to fill the room with the warm sunlight of a Virginian summer. It was so bright that Iain could see it even through his eyelids. Groaning, he tried to roll away from the light, but without thinking he put his weight on the stump where his hand should have been and the pain that shot through his right arm forced him to flop onto his back, swearing.

'Now Mr MacDonald,' the nurse said as she loomed over him. 'I won't have language like that in my ward. Now, there's a boy outside who wants to speak with you. Are you goin' to be civil or am I goin' to have to send him away?' Iain glared at her, but shook his head reluctantly. 'Good.'

She turned on her heel and strode back across the ward to open the door. 'All right son,' she said as a young lad of probably no more than fifteen stepped through the doorway. With a hand on his shoulder, the nurse steered the child towards Iain's bed with the warning, 'He's mighty cranky, so good luck.' She glared down at Iain, then moved away to attend to another patient.

Iain frowned at the wee boy standing next to his bed. He was wearing an ill-fitting Union Army overcoat, and looked even less healthy than Iain felt, with skin pale as a sheet and thin red hair plastered to his forehead with sweat. 'Who are you?' he asked brusquely, not really interested in this child.

'Your nephew,' he said quietly, and to Iain's surprise, in Gaelic. 'Duncan.'

'I beg your pardon?' Iain said, in English out of habit, before repeating himself in his mother tongue.

'I'm Margaret's son. She said I should find you,' the bairn mumbled.

'Well, congratulations,' Iain said and sat back, spreading his arms in a sardonic gesture of presentation, ignoring the shooting pain in his wounded left arm. 'What do you want?'

'I don't know.'

'You don't know?' Iain began to laugh, for the first time in a long while. 'So why did you go to all the effort of finding me, lad?'

'She told me to.'

'Well, why don't you go back to her in Cape Breton and leave me alone?'

'She's dead.'

Iain stopped laughing abruptly, and stared at the boy. 'What? When?'

'Last year. Consumption.'

Iain closed his eyes and took a deep breath, then opened them, and glared at him. 'Your mother has been dead to me for years. I don't need you to rake through things that were closed a long time ago. Why didn't you go to your Aunt Moira, or one of the brothers?'

'She said we don't see them anymore.'

Iain snorted. 'Well she finally came to her senses. Why the hell did she send you to me?'

Duncan shrugged again, then put his hand in one of the pockets of his overcoat. 'She wanted me to give you this.' He pulled out a creased envelope and reached forward to put it on the bed. Iain snatched it out of his hand and began to read:

My dearest Brother,

I owe you an apology, and it is long overdue. Probably too long, but if I am to make my peace with the Lord, I must first make my peace with you. I'm sorry that I didn't believe you. I'm sorry that I ~~abandoned~~ ~~betrayed~~ abandoned you all those years ago. I thought, and still think, that what I was doing was for your own good. However, I am sorry that it turned out the way it did.

I regret that I have waited so long to ask for your forgiveness, and I realise that you may no longer have any left to give.

I do not feel as though I have any right to ask you to do anything for me. You certainly do not owe me anything, but I am going to ask anyway. You will, by now, have met Duncan. He looks like Tam did, but he is nowhere near as strong. Even as a baby, as you might remember, he was sickly, and he has not improved in the years since. Will you watch over him, for me? I cannot, or would not, ask anyone else. Please, in memory of the love you once had for your twin?

Goodbye, Iain, for the last time. I'll see you in heaven,
All my Love,
Your sister,

Margaret.

Iain screwed the letter into a rough ball and let it drop to the floor, then at a loss for what to do next, he patted the edge of the bed to indicate that the boy should sit.

They sat in silence for a time, neither making eye contact with the other. 'How old are you now?' Iain asked eventually.

'Fourteen.'

'Ah.' He nodded. 'Yes, that would be about right.'

For fear of lapsing back into silence, Iain decided that drastic measures had to be taken. 'I'm sorry about your Ma', laddie.' Duncan nodded, the corners of his eye beginning to fill with tears. 'I don't know,' he said, speaking without really thinking about the words, 'I was so angry at her. I never tried to get back in touch. Maybe I thought that there would be time later. She was always such a survivor. I thought she'd outlive all of us.'

'Why were you angry with her?' Duncan asked.

'Your Ma' never told you?' Iain shook his head. 'No, I suppose she wouldn't have done.' He took a deep breath, then let it out in a long sigh. 'You know your Ma' and I are twins? Well, we were. So we were really close. Then she abandoned me when I really needed her. Or I felt like she had anyway. I was hurt and angry, and that blinded me.'

'What do you mean?'

'You were only a bairn, so you wouldn't remember what it was like.' He stopped, thinking, about how to continue but Duncan leaned forward eagerly.

'What what was like?'

'It's quite a long story,' Iain said, 'but I don't suppose it'd hurt to tell you. You know that we weren't born in Cape Breton, your Ma' and I? Nor were you, come to that. We all came across the sea from Scotland.'

'Aye, of course!' the boy said indignantly.

'Of course,' Iain repeated. 'Well, for the most part it began on the boat. Bits and pieces started long before that, but well, you'll see. Like most good stories, it started with a lass.' He paused, then added, 'Not that this is really a good story,' as an afterthought.

'Just tell me!' Duncan demanded, and Iain smiled.

'You know, you look like your Da', but at times you don't half sound like your Ma. Well, all right then.

'We were five, maybe six, days out of Greenock when I met her…'

We were five, maybe six, days out of Greenock when I met her. It happened entirely by accident. If my brothers hadn't shoved their way in front of me in the line for breakfast, I would probably never have noticed her, and my life would have taken a very different course. I reckon that there were nearly two hundred people on the boat, and for most of the journey we were all so dirty, and the living conditions so cramped, that I could have gone the entire voyage without once picking her out in the crowd.

So as I say, I was in the line for breakfast, and my bothers pushed in front of me. Literally. As Sorley – he was the next above me – took his place, he shoulder-barged me so hard that I overbalanced, and courtesy of a sudden listing of the boat, I ended up flat on my arse. I got to my feet as quick as I could, and found myself face to face with a lass of about my age. Trying quickly to brush the worst of the dust off my clothes, I apologised quietly.

'I'm sorry,' I said in Gaelic, assuming she was a Highlander. I hadn't met a single passenger that wasn't.

'It's fine,' the lassie replied, 'it happens.'

I nodded and gestured over my shoulder to my brothers. 'Especially with this lot around. I'm the youngest, so living in close quarters with them isn't exactly fun.'

'I know the feeling.' She smiled, and although there was no warmth behind the expression, I smiled back.

'I'm Iain,' I said, bowing my head self-consciously.

'Mhairi,' she said shortly, and nodded at me. Assuming that she had been returning my gesture, I smiled deeper. Her smooth forehead creased slightly into a confused frown, and after a moment I realised that she had been trying to indicate that the line had moved forward. There was now a gap of several feet between Sorley and myself. 'Sorry, I thought…' I broke off, and moved forward hurriedly, but as quietly as I could to not attract attention.

'Where are you travelling from?' I asked, after a few moments' silence.

'Sutherland.'

'Oh,' I said, and I couldn't help grimacing in sympathy. I'd heard of the things that had happened in Sutherland, of course I had. There probably wasn't a Highlander alive who hadn't heard, and thanked God that things were not quite that bad for them. 'I can understand why you're leaving. I'm from Skye.'

'Ah.'

We were almost at the front of the line now. Only my brothers were in front of us, but for some reason I felt compelled to keep talking to this lass. I don't know why. Perhaps it was because she was the first ray of light that I had seen since we'd been forced to leave our village, but for some reason I felt as though the most important thing for me in the world was to keep this conversation going for as long as I could. She was pretty enough, though I don't think that at the time I had realised that she was the most beautiful girl on the boat, let alone the most beautiful I'd ever seen. She didn't seem interested in telling me anything about herself, and she certainly wasn't interested in me, but somehow I knew that she was someone I needed to have in my life.

'Are you with your family?' I asked.

'Yes.'

'Me too,' I said, suddenly aware that this would have been obvious already. 'They were clearing our whole village out. My brothers didn't want to come, they said they'd find work in Portree or Dunvegan,' I continued, trying to salvage the situation, 'but when Angus got into trouble with the Landlord, Da' said he had to come, and what Angus does, the others do too. He's the eldest.' She didn't reply, so I carried on. 'Of course, my Ma' and my sisters didn't really want to come either, but my brothers were the most against it.' I sighed. 'I was thinking about leaving anyway, heading across the sea to make my fortune in Cape Breton, but it doesn't feel the same anymore. Not with them.'

She simply nodded at this, but after a moment, she too sighed deeply. 'I was going to go to Dundee,' she said wistfully, 'but I...' she broke off, her eyes widening as I felt someone's grip close on my shoulder. Turning my head, I caught sight of Angus as he pulled me around to face the angry-looking man waiting to serve breakfast, and pushed me forward.

'Pay attention, Sheep,' Angus growled, cuffing me on the head as he stalked off, Sorley and Donald in tow. All of them were laughing raucously. My eyes filled with tears, from the humiliation as much as the pain, and I angrily thrust out my bowl for a ladleful of porridge. The chef looked at me with disgust, and then proceeded to dollop less than half a serving of oats into my bowl.

'That's not fair!' I demanded, only to get a blank look off the man. Glaring, I repeated myself in English. 'Everyone else is getting a full bowl!'

'Everyone else is paying attention,' the chef spat back. 'Move it.'

Glaring at the man, I moved out of the way to allow Mhairi to step forward and receive her serving, an entire ladleful, complete with a lecherous look, I noticed. I was so angry that I began to stomp away, forgetting my decision to stick with the girl.

I stormed past the benches, straight out of the mess-hall and up the companionway that led onto the deck. I wandered along until I found a suitably empty and sheltered space to sit down to eat my meagre portion of oats.

There was only about four spoonful's worth of porridge in my bowl, and I'd probably swallowed two of them in my anger before I realised that I might not get any more food until dinner. I decided to ration what was left.

Staring at a spot several feet in front of me, I began to pick at my porridge slowly, still fuming over the way I had been treated by my brothers and the stupid sassenach chef. It was only the sound of a girl's voice nearby that penetrated the red fog of my anger.

'Do you mind if I sit down?' Mhairi asked quietly.

I swallowed the mouthful of porridge that I'd been savouring and nodded. 'Of course not,' I said with a smile.

'So, that was your brother?' she asked, once she had sat and arranged her skirts with as much dignity as possible.

'Yes,' I said shortly, stabbing my spoon back into the bowl, inadvertently flicking the small amount of oats that were left over the rim. Groaning in frustration, I tossed the tin bowl down, and then had to lunge to catch it as it began to bounce along the deck away from me.

Silently, Mhairi took the bowl out of my hands and spooned some of her portion into mine. 'As I was saying,' she began as she passed the bowl back, 'I was going away to Dundee. The minister referred me to an agency he said would find me a job as a maid in one of the big town houses. I was all set to go, but then—' she paused and sighed deeply. 'Well, it doesn't really matter anymore, does it?'

I couldn't think what to say so I nodded silently as I put the final spoonful of porridge into my mouth and began to chew thoughtfully.

At the sight of two figures walking along the deck towards us, I swallowed suddenly, coughing slightly in my haste, and, bending my neck forward to bury my head in my knees, brought my arms up to hide my face.

Bewildered, Mhairi stared from me to the two women, and back.

'Who are they?' she asked curiously.

'My sisters,' I mumbled through my arms. 'Don't draw attention to yourself.'

'What are you talking about?'

'Just don't let them notice me!' I said, more quickly this time, very aware of the fact that Moira and Katrine were getting closer.

'You really don't get along with your family, do you?'

'No!' I said, a little louder than I intended, and unfortunately, loud enough for Katrine to hear and recognise my voice.

'What are you doing, Sheep?' she drawled, stopping and turning to look at me, hands on hips. My youngest sister had been very quick to pick up Sorley's nickname for me, and had always taken the greatest relish in using it.

'Nothing,' I said, not looking at her. 'Just eating my breakfast.'

Katrine laughed obnoxiously. 'Donald says you're lucky you even got any today. He said you cried like a bairn, Sheep.'

'Hush, Katrine,' Moira said, and I was momentarily grateful to her. Momentarily. The sentiment vanished as she continued, looking down at Mhairi. 'Who do we have here Iain? I hope you're not bothering this poor lassie.'

'No,' I said indignantly, glaring at my older sister. 'We were just talking.'

'Well I'm sure she's got better things to do than listen to your nonsense.'

'It's fine,' Mhairi said, 'I'm the one that sat with him.'

'Why?' Katrine blurted out, then poked her tongue out at Moira's back as her older sister made a shushing sound.

'I wouldn't waste my time, or my breath, if I were you,' Moira said. 'My brother has never had anything to say in his life that is worth listening to.'

'He just goes "baa" like a daft wee lamb!' Katrine butted in with a giggle.

'Why won't you just leave me alone?' I said, and I could hear that my voice was edging on a shout. 'I wasn't bothering you.'

'You're always bothering me, Sheep,' Katrine said, but shrugged and began to resume her walk along the deck. 'Come on Moira. I'm sure we could find something more worthwhile to be doing than talking to our poor, useless brother.'

Moira took Katrine's arm and began to move off. 'Such as?' I heard her ask.

Sighing, as much to drown out Katrine's no doubt insulting response as out of frustration, I ran my hand through my hair and turned to look at Mhairi.

'I'm sorry about that.'

'It's all right,' she said, smiling. 'Is that why they call you Sheep,' she asked, 'because you bleat like one?'

'No,' I said bitterly. 'That's just a happy coincidence. They call me Sheep—' I groaned again, really not wanting to voice the hardly flattering explanation, 'because I'm wool-headed,' I tugged a strand of my distressingly curly hair to indicate, 'and wool-brained.'

Mhairi snorted with laughter, though at least she had the decency to blush when I frowned at her. The hint of colour in her cheeks only went to make her even more beautiful to me. 'Sorley, my brother, came up with it years ago. Even my Da' calls me it. Only Ma', Moira, and Margaret don't. Unless they're not thinking about what they're saying anyway.' I sighed again and got to my feet, turning to lean against the edge of the boat and look out at the ocean. 'Everything will be better when we get to Cape Breton.'

Mhairi, who had stood up and leant next to me, shrugged and made a non-committal noise. Then: 'Who's Margaret?'

'My other sister. My twin. She's the only person in my family I actually like.'

'Oh. Is she on the boat as well?'

'Aye, but it was a close thing. She was going to stay behind, but after Tam died, she felt it was best to come.'

'Tam?'

'Her husband. They were married about two years, but he got stabbed trying to break up a fight.'

'Oh. How terrible.'

'Aye. He was one of those "policemen" they've got in Glasgow, did you hear about them? They're like watchmen, employed by the city. Anyway, she met him at the kirk, and they got married soon after.'

'In Glasgow?'

'Aye, she was a governess down there, through an agency type thing, same as you said. She left Skye when we were sixteen, or thereabouts. She wasn't coming home, ever, but as I say, Tam died and it's hard for a widow in the city. Especially as young as she was, and with a bairn as well.'

'She has a baby?'

'Yeah, a wee laddie. Named Duncan. He's on the boat too, but he's only wee, so he doesn't exactly do much.'

'It's sad about his Da' though.'

'I know. Tam was a nice lad too.'

'You met him? I thought she never came back to Skye.'

'She didn't, but I took a trip to see her. My Da' was furious just when I asked to go. He said he couldn't afford to have one of his lads wandering off to the mainland and losing work. He couldn't stop me once I was away though. Didn't tell him I was leaving. I just upped and left, and worked my way there and back.'

'That seems a little selfish of you,' she said.

I shrugged. 'I suppose, but it's not like I was just wandering aimlessly. You can't understand what it's like, being away from your twin, unless you are one. Especially in my family.'

We stood in silence for a while, just watching the sea pass us by. It was a quiet day, the way I remember it. A few waves and the sky was grey and cloudy, and it was freezing, but at least it wasn't raining. Rain on the boat was a hellish thing. Rain on any boat is bad enough, but on *Elizabeth* it was ten times worse. Mainlanders not used to the sea, they'd panic, the women and bairns would be howling and even the men would be praying to the Almighty to spare them. Pitiful really, but you couldn't blame them because you were thinking it as well, deep down.

That day was calm though, and as we stood watching out over the railing, people were beginning to emerge, braving the openness of the deck.

This made me uncomfortable. In such a wide space as that, anyone could see me. Anyone, meaning my brothers, who'd likely be bored now, and looking for entertainment. Especially since all it would take would be for one of them to meet Katrine or Moira, and they'd know exactly where I was and what I was doing. I needed to get out of their way, and quickly.

'Do you want to go for a walk?' I asked.

'Aye,' Mhairi said, 'I'd like that.'

As we turned and began to walk along the deck, away from the direction that my sisters had been headed, I realised that I had not planned beyond that. 'Where do you want to go?' I asked, and I thought that I could feel my face flushing again, although it was so cold it was hard to tell.

'I don't know,' she said with a smile. 'I thought you had a plan.'

'Well, where are you boarding? Do your family have a cabin?'

The smile disappeared, and she frowned slightly. 'No. We're in the big communal quarters. My dad...' she paused. 'Well, we couldn't afford a cabin.'

'Oh.' I was at a loss for words. 'Ours is really nice,' I said lamely. 'Would you like to see it?'

She looked at me, unsure exactly what I was proposing. Determined not to make any more of a numpty of myself than I had already that morning, I explained. 'I think that Margaret and Duncan will be there. I'd like them to meet you.'

'Oh.' She smiled, though it seemed that under the realisation on her face, there was also a look of relief. It bothered me a little, that look, as though she thought I was a threat, or worse, as though she felt repulsed by me. Suppressing that thought I led the way to the cabin that my entire family would be calling home for at least the next month.

Every day after that, Mhairi and I spent more and more time together, until, less than a week later, we were spending every spare moment we had in each other's company. There are a lot of spare moments when you're confined to a boat in the middle of the Atlantic. Each day, after getting up before the rest of my family to avoid the usual bullying, I would make my way across the ship to meet her at the sleeping quarters. Then we would head up to the mess for breakfast. We would always eat together, alone except for the rare occasions when Margaret joined us, having left Duncan – I mean you, of course – with Ma' or a sister. Then, if it was nice weather, Mhairi and I would generally just wander the ship, talking about nothing in particular. If not, we would find as sheltered and secluded a spot as we could, and do the same thing. Increasingly, we were doing more than just chatting too. Oh, nothing too wayward, not at that point, but we were definitely becoming closer.

It was probably clear to everyone what was happening between us but I really didn't care. We were in love. At least, I know that I was, and I like to think she was as well, though she never said as much. Mhairi never said much about herself really. She was happy to talk about me, or about impersonal things, but she would always turn away questions about her past, and she kept me as far away from her family as she could. I didn't meet them, and I didn't even know how many people she was travelling with. She had mentioned her father, and her sister, and someone named Ruaraidh. I assumed he was a brother, but he could just as easily have been a brother-in-law or a cousin. Looking back, I suppose that I should have suspected something was amiss, but it's not as though I was going out of my way to show her off to my family either. And, well, I was in love, and you just don't think about things like that when you're in love.

Anyway, as I say, things were getting serious and eventually we started dodging the boat's curfew. All passengers were supposed to be in their beds by the ninth bell. At the start of the journey, people were quite prepared to break this rule, but after a few days, the crew taught everyone to stick to it. Dodging it – the curfew – involved a fair amount of sneaking around, and even so we got caught a couple of times. It just added to the excitement, even if the beatings weren't much fun. I didn't mind so much. I was used to them from my brothers anyway, but it hurt me more to see the bastard sassenachs raising a fist to Mhairi, though they did let her off lightly compared to me. She only got a couple of slaps each time, rather than the full-on punches that I was treated to.

We managed to laugh it off though, and the threat of a little beating certainly wasn't going to stop us from seeing each other. Not when we were as in love as we were. Nor would my family. I don't know about Mhairi, but certainly every time I returned to the cabin late, someone would give me a hard time about it. Katrine would mock me, while Moira just stood there looking at me disapprovingly. Da' would normally just give me a lecture on being a responsible adult, and of the dangers of not following the Lord's path. A couple of times though, when I came back especially late, or escorted by whichever crewmember had found us, he would roar loud enough that he woke you up, and then, accompanied by your yelling, would accuse me of endangering the family, and especially my mother, and of being selfish, and so on and so forth. That was hardly a change from the way he had spoken to me back home on the croft in Skye, and it had become boring to listen to long before we boarded *Elizabeth*. My brothers wouldn't talk to me, instead they'd express their disapproval with their fists. Again, as usual. Ma' wouldn't say anything, of course.

I say of course, but have I told you about my Ma' yet? No? Has anyone else? I'm not surprised. Well, she never travelled well by boat, not since she was a lass, she used to say. She used to feel sick just standing on a boat sitting in the harbour at Suisinish, so you can imagine what she was like on an ocean-going ship. And we didn't know it at the beginning, but she was sick beneath that as well, and that made everything worse. She started seeing blood when she was sick, less than a week into the journey, probably even before I met Mhairi, though I can't remember for sure.

We'd never got on too well; like everyone else there was just something about me that rubbed her up the wrong way. Still, when your mother gets sick, when you have to watch it happening and the faint smell of illness never really stops permeating the cabin, it affects you. We all had to take turns sitting with her, though I tried to get out of it as much as I could. I still did enough, but it was so dull, and I had someone else to meet with, so I'd often "forget" to go back to the cabin, or convince Margaret to swap. That was probably just another reason why I wound everyone up during the journey, now that I think about it.

As I say though, it wasn't as if I never went to keep her company, and we had some of the best conversations we'd ever had in that cabin, when she wasn't vomiting. She told my stories about when she and Da' were younger, how they met, things like that. What was most interesting though was what life was like before they started Clearing us, though she didn't like to talk about that too much. She said it was too depressing.

In turn, she asked me to teach her English. I tried to put her off the idea, but she was adamant. She said that if she'd been able to speak English, she might have been able to convince the Factor to let us stay, and after that, how could I say no? Even though it wasn't true. I wasn't the best teacher, I didn't have the patience, especially once I met Mhairi, but I tried.

One day, when I was in the middle of a "lesson", if you can call it that, instead of repeating back to me what I'd just said, she asked 'When are you going to introduce her to me?'

'Sorry?' I was surprised, more that she knew about Mhairi than that she wanted to meet her.

'This lassie they say you're spending all your time with. I'd like to meet her.'

'I don't know,' I said guardedly, 'She's quite shy.'

'Oh. I see.' Her face fell.

'I can ask,' I said, mostly because she looked so sad, rather than because I wanted her to meet Mhairi, 'but it's up to her.'

'Of course. I just want to see at least one of my bairns happy before I die.'

This took me by surprise. 'Ma', you're not going to die.'

She looked at me, in the way that only a mother can, though usually they stop using it once their bairn gets past the age of ten. The look that says "I know I'm right and everything's going to be awful forever, but I'll let you think that it isn't, because I love you."

'You're not!' I insisted. 'It's just sea-sickness.'

I can't remember now if I was just trying protest to make her feel better, or if I actually believed that she was going to be all right. Either way she was correct, but that comes later in the story.

I ended up promising that I would ask Mhairi if she would mind coming to see my Ma'. That made her smile, but I don't think she meant it. I know that when I smiled back at her, as we tried to begin our lesson again, I didn't mean it. When the movement of the ship suddenly got too much for her, and I had to tend to her as if she were my bairn, rather than the other way round, I felt scared, in a way that I don't think I'd ever felt before.

I upped my efforts to avoid the meetings after that. It was too uncomfortable for me, and I definitely didn't ask Mhairi to come. I didn't want Ma' to scare her off.

As her condition got worse, any time anything went wrong, or one of us, by which I mean me, did something even remotely out of line, either my Da' or Moira would accuse us of upsetting my Ma', to try and make me feel worse about myself. I hated it, and though I'm really not proud of it now, I found myself starting to blame her for giving them more ammunition against me.

In general though, when I could get out of these sessions and forget about my Ma', I was blissfully happy for the first time I could remember.

One day, about two weeks into the voyage, everything went to hell.

It didn't seem like much when it started, it was just a bit of a dark sky. Living in Scotland, you were used to that, so none of us thought too much of it at first. Clouds like that usually get blown away before they do too much damage. Usually. The rain started about lunchtime, and I don't think I've ever seen it coming down so heavily before or since. And the wind! It was like being inside a nightmare. Remember what I said about mainlanders who were afraid of the sea? I stand by that point normally, but this was not a normal storm. Everyone was afraid for their lives that day. There were three ministers among the passengers, and being as how they were all from different Kirks, they couldn't agree on anything at all. They normally avoided each other, and when they did meet there would almost always be a hell of a shouting match. During the storm though, they put aside their differences, and they brought everyone into the sleeping room to lead us all in prayer. I have to say it helped, though maybe not in the sense they intended. Kneeling there, next to Mhairi and away from my family, I felt far more secure than I would have done if I'd been forced to stay in the cramped cabin with them for two days and having to listen to their arguments and insults overlaying the rain battering the ship, the wind blasting through her sails, all the while desperately hoping that we would live to see Cape Breton.

Two days. That's how long the storm lasted. There were some deaths, though I forget how many. They were mostly crew members, so none of the Highlanders really cared. Only three of us died. One wee bairn was swept over the edge of the boat on the first night, an old woman from Benbecula who was, for some reason only she and God knew, travelling on her own, fell down some steps, and then there was a man from Mull. No one knows what happened to him, but we all knew that his wife spent days in hysterics that could probably have been heard back in Tobermory. The ministers held funerals for all three of them, though only the old woman was actually there in person as it were. It was a shock to see them just tip her corpse over the edge of the boat. I vaguely remembered my Grandda' telling us that when Admiral Nelson died, they brought his body back to London in a barrel of wine, and as I'd not spent too long thinking about people dying at sea, I assumed they did that with everyone, in spite of the fact I grew up on the coast around fishermen.

The night after the storm, when we were finally able to see the stars again, it turned out that not only had *Elizabeth* miraculously managed to survive, but the wind had not blown her too far off course. In fact, it had even given us a little bit of an extra push. The Captain estimated that we were about halfway through the journey, nearly two days ahead of schedule. In response to this news, and to celebrate the fact that we weren't all languishing on the bottom of the ocean, it was decided that we needed a shindig. It took a bit of convincing the crew, but after most of the families pooled their resources and bartered them in exchange for them to letting us have a cèilidh in the main sleeping quarters. It cost about half of our whiskey and tobacco reserves, and a fair amount of coin as well, but everyone felt that it was necessary for us to celebrate coming out of the dark.

Almost all of the passengers spent the day of the cèilidh preparing the hall. I say almost, because sick folk like Ma', and those with bairns like Margaret obviously didn't. Mhairi and I had made ourselves scarce as well, retreating to one of the far off corners that had become one of our most frequently visited hideaways. By the time we emerged and made our way over to the impromptu cèilidh hall, it was barely recognisable.

The hammocks and sleeping mats had all been stowed away out of sight and, in their place, all of the benches had been brought down from the mess hall and arranged along the sides of the room. A few crates had been pushed together at the head of the hall to provide a stage as well. There were a handful of men standing on it, already playing their instruments and a few people had begun to dance. Clustered at the edge of the stage, a larger group of men were tuning their fiddles and filling their pipes. It's interesting the things that people thought were important to take with them to the New World. Anyway, most of the rest of the passengers that weren't already dancing were sitting on the benches. I spotted my family sitting in one corner, though my Ma' was not with them. Her condition had worsened with the storm, and when I'd left the cabin that morning she'd been unable to hold herself up. Even you were there, sitting propped up on you Ma's lap, bouncing in time to the music. Taking Mhairi's hand, I led her around the hall, away from my family as if I hadn't noticed them, until we found room to squeeze onto a bench.

Truth be told, I don't remember much of what happened during the cèilidh itself, and it's what happened afterwards that's important to this story. There was music, people danced, and drank, though as I say, we'd traded most of our whisky away. I think I remember that Mhairi's eyes kept being drawn one of the pipers, an anxious look in her eyes, but maybe it's just my mind playing tricks with me, getting confused and trying to make sense of what came later. For the most part though, we were too engrossed in each other to pay attention to anyone else, except at one point, when we were interrupted by my siblings descending upon us en masse.

Mhairi had been in the middle of telling me the exciting news, which she had somehow forgotten to tell me until then, that the elusive Ruaraidh had won a cabin off of another family in a game of dice, when suddenly we were aware that there was a large crowd of people standing next to us. Casting a glance up, I found myself looking straight at Katrine, who was looming, arms folded and glaring down at me, flanked by Moira and my brothers.

'What do you want?' I asked.

'Da' wants to know why you're not sitting with us?'

'And it takes all five of you to ask that question?'

'Watch it, Sheep,' Angus said, looking at me threateningly.

I glared back. 'I'm just sitting here with Mhairi. I don't have to sit with you if I don't want to.'

'You should come over and sit with Ma'. She wants to talk to you.'

I looked at her in confusion. 'Ma's back in the cabin.'

'Shows how much attention you were paying to your family,' Katrine said, disgust coating her voice like grease, as she stepped aside to allow me to see across the hall. Lo and behold there she Ma', still looking very pale but sitting propped up between my Da' and Margaret, who still had you on her knee.

I shrugged. 'Well, she'll just have to wait. I'm in the middle of a conversation. I'll maybe wander over later.' Moira gasped slightly, as if I'd just slapped her, Katrine pursed her lips, and the boys grunted to each other unintelligibly. 'Now, if you'll excuse me?' I turned away from them to face Mhairi. Having taken my eyes off them, I knew nothing of the punch Angus threw at my shoulder until it connected. With a yelp of pain, I turned back in time to see Katrine put a hand on Angus' shoulder, and him drop his fist.

'Come on,' she said, looking somewhat tiny in comparison to our bulky older brother, who, after one last glare at me, turned, shrugging her hand off his shoulder, and stalked back across the room, the rest of the siblings in tow, carefully dodging the couples dancing the Gay Gordons.

Satisfied with my victory, I turned back to Mhairi, who was looking at me with an odd expression on her face.

'What?'

'Why didn't you go back to your Ma'?' she asked.

I shrugged. 'I sat with her for about three hours earlier on. She'll survive an evening without talking to me.'

'I thought you said she was ill?'

'Look, what does it matter?' I said, starting to get annoyed. 'If I go over there, I'll just have to suffer being around my brothers and sisters. I'd be miserable. I'd much rather be here with you and happy. Do you understand that?'

Mhairi stared at me, then nodded silently.

Even though she was agreeing with me, I still felt as if she was trying to make me uncomfortable. With a big sigh, I got to my feet. 'It's too hot in here, and I need some fresh air. Do you want to come for a walk with me?' Mhairi shrugged, and got to her feet.

Hand-in-hand we skirted the edge of the dance floor, rather than crudely cutting across it as my siblings had, and headed for the door. I remember thinking that I could feel a prickling of the hairs on the back of my neck, as though eight pairs of eyes were following us, boring into me with accusing looks. I quashed the sensation, which was probably a figment of my guilt, and we climbed the companionway that led out of the hall.

It was already dark outside, though it didn't feel particularly late. We were hoping that, what with the cèilidh, nobody would be caring about the curfew. Even so, we still kept fairly quiet as we walked. I can't remember now whether I had planned it or if we just ended up there by accident, but after a few minutes walking, I found that we had arrived at the door to my family's cabin.

'What are we doing here?' Mhairi asked.

'Well everybody is down at the cèilidh, so we won't be disturbed if we're in here, will we?' I asked, pushing the door open and gesturing for her to go in. A little hesitantly, Mhairi entered the cabin, and I followed, closing the door firmly behind us.

I'm not going to tell you what happened next, because, well, you're still too young. Suffice to say, things had become a lot more personal, in spite of, or perhaps because of, our little argument. We emerged from the cabin about twenty minutes later and I was all of a sudden very conscious of the fact that there had been nothing stopping any of my family coming back to the cabin. I offered to take Mhairi back to the cèilidh, but she said she'd rather carry on walking around the ship. So we did. With my arm wrapped around her waist, we flitted across the ship with no real purpose or destination in mind.

Eventually, we ended up at one of our favourite haunts, somewhere we could see the stars but still be sheltered from the wind, and we lay down, holding each other tightly, enjoying the renewed closeness of our bodies. At some point we must have fallen asleep, because the next thing I knew was the sound of one of the crew yelling at us in English.

'What the hell are you two doing out here again?' The man shouted, before reaching down and grabbing each of us by the shoulders and pulling us to our feet before we had really come to our senses. Once I was able to focus my eyes on the figure before us, my stomach dropped. We had only run into contact with the First Mate once before, but that had been more than enough for me. The man was barely human, monstrous in size and in temper, and he could punch harder than anyone I'd ever known, even Angus.

'I told you last time, if I caught you out after curfew again, you'd regret it. And the way I hear it, you've been caught by others more than once since. So,' he paused to roll up his sleeves, 'I'm just going to have to make sure you remember it this time.'

It was the worst beating any of the crew had given either of us. I'd never known pain like it, and I don't think I have again, until I lost my hand at least. Once he had finished with me, leaving me crumpled in a heap on the floor, I heard him step towards Mhairi. It was the most horrible thing I'd ever heard in my life. I still sometimes hear the sound of her agony in my nightmares. The worst thing of all was that I was so broken, and so afraid of death, because I was sure that the mate had left me close to it already, that I wouldn't have moved to save her, even if I could have. Eventually, once Mhairi's screams had subsided into agonised sobs, I felt someone grabbing my shoulders and dragging me upright. With barely enough strength left to stand, I allowed myself to be led by the unseen figure, vaguely aware of the fact I could see the Mate in front of me leading Mhairi the same way. So dazed was I that I did not know where we were until a door opened, and I was able to focus my eyes on a massive figure, almost as tall as the Mate, though half as wide. It was the piper that Mhairi had been looking at during the cèilidh. I saw the Mate thrust Mhairi over to the man, gesticulating, and talking loudly and slowly, though my mind was too scrambled to make sense of the words. The man clearly didn't understand either, and simply glared at the Mate. As the man pushed Mhairi into the room, I tried to cry out in protest, though I don't think I made much more than a faint gurgling, as the shooting pain that ran through my chest as I did so cut me off. Then, all of a sudden, we were moving again, and seemingly in no time at all, I found myself being thrust into my Da's arms. I was, I think, aware of Margaret's voice, talking to the Mate in English, though I maybe dreamed that, because I don't remember a single thing after it.

I don't know how long I was unconscious, but however much time it was, I reckon it wasn't long enough. I could tell, from the moment I blearily opened my eyes, groaning, that something had happened while I was out of it. From the way that my brothers were glaring at me, with even more distaste than they normally wore, to the red rims around Katrine and Moira's eyes, and more shockingly, around my Da's. I'd never once seen my Da' cry, not even when we were forced out of the village and were reduced to sleeping rough in Dunvegan. I knew it wasn't me he'd been crying over, and even though there was only one thing that could even possibly have made my Da' cry, I still heard myself asking what the matter with everyone was.

I knew, as I was saying it, that it was the stupidest sentence I had ever said in my life, and looking back, that's saying something. Once it was out though, I couldn't take it back, and had to put up with the abuse that was levelled at me, which, again in retrospect, I more than deserved. I was able to discover that it was a combination of the dejection of my ignoring her at the cèilidh, grief over my condition and worry that the crew would somehow try to punish the rest of the family even more that finally pushed my Ma's infirmity to the edge. After falling asleep the afternoon after the cèilidh, she never woke up again. This information was accompanied by a flood of abuse from everyone, not only of my character, but also Mhairi's as well, before turning back onto me. I don't know how long I was subjected to that, but it felt like hours. It only stopped when the door opened, allowing Margaret, and you to enter the cabin.

'All right,' she shouted, audible even over the sound of the insults. 'Everyone just calm down. Go and get some fresh air, all of you, or something to eat for the love of God!'

'You're just going to comfort that bastard!' Sorley muttered bitterly.

'None of you have left the cabin in days,' she said, more quietly, placing a comforting hand on Da's shoulder. 'Please, for your own sakes go outside. Shouting at Iain isn't going to make anything better.'

Grudgingly, the rest of the family stood up one by one and slowly made their way outside. As Donald shut the door behind him, Margaret walked over towards me, still carrying you, and leant against the wall.

'You've really done it this time little brother,' she said after a while.

'I didn't mean to!' I said angrily, though I couldn't tell if the tears forming in my eyes were from anger, the pain that shot through my chest as I tried to move, or from grief. 'It's not like I planned this.'

'I know,' she reached out with her free hand and rubbed my head softly. 'But you did it, and you need to find some way to do right by them.'

'Why?' I demanded, shaking my head to escape her reach, ignoring the pain. 'I'll pray for Ma', of course I will, but I don't owe any of them anything. Not a single one of them cares about me.'

'You've not exactly made yourself easy to care about, Iain,' she said firmly.

'Because of Mhairi? What about everything Donald did with whatever her name was? Or Angus with Catriona MacLeod? The Factor's daughter over in Dunvegan? They caused just as many problems as I did!'

'It's partly that, but I meant in general. You've never tried to be likeable.'

I glared at her. I suppose now that she was right, but at the time... Well, nobody wants to hear that, and I was feeling particularly bitter from getting a verbal beating before I'd even properly recovered from the physical one.

'What happened to Mhairi?' I asked, frowning at the faint sigh of frustration that Margaret wasn't able to fully suppress.

Margaret looked at me for a while, rubbing the side of her face thoughtfully, as though debating with herself what answer to give. 'I don't know,' she said after a while.

'How can you not know?'

'I've not seen her since the cèilidh.'

'Didn't it occur to you that I'd want to know? You couldn't have looked?'

She frowned. 'Yes,' she said curtly, 'and I did look for her, but I couldn't find any sign of her on the boat.'

'You obviously didn't look hard enough,' I said. With a great effort, I sat up and climbed off the bed, limping towards the pile of clothes that were sitting on a chair across the cabin, the bloodstains still faintly visible. 'I thought you were supposed to be the one person in this family who actually liked me.' I paused, as you began to cry, but then continued, increasing my volume to be heard over your wails. 'But now you're blaming me for things I had no control of, and you can't even manage to do the one that thing that would make my life tolerable!'

'I was looking after you while you were unconscious!' Margaret said, more quietly so as not to upset you, though with just as much viciousness in her tone.

'And a fine job you did,' I said as I pulled on my shoes, trying my hardest not to wince in agony as I bent over. 'You couldn't have been trying to make the rest of them see reason? You've always been so good at making people think straight, but somehow it's mysteriously failed you now!'

'I can't always fight your battles for you Iain,' she said, and I could hear that she was crying now, though I couldn't bear to look up and see her face.

'Well now you won't have to.' I strode to the door as confidently as I could, and wrenched it open. 'I'm going to find Mhairi, and then I'll keep myself right the rest of the journey. Once we reach Cape Breton, you'll never have to see me again.'

I slammed the door behind me, your cries still audible through the wood, and hobbled off in search of Mhairi.

Apart from a few sneers here and there on the last two weeks of the journey, that was the last time I spoke to any of my family.

'...That was the last time I spoke to any of my family.'

The ward was silent again, except for the sound of the man by the door breathing, though even this seemed less rasping than it had earlier on. There weren't even any sounds coming from outside now. Night had fallen, and at some point the nurse had been back in to close the windows and light the single oil lamp that hung in the middle of the room.

As Iain told the story, Duncan had climbed up onto the bed and, wrapping himself with the thin sheet curled up next to Iain, where he was still staring up at him, wide-eyed with rapt attention.

'Did you find Mhairi?' Duncan said eventually.

'No,' Iain said hoarsely, reaching up to rub away the tears that had formed in his eyes. 'I looked, and looked, but there was no sign of her.'

'What about her family?'

'I got another beating when I went to find out. From Ruaraidh this time, warning me to keep away from the whole family. He said I'd caused enough trouble for them already.'

'Did anyone else know?'

Iain sighed. 'No one I spoke to. Not even any of the crew, and asking them got me more than a few bruises as well.'

'What do you think happened?'

'I don't know any more. At the time, I came up with hundreds of theories. She'd died from the beating the First Mate gave us, Ruaraidh or her Da' had taken their drunken anger out on her, she'd jumped overboard, I even ended up thinking bitterly that Angus or one of the others had done something to her. I'm not proud of that, just so you know. But I expect she was hiding in their cabin. When we landed, I waited at the docks for hours, waiting to see her walking down the gangplank, but nothing. When it started to snow, I picked up my bag, which I'd stolen from one of the other passengers and filled by sneaking into the family cabin to take what I could, then I headed away in search of somewhere to sleep, or a way of getting further away from my family.' Iain reached up his remaining hand and ran it through his hair, stopping as he felt his nephew's head suddenly resting on his uninjured arm, eyes closed and beginning to doze. 'But that's another story for another day.'

THE AIR AT KNIGHTSTEED

Darren Everett

THE AIR AT KNIGHTSTEED

A S THE STORY GOES, THERE WERE THREE WAYS IN WHICH A CHILD might come to live in the Copper City.

The first was in the way that is most natural – that is, as the product of a gentleman and his lady, in love; the second was on the not-so-uncommon occasion that one became lost on the roads outside the city and the Hall of the Chapels deemed it necessary to offer succour within its walls; and the third was when Lady Emma of the Knightsteed estate wrote a letter to the First Lord of the Treasury at Piccadilly, London, to request a son.

At that time relations between Britannia and the free city-state of Copper were civil – indeed, before madness befell him, His Majesty signed an agreement with the city's Marquis to allow the city to extend its northern borders into a forest belonging to the crown. Therefore, the Duke of Portland, First Lord of the Treasury, responded immediately to Lady Emma in order to ascertain the age, social class and lineage of the son she desired. It is said that Emma replied simply: 'Oh, you know the sort, William[1]; one that will grow into a fine gentleman should do.'

---

[1] William Henry Cavendish-Bentinck, 3rd Duke of Portland. A reference in *Copper & Verdigris* to a dalliance between Lady Emma and His Grace in their youth is almost certainly untrue.

So, while it remains unknown how Portland acquired the boy, it was on the second Thursday of October 1808 that Lady Emma's heir was dispatched to Knightsteed.

It would be fair to say that Lady Emma was not particularly fond of Thursdays. Her husband had been hanged for crimes against the state on a Thursday, and while she may not have found this disagreeable in itself, the entire affair had surely been something of an embarrassment. In a letter to a friend, Mrs Crockoll, Emma had this to say:

> It has been more than forty years, Enid – and truth to tell, nothing has occurred on a Thursday since to alter my opinion. I find it the dullest of the weekdays, surpassed only by Sunday afternoons. Trust William, then, to despatch my boy on this of all days. And in October, of all the months!

In fact, she found Thursdays so objectionable that she would refuse to leave the house or entertain guests, and if pressed to reply to correspondence she would keep it concise to the extent of leaving sentences unfinished and closings unsigned.

It is probable, therefore, that Lady Emma was not in the best of moods on that day and she was clearly underwhelmed with her boy. Nine years old, he was "lanky and pale of complexion [...] quite obviously the runt of the litter" with "a weak chin, ginger hair, and a shortness of breath that makes him wheeze like an old mongrel dog".

The boy's breathing problems were in fact more severe than Emma made out in her writings. Before his arrival at Knightsteed, he had been caught in a fire at St Bartholomew's Hospital in London which claimed seventeen lives; while the boy survived, it is possible that the smoke he inhaled caused him long-term respiratory difficulties.[2]

Their first exchange was transcribed by Lady Emma:

EMMA: What is your name, boy?
BOY: I don't have one, miss. I was told you'd be
        naming me.

---

[2] This theory does not explain why the boy was at the hospital to begin with; it has been suggested elsewhere that the boy had health problems before the fire started, and it was only because of his shortness of breath that he did not inhale as much smoke as the seventeen unfortunate children who shared the ward with him.

EMMA: I was never pleased with the name my father gave me. You shall choose your own, when you have come of age and have proven yourself to be a gentleman.

BOY: So what will you call me till then?

EMMA: Until then, I shall call you "boy".

For several days, she was undecided as whether to keep the boy or return him to London – perhaps another reason for her disinclination to name him. Mrs Crockoll attended a function at Knightsteed at the end of October and may have persuaded Lady Emma to accept the boy as her heir. Their conversation is not recorded in detail, but Mrs Crockoll appears to have drawn attention to certain pale, nervous, and possibly inbred male members of high society who were present at the party, and suggested that the child was well-qualified, therefore, to become a gentleman.

"All the same, I imagine it will be no mean feat; frankly I do not think you are up to it" is the phrase attributed to Mrs Crockoll in Lady Emma's journal – the deciding factor, we can assume, in her acceptance of the boy, history having shown time and again that Lady Emma could never turn down a challenge.

Though she would not admit to it, Lady Emma had not the foggiest idea of how to raise a child into a gentleman. She may have thought it was a natural progression for a boy – though Mrs Crockoll's words must have put her right, for the very next day she commenced his tuition.

This period is well-documented, not least because, despite his age, the boy was already a keen writer – something of which Lady Emma would have approved, had she known.[3] The following conversation has been taken from his journal:

EMMA: First things first, boy. You have a distinct lack of chin. You will grow a beard so I don't have to look at it.

BOY: Yes, miss. [Pause.] How do I grow a beard,

---

[3] As we will discover later, almost a year would pass before Lady Emma came across her boy's journals.

miss?

EMMA: [Firmly.] We shall speak to the gardener. He has marvellous whiskers.[4]

The curriculum Lady Emma followed seems to have been based on a combination of her own interests and vague memories of her father's favourite pastimes.

For instance, since the death of her husband, Emma had developed a taste for fine whisky; with no convenient trauma on the horizon, she did not feel it necessary to delay the boy's introduction to alcohol, and they would spend each morning partaking of the contents of a bottle of single malt.[5]

Her father had been an accomplished swordsman, so after breakfast Lady Emma would instruct her boy in the ways of fencing, specialising in use of the épée. (Her father had favoured the foil which targets the torso, neck and groin; Emma found it more liberating to attack the entire body, hence her choice of weapon.) Emma was naturally left-handed, and in her childhood her father had bound this hand behind her back to encourage use of her right hand; it is said that she was somewhat disappointed to discover that her boy was already right-handed, so she bound this arm and made him fence with his left.

Lady Emma had never learnt to swim, but she considered it an activity worthy of a gentleman; after their daily duel she would take him to the lakes behind Knightsteed House. As noted in the boy's journal,

> I think M is pleased at how quick I have got good at Fencing despite my best hand being tied up. This morning she took me to the Big Lake & pushed me into the water. It was cold. Only when I had sunk to the bottom did I notice something. She had tied both my hands behind my back. M is a Fine Lady even though she is Old. She is always pushing me to better myself.[6]

---

[4] The outcome of this conversation is not recorded; however, in his adult life the boy would wear a beard in the imperial fashion.

[5] Emma was a firm believer that "to truly appreciate whisky, it must be drunk before one's fast is broken, so as not to taint the taste buds with morning foodstuffs such as kidneys, kippers and kedgeree".

[6] "M" refers, of course, to Lady Emma, and is likely an abbreviation of "Miss" or "Mistress".

Lady Emma's father and grandfather had both enjoyed foxhunting – indeed, it had been her father's favourite sport – and although she felt it might be an important component in the construction of a gentleman, she could not bring herself to teach this to her boy. She had vague recollections of sitting with her uncle on the riverbank as a small girl, angling for trout; considering this a much nobler pastime, she resolved to teach her boy to fish instead.

Each afternoon, Lady Emma arranged for a rickshaw to take them into the centre of the city, to the largest of the nameless Copper canals, and they would sit on the jetty by Five Irons Brewery. It is not recorded whether they ever caught any fish, but it is clear that this was the boy's favourite part of the day. Lady Emma writes:

> Usually the solemnest of creatures, our trips into Five Irons bring him out of himself. While I don't hold with unnecessary effervescence, his moods are quite infectious and I almost smiled at his delight as we approached Bazeley Gardens, and the gaily-coloured Peruvian lilies and snapdragons upon display there. Having lived here for nearly six decades, one becomes almost blind to the splendour this city can offer. All the same, I clipped his ear and he duly curbed his enthusiasm.

Dated March of the following year, the boy had this to say:

> This is truly an Amazing City. I have forgot London (what it looks like) but I do not grieve because there is so much to see Here. The houses near the Canal are all painted in Different Colours. My favourite one is the Theatre which M says I shall go to when I am a gentleman. The Air is most clean & I find it better to breathe here than in London but M says it is the whisky & it is putting hairs on my chest.[7]
>
>   This afternoon we sat on the jetty & M told me Tales of the City like she always does when we are fishing. Today she spoke of the Hall of the Chapels & the s___ fox.[8] We did not catch any fish but we will bring

---

[7] The Copper City – being a city only in the strictest sense because of its cathedral, the Church of Sang-Clutch – was rather more rural than nineteenth century London, being less than a third of its size, and not subject to its heavy fogs and pollutants.

[8] Many of the boy's journals are water-damaged and in some instances his words are illegible. In this case, the missing word is widely accepted as "slow".

Cook's treacle sponge as bait tomorrow. M says it is World-Renowned
and it will surely draw the Little Buggers in.

Finally, before retiring at the end of the day, Lady Emma would take the boy to the ballroom and teach him to dance, favouring classical steps such the waltz and the minuet.

This curriculum was adhered to religiously on a daily basis, save for Thursdays ("How we can be expected to train on such a *dull* day?") and Sundays ("I have never believed in a supreme deity, Enid, but one does keep up with the gossip at church gatherings").

Lady Emma's stories of the city, told on the banks of the canal as they fished, had a lasting effect on the boy. He wrote down many of her tales, though it is clear that he was interested the most in those pertaining to the Hall of the Chapels.

For us to understand the lure of the mysterious Chapels, it is worth turning to *Copper & Verdigris*. Said to have been compiled by the city's fifth Marquis, Lord Lucius Deganos, it is little more than a collection of fables and romances; nevertheless, despite some far-fetched passages and many internal inconsistencies, this is the most comprehensive text available to us regarding the history of the Copper City, and it includes a score of previously uncollected Chapel tales.

In an early chapter, a young woman named Stone awakens to find herself in a great hall. Exhausted and uncertain as to her whereabouts, she explores her surroundings. Upon a daïs in the centre of the hall is a low granite altar, laden with fruit. Nine large rocks surround this table "like hungry guests preparing to dine". There are no walls – tarnished copper pillars support a high beamed roof – and outside, Stone can see the cobbled streets of Grasstown, one of the most affluent areas of the city. Somewhat confusingly, the story then describes this location in some detail, suggesting that Stone is familiar with this place, only to return to its description of the hall and her concerns at being "lost in an unknown clime".

At this point in the story, she becomes aware of a man standing in the shadows of the large rocks. He is leaning on a walking cane, his

---

as in the style of foxtrot dance that Lady Emma may have taught him in preparation for becoming a gentleman. However, the foxtrot was not commonly danced until the early decades of the twentieth century.

head angled away from Stone. Throughout the following conversation, he remains in the shadows and does not allow Stone to see his face:

MAN:	This here is the Hall of the Chapels. Centre of the city, smack bang in the middle.[9]
STONE:	[Confused.] I don't understand. Is this Gondal? I was lost in the snow on the moor…
MAN:	These rocks, them's the Chapels. They rescued you. Important part of this city, these rocks. Known anyone who's gone missing? Vanished off the face of the world? This is where they come, brung here by the Chapels. Bairns born in the city come here, too, to be named. Most important rocks you'll ever see, they are.
STONE:	I need to get back… I'm so tired. I'm so hungry.
MAN:	Hands off the food! You eat from the table, the Chapels'll wake up and start their slow dance. Don't touch. Keep quiet. Let them lie.

This was already a popular story before it was collected in *Copper & Verdigris*, and was quite likely told by Lady Emma to her boy on the banks of the canal. It features many of the hallmarks associated with the Chapel tales: the nine sleeping giants, the altar of fruit, the copper pillars and the "slow dance". Another prevalent characteristic of these tales is the "lame man" or "faceless man" – possibly the same character who appears to Stone in this story.

Occurring less frequently, yet still mentioned in at least half a dozen of the Chapel tales, are references to both chapel-found and city-born children; it is this in particular that seems to have obsessed Lady Emma's boy. Although his journals contain no explanation for this obsession, a later chapter of *Copper & Verdigris* – "The Lady and the Bee" – provides, despite an air of melodrama throughout, some

---

[9] Historically the centre of the city, though in 1756 (by British reckoning) the city extended its northern borders. The site that now lies central is Black Parade, home and office of the Marquis.

interesting conjecture on the reasons for his fascination.

The Bee[10] would follow the Lady everywhere, even to the extent of sleeping at the foot of her bed (clearly untrue as the journals of both Emma and the boy refer to his bedroom being in the loft of the house whereas hers was on the ground floor). On the days she attended church, he would fret anxiously about the house, awaiting her return.

It is on these days that, irritated by his moping, the Knightsteed staff would send the boy out to play. There were many children who played in the fields surrounding the Lady's house; she was an eccentric old woman and the children, thinking her to be a witch, would loiter in the hope of witnessing some act of magic. To be confronted by the sickly-looking Bee must surely have been a disappointment and the children did not take kindly to him, drawing attention to the fact he was neither city-born nor chapel-found. "The Bee does not belong" became their slogan; the Bee withdrew into himself and remained inside, exploring the halls and rooms of the Lady's house.

It is said that during one of the Lady's absences the lonely Bee discovered a secret hatch beneath her bed, under which was a small recess containing "many wonders the Bee had not spied before: a great glass Cyclops eye, fringed with long dark lashes; a large black umbrella with a whangee handle; an early draft of the novel *Fernando De Samara* by Ellis Bell[11]; a pair of tall-heeled boots; and a chipped champagne coupe".

Amongst this wondrous bric-a-brac was a small pamphlet written in the Lady's hand, detailing her first visit to the Hall of the Chapels. The Bee, "with hands trembling, for the Lady's past was a secret to him" read this pamphlet during his mistress's absence. The contents of this pamphlet are not reproduced, but there are references to "a sombre dance of giants" which was a threat to the Lady. She appears to have stood her ground and banished the giants with a single, magical word – which, interestingly, *is* reproduced, albeit elsewhere.

Copper & Verdigris is accepted widely to contain little historical accuracy. Strange, then, that the boy's own writings should lend

---

[10] *Copper & Verdigris* does not refer to Emma or the boy by name, and there is no indication as to the relevance of using "the Bee" to describe the boy. (Of course, though it is merely coincidence, some years after the publication of this text, the name that the boy chose for himself began with the letter B.)

[11] The pen name of Emily Brontë; an early draft indeed, as she would not be born for another decade. *Copper & Verdigris* contains many such inconsistencies.

credence to such a text: in one of his journals, mention is made of Lady Emma's fabled visit to the Chapels. The boy suggests that he had seen the magical word written down and describes it as "a Symbol which makes Me think of the French playing card suit of *Piques* [spades] with a Small Inkblot before & after". He suggests:

> *If M can stand Fearless before the Giants then I think I can too. I am training to be a Gentleman but it is a useless task. I am not City-Born & I am not Chapel-Found & it is clear that I do not Belong. I shall stand fearless before the Giants & demand that they Name me as one of Their Own. Only then can I be the Gentleman that M desires.*

Some historians have suggested that it is in this moment that the boy took his first brave steps as a true gentleman; others consider it merely a display of childhood folly.

It is widely accepted that the boy set out for the centre of the city on the morning of 3 September 1809[12] – one year to the day since the fire at St Bartholomew's Hospital in London. Lady Emma would have been at church so the boy almost certainly slipped away unnoticed. How he made his way to the Hall of the Chapels is not recorded, but it is probable that he took a rickshaw as was usual for his and Lady Emma's fishing trips to Five Irons.

What was going through his mind as he approached the Hall? *Copper & Verdigris* assures us he was, for the time being at least, true to his intentions: "fearless and bold". However, if we turn to the boy's journals, an entry written several days after his visit to the Chapels admits:

> *No matter how hard I tried to be Brave all I could think was that I would have to Awaken the Giants. I was afeared of the Slow Dance & what would Happen should the Giants dance it.*

The streets of Grasstown were quiet – as it was a Sunday, and raining heavily, it is likely that most people were at church or in their homes – so the boy entered the Hall of the Chapels unnoticed. *Copper & Verdigris* tells us that he was somewhat surprised, therefore, when the sound of

---

[12] By British reckoning, of course. Being a free city-state, Copper chose not to adopt the Gregorian calendar and to this day uses its own civil dating system.

someone clearing his throat came from the shadows. The lame man, it would seem, had been expecting him.

MAN:	Took your time, didn't you? They told me you'd be coming. Just didn't think I'd have to wait this long, is all.
BOY:	[Shocked.] Who are you? Why're you wearing a mask?
MAN:	Faceless, see? And show some respect to your elders, lad. Call me... call me Mister E. Course, should be Mister O. You know, strictly speaking. But E's got a ring to it.
BOY:	Why are you here? I came to... *Mystery*?
MAN:	Give the boy a prize! I know why you're here, lad. Chapels told me. Look, I got an appointment with my old lady, places to be and all that, so let's make this quick. You wake the rocks, you get two things: an audience with the Chapels, granted. But you got to dance with them too, and that's not so peachy.
BOY:	I don't understand you. Please leave me alone.
MAN:	Listen to my words! You mustn't dance! Me, I've got the moves. I can keep to the way. But you can't. The fox is too fast and it'll take you away.

In the boy's journal, however, there is no mention of the lame man. The boy walked slowly to the centre of the hall and stepped onto the daïs. The altar was laden with fruit – mainly ivy and holly berries – and mistletoe hung low from the beams above. Before addressing the giants, he bowed nine times, once for each of them.

He has not transcribed his exact words, only that his initial pleas for their help were ignored. Remembering the story of Stone, the girl who was warned not to eat the fruit lest she rouse the giants, he turned to the altar and took a handful of purple berries, only to discover that they were carefully painted pebbles. It was only then that he noticed the goblets, practically buried beneath the fruit; there were nine – "a chalice for each Chapel" – and they were overflowing with the rain that fell between the wide beams of the roof.

The Family Way

The following extract – the source of which is easily identifiable by its somewhat sensational style – explains what occurred next:

> He lifted the cup closest to him and, with a silent prayer, raised it to his trembling lips. Just as he supped its contents, there came an almighty groan: the giants were waking! The Bee stumbled backwards, dropping the cup and sprawling clumsily upon the low table of the Chapels, scattering fruit in all directions. He screamed in fear, for he was but a child, and the word he screamed was 'Mistress!'
>
> Then the giants spoke. Their words were a backward echo, starting low:
>
> *…chapels…*
> *…the chapels…*
> *Who dares disturb the Chapels?*
>
> When the giants speak, one must respond or risk their wrath. 'I haven't got a name, sirs,' the Bee stammered. 'I've come to ask a boon from you.'
>
> *…request…*
> *…your request…*
> *Speak your request, boy.*
>
> The Bee took a deep breath. 'I want you to make me a gentleman.'

Before we go much further, it is worth pointing out that while a similar description of events appears in the boy's journal, it is with the following caveat:

> *I felt the Dizziness of Fear & it was then that I considered the Chalice I had drunk from. Was I dizzy because I was Frightened or was this the dizziness of Breaking Fast?*[13] *Had the Chalice been full of rain water or had it contained some other Substance? I knew only that my words were slurred. I tried to say that I wanted to Belong in the City. The Giants told me they could not Change they could only Show. I do not remember for sure what Came Next. All I can say with Certainty is that I had a Dream or a Vision. I saw a Great Many Things.*
>
> *I saw myself bound in chains & locked within a Crate or Coffin. They were Drowning me in the Canal. They were the Hourmen. I duelled with*

---

[13] Remember that it was Lady Emma's custom to drink a bottle of whisky at breakfast.

a Thin Man in a burning ballroom. A lantern clock lay shattered between us. He stood at the hour of Six & I opposed him at Midnight. M was a young lady standing before a Grave in a London made of Steel and Glass. Magnolia snow had fallen on the Copper City.

On this rare occasion, *Copper & Verdigris* provides a simpler narrative:

The giants shewed him fire and smog, and water and blue sky.
...life...
...a life in each...
You have a life in each, boy. But you will belong in neither.

Both accounts veer towards the fantastical and it is regrettable that no other report exists. It is quite possible the water in the goblet was poisoned and induced hallucinations in the boy, as suggested in his journal. Several historians have proposed that the pebbles painted to resemble ivy and holly berries – fruit toxic to humans – represent a warning against the tainted water.

A warning, evidently, that the boy did not heed. He came to the Hall without the permission of his mistress. He dared to rouse the Chapels and bid that they make him a gentleman. He risked the wrath of the giants knowing the repercussions.

It would seem, unfortunately, that he did not consider those repercussions until it was too late.

Copper & Verdigris tells us that "the very ground quaked as the giants circled the Bee". The boy's journal describes his overwhelming terror at the "sound of Drums & the grinding of Stone" as the Chapels closed upon him. The slow dance had started.

It is as this point that Lady Emma arrived. There are two versions of the events that occurred next. The less trustworthy source suggests that

[she] stood tall and the Chapels seemed to shrink beneath her gaze. A great wind picked up and her cloak thrashed around her like a living thing. The very moonlight slunk back, leaving her in shadow. There was a moment of tension as the Chapels' slow dance shook the hall... and then the Lady raised her arms and spoke a single word which struck the Chapels like a bolt of lightning and stilled them forever, a magic word of immeasurable

power, and that word was "♠"

The other version, as written by the boy, provides a more concise (and credible) description of events:

> There was no storm or melodrama or Magic Words. That was not her way. She just took my hand in Hers & said: 'Let the boy be, you stone-faced tarts, or you'll have me to deal with.'

There is little more to tell of Lady Emma's boy. The history books chart his life from his coming of age in some detail, but of his remaining childhood there is limited information available to us, as the journals he kept between then and his twenty-first birthday[14] were lost in the flooding of Knightsteed some years later.

What does remain, however, are two final items of correspondence from Lady Emma to Mrs Crockoll. From the first of these letters we can gather that, during their return to Knightsteed, Emma and her boy conversed at some length. The boy asked his mistress how she had ascertained his whereabouts, and in response she flourished the journal she had found in his room which had detailed his intentions. Being a keen writer herself, it appears that she was delighted to discover her boy's interest in journal-keeping and it is possible that she did not reprimand him as severely as she would have for his foolishness in approaching the Chapels. The following exchange is worth quoting in full:

BOY:	I've let you down, miss. I'm not a gentleman and I don't belong here.
EMMA:	[A rare smile.] Look on the bright side, boy. For what it may be worth, I don't belong here either.
BOY:	Really?
EMMA:	Of course, the trick is not to let anybody know.
BOY:	Miss? Do you still want me to be a gentleman?
EMMA:	No. [A sniff. She clips her boy's ear, as is her way.] We'll have to work on your handwriting, though.

---

[14] When he left Lady Emma's house and moved into Mourning Star.

In the second of the two letters, we learn that shortly after his experiences in the Hall of the Chapels, the boy made an important discovery: just as there were three ways for a child to come to live in the Copper City, there were three ways in which one could leave. The letter is listless in tone, however, and Lady Emma neglects to explain further. We can safely assume it was written on a Thursday.

BEHIND A THOUSAND SHIPS

Meghan Hawkes

Meghan Hawkes is a writer, freelance illustrator, shameless book-addict, and history enthusiast. She has previously been published through Chalk Path Books with the story VALE OF YEARS, *included in* THE LAST POST.

Feel free to view some of her other work at www.meghanhawkesillustration.com.

BEHIND A THOUSAND SHIPS

I WAS NINE YEARS OLD WHEN MY MOTHER WAS TAKEN AWAY. MANY things have been said of this. Some claim that she went of her own accord, willingly abandoning us for a young lover. Others say that she was bewitched by the gods and spirited away. And others yet, in quieter tones, with cautious sideways glances towards me, that she was taken by force and violence in the middle of the night.

No matter what the nature of the telling, however, there is a single constant in every tale: that it was her terrible beauty to blame. That, in some way, it was her fault for being so magnificent.

I have seen them sometimes looking at me, studying my face and figure as though something of her will suddenly blossom in me and start the whole horrid business anew. Those were nightmarish, bloody days, and I understand their fears, but I am not my mother. I am not foolish enough to think myself unlovely – no child of my mother's blood could ever be called that – but no one could compare with her luminous skin, golden hair, and starry eyne. She was the most beautiful woman to have ever walked the earth. I have never heard anyone dispute that.

She was rare as a pearl, and has been called many things: Helen, child of the King of the Gods, queen and wife of the mighty Menelaus of Sparta, and the cause of the bloodiest war the world has ever known. But, whatever may have been the truth, she was my mother. And I loved her.

Up until my ninth summer, I had lived in the warm idyll of a dream. My earliest years remain with me as but the faded strains of a song – half-snatches of tunes and words, part forgot – and yet I do recall that they were happy years. It might have been said then that the Fates had blessed us.

How naïve we that set ourselves apart from the woes of others.

There are specific instances that remain more clear in my memory, thanks be to Mnemosyne for her gifts. Simple moments and impressions, perhaps, but ones that my heart has cherished.

I remember, for instance, the sight of my mother at her loom, her every movement graceful and sure.

She would often sing at her weaving, and her voice was warm and enveloping like the sun on the first morn of summer. One of my earliest true memories is of sitting in her lap as she guided my small hands through the task of weaving. It took both my hands to grasp the shuttle, though her fingers wrapped gently around mine to hold it steady, and she taught me to lead it through the warp threads and pull it tight. It seemed a special magic to me, to be making cloth out of string, as though my mother were one of the Fates themselves, weaving the measure of our lives. If I close my eyes, I can still feel the calm room around me, hear my mother's quiet voice in my ear over the rhythmic clack of the loom, and smell the sweet summer air.

My mother always smelled of apple blossoms.

Undoubtedly the bards have already crafted many tales about my mother. I have heard a few, though they tend to be kind enough to avoid the more lengthy mentions in my presence. They are surely well told, but I am not as sure that they are the truth.

I am no bard or poet, merely a woman who has a memory and a desire to pass it on. I should like my mother to be remembered. Though, I do not know what her story should be. Gods grant that I tell it well. Sing, o Muse. I have burnt incense in offering to both Clio and Melpomene. Perhaps they will take pity on their earthly cousin and grant me a measure of skill to tell it right.

I should, perhaps, offer a bit of history.

My grandmother was Queen Leda, wife of the bold King

Tyndareus of Sparta. The people say that Zeus, enamoured of her beauty, changed himself into the shape of a swan and forced his attentions on her. Afterwards, she birthed two giant eggs. When the eggs hatched, they yielded two girls and two boys. That is the story of my mother's birth.

So far as I know, none have ever asked the truth of it. My grandmother was a proud and noble woman, and my grandfather – as Tyndareus always held himself to be, regardless of what was said – a wise and fair man. To have asked them such a question would be an unthinkable insult. But the story remains that Leda bore to the swan Zeus four children, and of them my mother was most favoured by the gods.

They say she was beautiful from the very moment of her birth, and I do not doubt it. No one who saw her ever could. Her beauty was of a sort that people would be startled into silent awe at the very sight of her. Though her brothers and sisters were said to be very comely as well, none could compare.

My mother's sister Clytemnestra was wed to the great king Agamemnon, which makes her my aunt twice over for he is my father's brother. It is said that she murdered him. I cannot speak as to the truth of that. I met her only once, and she seemed very regal and very cold. My mother's brothers are unknown to me entirely, though on the rare occasions she spoke of them it was always with affection. They are buried at Therapne, where my mother was eventually laid to rest. Someday my father will join her there, Charon grant him safe passage.

My father said that his first glimpse of my mother felt as though it were the first time he had seen the sun.

He and my uncle were in exile from Mycenae after the murder of their father, Atreus, and sought allies to regain his throne. It made a great deal of sense that they travelled to Sparta, for our warriors' prowess is well known and my grandfather was a very fair man.

Tydareus welcomed them in with expansive hospitality, and listened to their tale. My father said that no sooner had they finished speaking but Helen entered, and he forgot how to breathe. He watched her, transfixed, and she looked back and smiled. He decided then and there that he would give the gods anything if she would agree to be his wife.

The time was not right for marriage, not with war looming so readily over their heads, so my father was forced to ignore his love for my mother for another two years. During that time, Nike granted them victory over their foes, and mighty Agamemnon was restored to the throne of Mycenae with Clytemnestra as his queen. Then my father returned to Sparta, to court Helen at last.

This is a story that has been told many times, and I will never doubt the truth of it.

Forty-five men had come to woo my mother, for word of her beauty had spread far and wide. She was courted by kings and princes aplenty, the sons of the greatest men in all of Achaea. They brought rare and wondrous gifts, and exhibited many feats of strength. They battled amongst themselves, hunted wondrous beasts, and tried to move the very mountains of Sparta. Ajax, son of Telamon fought for fair Helen's favour. So too did Menestheus of Athens; and bold Odysseus of Ithaca; poor, doomed Patroclus; and countless others – heroes, all. But my mother remembered great Menelaus, my father, and was resolved to take no other. King Tyndareus knew not what to do, for how could he turn down any of those great men without causing offence? My grandfather had no desire to start such a war, and greatly feared what it could mean if so many armies rose against each other.

In the end, it was Odysseus who came up with the answer. He proposed that all the suitors be forced to make a pact to uphold whatever choice fair Helen made. No man could take from the chosen his lawful wife, and should any attempt to do so the others would all be obliged to fight for her safe return. They would protect her marriage as though the gods themselves had decreed it.

They sacrificed a bull to Zeus, and swore upon their honours, and so the pact was made.

My mother used to laugh when this story was told.

'Dramatic boys,' she would say. 'They make many pretty vows, but none could ever doubt that your father was the best man. Hyperion himself could not have moved me so.'

Then my father would kiss her, and they both would laugh again.

Once, when I was very small, one of my father's hounds died and orphaned a litter of puppies yet to be weaned. My mother soaked old cloths in goat's milk, and patiently suckled each one until they were old enough to chew. Even then, she gave them scraps of her own meals, and kissed their downy heads as they ate.

It made my father laugh to see her, but he let her do as she would with them. He could never deny her anything.

I remember playing with the pups. They were terribly small, but such dogs are beloved of Maira and thus they thrived. There were three of them – two males and a female. My mother named them for her brothers and sister, and laughed when they mouthed her fingers or licked her face.

Small child that I was, I revelled in the presence of such tame beasts. My father's hounds were magnificent, but they were trained for battle, for the hunt, and for violence. They were not the companions of a small girl. My mother's pups, however, were ideal. They followed us loyally from task to task, stretching themselves lazily across the threshold of every room. At night, they would doze with their heavy heads in our laps. During the day, they were ever my constant playfellows.

Aethra, my mother's serving-woman, was convinced the pups would die, and firmly of the mind that we should abandon them to do so. She did not understand my mother's innocent devotion.

'If the gods desire them to live, then live they shall,' she said crossly, 'but better to let them alone and not waste cream on foolish hopes.'

I do not doubt that others of the household agreed, though none so boldly as Aethra. My mother only smiled and shook her head.

'Surely kindness is never a foolish course,' she said.

Disagreement tightened Aethra's face, but she did not argue further.

Castor and Polydeuces eventually grew to be trained with the rest of my father's hounds. Clytemnestra was permitted to stay with my mother and myself, and a more faithful creature the gods have never seen.

She died the night my mother was taken, stabbed through the heart, with blood on her teeth.

The prince Paris I shall hate for all my days.

I know he is long dead, but I would still gladly tear out his heart and feed it to my father's hounds. I would take great pleasure in watching Castor and Polydeuces dine on such despised flesh.

They say a seer told King Priam that if Paris lived, he would bring about the fall of Troy. Priam despaired over this, for what man wants to kill his child? But he was a king, and had to care for the fate of all his people. Rather than strike the blow himself, he left the babe on a mountainside in offering to the gods and asked that his death spare all of Troy from disaster.

The story should have ended there.

Instead, a shepherd found the child and, out of pity, raised him as his own. So Paris grew to manhood as a shepherd's son until the gods themselves stepped in. I have heard it said that Hera, Athena, and Aphrodite all came to him, and demanded that he judge which of them was fairest of all. Why they asked such a question of a mortal shepherd-prince is beyond my understanding, but none can know the thoughts of the gods.

The three goddesses offered him many things to sway his judgment on themselves. In the end, he picked Aphrodite. She had promised him my mother.

And so we come to the crux of the matter. Whether impelled by the gods, or driven by his own jealous wants, Paris stole Helen from Sparta and brought her to Troy.

How Eris must have laughed at the ensuing chaos.

My memories of that night are scattered and sharp. My father was holding a feast. I could hear the music and gaiety from where I was meant to be asleep, and stayed wide awake to listen. I remember peeking out the door and catching a glimpse of my mother before Aethra caught me up and shooed me back to bed. It was to be my last true sight of my mother, and I shall keep it unto the crossing of the River Lethe, which steeps all souls in forgetfulness.

She was laughing at something my father had whispered into her ear, head tilted back and curls glistening like molten gold in the torchlight. Her cheeks had been flushed with wine and merriment, and her richly purple chiton was slightly ruffled from dancing. I remember the glint of gold at her arms, the shimmering rustle of silk, the gentle hand that caressed my father's cheek. She looked joyful and divine and very much in love.

I must have fallen asleep at some point, for I remember waking after the feast had ended to the sounds of shouting. There was such a din that it seemed as though every warrior in Sparta had come into my father's home, and was preparing to fight. They yelled and pounded their shields, and somewhere in the midst of it I heard my mother scream, followed by my father's anguished cry of her name. I could smell smoke, strong and acrid in my nose, and was terribly afraid.

No one came for me until mid-morning, by which time I had huddled in the corner and was weeping. I did not know what to think. I worried that my parents had been slain, that war had come and I was the only survivor.

When at last my father entered the room, I threw myself into his arms, too relieved at his presence to wonder why he had come and not my mother. His hand shook as he stroked my hair. Then he pulled back, and bent down to look at me straight.

'Hermione,' he said, and I froze in fear at the unaccustomed grief in his tone.

'They have taken your mother. She is gone.'

I have surprisingly little of my mother in my mien. Oft have I gazed at my mirror in the quiet night, trying to find some small trace of her.

What I have discovered is this: her slender neck, her almond eyes, and a hint of her smile. Yet, the oval of my face is not so smooth as hers, the shape of my nose not so fine, nor my lips so tender soft. I am naught but the shadow of my mother – drawn with her airy lines, and filled with my father's earthen hues. But sometimes, if the firelight is right, I can see the echo of her in my face. We are most alike in sorrow, and her image brings me tears.

Once, not long before her death, Queen Leda laid her hands on my cheeks and stared long into my eyes. It was the closest I had ever seen my grandmother to weeping. She had remained strong and composed as Hera herself even when she buried her husband and sons. Yet, that day, as she searched my face, I saw the glimmer of moisture in her eyes.

'I wish she had looked more like you,' she said quietly. 'Protect me from the gods' jealousy, but she was lovelier than Aphrodite herself. How could she not have suffered for that?'

I knew not what to say in response. After a moment, Leda smiled and her tears were hidden away.

'You are lovely enough for yourself, child. Go to your weaving. I shall retire, for the day is very hot.'

I nodded and moved away, but watched from the shadows for a moment as her hand passed over her eyes. I understood her then, and prayed for both of my parents to come safely home.

* * *

The days following my mother's abduction were unbearably tense.

It was for just such an occurrence that Odysseus' pact had been forged, but it seemed none had ever expected it to come to pass. The time it took to send messengers to the forty-five kings, and for them to then travel to Sparta, seemed interminable. My father spent those days pacing the courtyard in agitation. I was afraid to cross his perturbed path, but watched from the doorway and whispered prayers under my breath.

The grief on my father's face was terrible.

At last they all arrived and assembled under my father's roof. So many great men, all full of anger, all trying to talk above each other and be heard. Many of them did not wish to go to war. Some claimed that the pact had been to protect against one another, not a Trojan prince. Some argued that surely Helen had gone of her own accord and not been stolen away at all. The first man to say such a thing, my father nearly killed on the spot. It was only Odysseus' intervention that spared him.

At the end of the day, my uncle stood before them, and all fell silent. None dared argue with the great king Agamemnon of Mycenae.

'It was agreed,' he said, eyes sweeping over the crowd and voice ringing with authority, 'that every man here would safeguard the marriage of Helen to Menelaus. No conditions or excuses were given. Are you not men of your word? There is a great dishonour done against that marriage here.

'Of equal import is the dishonour against the gods. Young Paris was a guest of this house. He violated sacred hospitality. He perpetrated violence against his host, and against a great queen. He offended the gods, went against the edicts of Zeus himself. It is Paris of Troy who has done this, and he must answer for it.'

There had been a rumble of anger among the men at the talk of Paris' offences, and they knew that Agamemnon spoke truth. Nestor stepped forward as my uncle sat down, and addressed them.

'A war it is to be, may Nike grant us victory. Now we must decide what war we shall wage. Offer your praises to Ares and Athena, and let us talk.'

It was seven more days before all matters were settled to every man's satisfaction. They argued over the number of men and ships, over whether there was enough food, the quality of weapons. There were great disputes over the tactics, whether to settle in for a siege or simply attack in full glory of the gods. The swiftest routes were plotted, disputed, plotted again; and many vowed to raze farms and ships to limit Troy's stores. Each man had to have his say, and each man had to argue every point. It was very slow going, but in the end they all agreed.

And so, a thousand ships set sail for Troy.

For ten years, we knew nothing of my parents' fate. We had to assume that they both lived, and the war raged on, for we heard no word and no men returned.

The first year was the worst. Our entire household was always on edge, fearing the day that a messenger would return with devastating news. The same held true throughout all of Sparta. Perhaps across all of Achaea. We jumped at every sound, chased every shadow, and worried away the hours that we should have been working. There was a very poor harvest that year.

Still, life continues in spite of us. Gradually, its natural rhythms crept back into life. People returned to their fields and to their looms. Work went more slowly with so many men gone, but it continued nonetheless. Libations were left for Demeter, and the wheat grew tall. Come the harvest, we reaped what bitter seeds we had sown.

Tyndareus retook the throne he had so willingly yielded to my father, and ruled quietly. There were very few disputes.

But there was still so much missing, a gaping hole in the very heart of Sparta.

Many looked to me to lead my father's household in his absence, for there were so very few of my family line there remained. But I was yet a child, by no one's imagination grown or wise, and I was afraid. Until that summer, I had been idle and cosseted and knew nothing of my mother's duties as the lady of our home. I still woke in the nights calling for my mother's calming embrace.

In the end, Leda took the time from her own household to show me the running of mine. She taught me early on to bury fear and to appear wise. She counselled me in frugality, taught me to calculate our stores, to manage disputes and soothe injured prides. She took me to do honour to Hestia, and ask for her guidance. We left her a libation of wine, and promised to keep the hearth burning. In silence, I asked her to return my parents alive that our home might be whole and happy.

It was a mother's task that Leda took on, performed in her daughter's stead, and she gave me all the knowledge she could.

I learned the ways of the kitchen and stillroom, of the weaving room, the storerooms, the workrooms, and the guest rooms. I learned the value of gold and jewels, of linens, of wines. I learned the importance of hospitality – sacred to the gods, Zeus bless our travellers and friends – the politics of guests, and the art of preparing a feast. By my thirteenth summer, I governed the household with enough economy and grace that even Leda herself was proud.

'You do great credit to your father's home,' she said, and her rare approval filled me with joy at the achievement. My grandmother was stern and noble, and a single smile from her was worth many words of praise.

Much of my brother's care fell to me in those years as well. Aethra wept bitterly after my mother's abduction, and could not look at either of us without once more showering us in tears. Eventually, she kept mostly to the kitchens and avoided us entirely.

I took over feeding my brother, watching over him as he played, and tucking him into bed. I cozed from him his first attempts at words. He said 'Hermione' before all else. And, it was I who stood witness to his first, faltering steps in the courtyard.

Nikostratos still has all the love my heart can hold, and I shall always remember how he tottered towards me with his arms outstretched. It was a cloudy day, but hot and close with late summer heat. I had for but a moment seated my brother on the ground to retrieve some water for us both. When I turned back around, he had brought himself to his feet and was determinedly stumbling the few small steps to my side.

Once there, he grasped my skirts with a cry of triumph that would have suited any great hero in battle, and promptly fell back to the ground. Rather than tears, as most children's falls produce, this resulted in a loud burst of laughter. I could not help but laugh right alongside him, so proud and amazed was I.

After that, Nikostratos quickly apprehended the art of walking and running. I spent much time chasing him out of mischief. He was always such an energetic boy, prone to violent fits of anger but with a great kindness in him. When the time came, I secured him the best teacher I could find. Aberkios was an aged man, but so were all who had been left behind in the war. He was still swift in mind and body, and had the patience to handle my brother's wild ways. Nikostratos loved him dearly.

Those were lonely, painful years, but there were moments of great beauty and happiness as well. Such is the way of the world.

Then, at last, the war ended.

I have heard it said that, after ten long years of war, my father was prepared to strike my mother dead. When the great city of Troy finally fell and the Achaean men roamed the streets, he had his sword in hand to do the deed. My mother prostrated herself before him, welcoming of her fate. Yet, when he was faced with her loveliness and sorrow, he could not bring himself to strike the final blow. He could not, in the last, convince himself of her guilt.

Over the years, I have imagined this scene many times. I can see in my mind's eye the struggle in my father's form as he lifted the sword. I can see the quiet trembling of my mother's shoulders, the way she clenched her eyes tightly shut, and the single tear that escaped. I can hear the deafening clatter of my father's weapon falling from his nerveless hand. And, most of all, I can see him embracing her and weeping in the middle of the ruined city.

At the end of the war, it was love that made him bring her home.

They told me that Paris had a wife, a nymph named Oenone who had the rare gift of healing. I have wondered, sometimes, what became of her. If they had any children, if her life was filled with sorrow or anger, if she was a casualty of the war her husband started over another woman. If the gods gave her any warning before her life was torn asunder. Oenone is in my thoughts tonight, Eleos embrace her and grant her kindness in this life, and I hope that she has found some measure of peace.

For myself, I am restless and sad this night, when I ought to be joyful. Tomorrow, my brother Nikostratos shall be wed. His bride is Pisidice of Pylos, daughter of the wise Nestor. She is a sweet and moderate girl, and it is hoped that her gentle influence will calm my brother's passions. He has the fire of youth in his veins, and is much beloved of Ares.

Still, he seems to hold for her a tender affection, and the omens bode well for the marriage. The full moon shines for the fourth of Gamelion, the seers see no ill omens, and all due offerings have been made to Artemis and Aphrodite. Good Nestor held such a feast this evening that I do not see how tomorrow could possibly surpass the gaiety and celebration. Bards and musicians abounded, wine and laughter flowed freely, and all ate more than their fill of fine foods. He gives his daughter gladly to our house, with much talk of the greatness of both my father and brother. For all his losses in those terrible ten years, he makes no mention of the pain our house has caused all Achaeans. Nor has anyone else.

That has not, however, banished it from our thoughts. Nikostratos sought me out after the feast, and clasped my hands in his.

'Hermione,' he said, sounding less certain than I can remember since he was but a small boy. 'Have I your blessing in this marriage?'

'Silly boy,' I told him. 'Of course you do. Pisidice is fine and fair, and I do not doubt she shall make a fine wife.'

'But shall I make a fine husband?' he asked, face part hidden by shadow. He paused then, but I know my brother well enough to wait until he came to his true point. At length, he said:

'I do not much remember our mother. If any has been such a thing to me, it has always been you. But you are our father's daughter, not his wife. And, though it has been agreed that you shall marry Neoptolemus, it is yet to come and I have never seen you in such a role. I do not know how a man acts to a wife.'

I forced myself to laugh, though it pained me to hear him say that he did not remember our mother.

'You have seen other husbands and other wives,' I said. 'And you were not so young as to forget the kind strength of Tyndareus to bold Leda. Follow their example, trust the gods, and, if there is a doubt, listen to your wife. She will undoubtedly have thoughts of her own.'

He smiled then, and released my hands.

'You are wise, sister. I thank you.'

Then he bade me good night, and kissed my forehead as I had always done for him in childhood. It brought tears to my eyes to find him so fond, where of late he has been warlike and brusque. I watched him walk away, and now I have returned to the room granted to the women of Menelaus' house. The fire is burning low, and I can hear the quiet sleeping breaths of the others, but Hypnos still grants me no slumber. Perhaps the gods desire me to write this story. Someone must remember Helen, if even her son cannot.

It is not his fault. Young though I was at the time of her abduction, Nikostratos was even younger – barely more than a babe in arms. When our father first returned after the ten long years of the war, Nikostratos ran from him as from a stranger and hid behind my skirts. He had to learn our father's presence, and his place in our lives, by slow turns.

And even more, the woman who came home with Menelaus was not truly our mother. She was a pale, otherworldly ghost more than a woman – luminous in her grief, and still and silent as marble. She did not sing, nor laugh, nor smile. She did not dance or weave. She simply sat in the courtyard and looked up at the sun, faded and sad and still redolent of apple blossoms.

In the stories, I've heard it said in whispers that Helen was finally driven from Sparta. That she lives now in the mountains, naked and mad as the Oracle at Delphi, dispensing dire predictions to unwary travellers. It is a dramatic image, one that makes listeners gasp with scandalized delight, but it is not true. The simple truth is that she faded away and died within the year. My father grieved over her renewed loss, but I could not. To me, Helen of Sparta had never returned and all my mourning had been done. I do not believe Nikostratos felt anything but relief.

We buried her, as I have said, near her brothers and observed all due funeral rights. The motions seemed empty to me, and many of our kindred seemed to resent their practice.

They say of Spartan women that we are strong and fierce, and rejoice when our men are slain in glorious battle. It is not so. We are taught the honour of a strong warrior, and we do celebrate their victories and greatness, but in truth what women would not prefer her husband or son, father or brother, to return home? So many did not return from Troy, and it was so many years to spend in fearful wonder of their fates. I could not begrudge the women their need to blame. I had not the energy to try.

'Harlot,' they whispered. '*She brought us bitter war, stole our sons, and now is gone forever.*'

I pretended not to hear. They were angry, and full of grief, and I had nothing left to fight them with. I did not even have my mother's soothing voice and gentle touch, though I had waited so very long to have those tender comforts back. Instead, I stood solemn-faced in the procession, and tried to summon any reaction at all. Then, I returned to be the lady of my father's household, and life continued as it had for the past ten years.

It was another year before I finally wept and laid my sorrow to rest in Penthos' care, and by then my mother had become more myth than truth. I think the people like her better that way. Yet, my tale is meant to impart a bit of that hidden truth, for truth it is: Helen of Sparta was a woman – a mother and a wife of extreme kindness and grace. She lived, and she was loved.

IRIS

Peter Kendell

IRIS

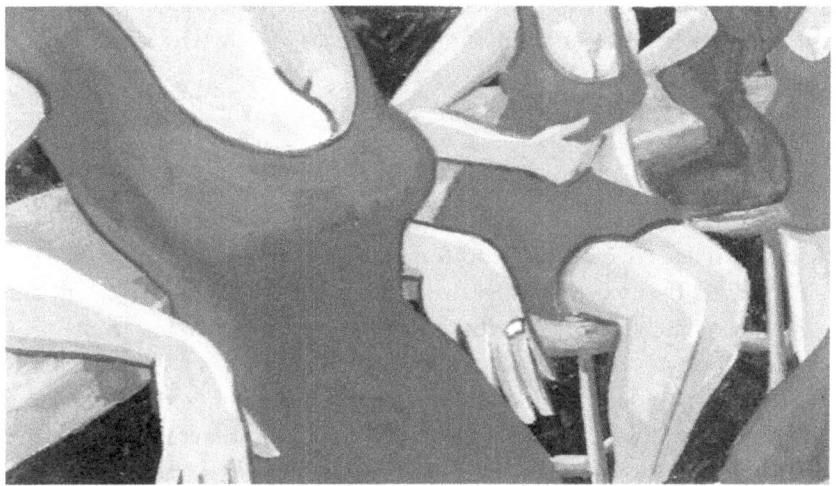

IRIS HAS COME TO THE POINT WHERE SHE HAS TO MAKE A CHOICE. THESE days her life is so full of blue and grey that she fears she may drown in it. Is this all there is to be, for the rest of time, she asks? No, of course not, don't be so dumb. There is, she knows, no real cause for her fear. Her days are full. She makes cakes, she keeps house, she helps at the thrift store, she goes to church, she meets with the other church wives, she, like them, is a good wife. But that is no good now. She needs more. She needs a change. And she is sick of death.

She could find a new man. That might be fun. But wait; she has a man right now – a fine man – and she should be glad of this, and of him. Ben is kind and he is a good dad to Sam. It is not his fault that he is so dull – it is the fault of the world that made him. This she says in her mind. And so it is true.

If she could take a break – that might do it. Go on a road trip. Just her. Take the car and head off, like Ben did that time with Ryan. But just her. That would be fun. She could drive and drive and stop just when she felt like it. She could make her own choice of when to stop and where to go, when to drive on and when to stay in one place and spend a day or two with the folks who live there. Free to be, just for a day or two, a new Iris, one with no spouse, no kids and no ties.

She sits on the bed in the room at the top of the house – Sam's room

– and the thought comes to her that she could take a new name as well. That would seal it. She would be a blank, a void, a space to be filled, like a tin with cakes or a vase with blooms. A new name; that would mean a new Iris, in – and why not? – a new town in a new state.

Yes, she says to the quiet air of the quiet house. I will do it!

Iris knows that Ben would miss the car if she went off in it. He needs it to get to work. Worse, it would brand her. She can see it now. Yes, Ben will say, it's a Toyota Prius and the plate is— and he will give the cops all the facts they need to track Iris down. They will put out a call and when they catch up with her they will cuff her and lock her in the cells. She will be put on trial in court as a car thief. This is all quite clear in her mind. Iris is not a thief, and so she waits for Ben and Sam to leave the house and then she packs her clothes, calls a cab to take her to town and rents a car with her own card. She signs her old name – for the last time? It has been some time since she was last at the wheel and so she drives with great care.

   The road leads north. That is not the way she meant to go – which way had she meant? – but it will do. North, South, East or West; they are all the same to her. All she wants to do is drive. To start with the road is full of cars and trucks, but as she drives on it grows more sparse. Soon the road is all hers. She can do what she likes – drive in the wrong lane, say. But she does not. She takes great pains to make sure that she does not stand out. She does not want the cops to flag her down.

She drives for eight hours, but as it grows dark she pulls up at an inn and stops for the night. The boy at the desk has an odd way with him but she does not let it put her off. She knows he will not harm her. She takes the key with a smile, goes to her room, kicks off her shoes and lies on the bed. She has a wash. She stares at the tube for an hour or so. She goes out to eat and chat to the staff. They talk with her. It is their job.

   There is a bar next door so she looks in there and has a drink. She sits on a bar stool, next to the whores, and waits for a man to pick her up. But the men in the bar do not pick her up or try to buy her a drink. They can tell she is not a whore, but a man's wife. They see the ring on her left hand. The old Iris would have liked that. This new Iris is not so sure. Soon they ask her to leave. She is bad for trade. She puts the men off.

Back at the inn, she goes to bed and tries to rest. She is worn out from the drive, but sleep is slow to come. She is just on the edge of sleep when she thinks of her cell. It could help the cops to track her, like the car. She gets up and takes the phone from her purse, pulls out the sim card and breaks it in two. She hopes it is not too late to do this. She will buy a new sim in due course. She cuts up her bank cards and throws the shards in the trash. That done, she goes back to bed and goes to sleep at last. When she sets out the next day she is still tired, and it is only the buzz she still feels – look at me, a slut who hangs out in bars! – that keeps her sharp and safe at the wheel.

The next day is much like the first. She drives, she stops for gas, she eats, she stays at an inn. And the next day and the next. At the end of each day, she takes off her ring and hangs out in a bar. She learns some of the ways of the whore. She pulls up her skirt and shows her legs. She wears a low top. She smiles a come-on smile. And she has good luck, or bad. Some days she gets to eat, some not. No two days are the same. She is picked up, or she is not picked up. She has sex with a strange man, or she does not. She goes back to her room or she stays at the man's place. One man hires her at a time, or more than one. She serves them and they pay her in cash. Now she leaves no trail for Ben or the cops. Two weeks pass, and she hands back the hire car and buys an old truck from a small ad. She pays in bills.

Iris takes a new name. She is called Lisa now. She sells the ring. She buys new clothes, new shoes. Her new look says, this is not a nice girl. This girl is up for a good time. You can have her if you pay. The johns like her as she is fresh on the scene.

More times than she can count, a man rapes Lisa. Once he has raped her, the man stabs her or shoots her or crushes her throat with his thumbs, and dumps her corpse at the back of a spare lot, or in a creek, or in a trash can for the dogs and rats to maul. The cops do not find the man in the case, of course. Why should they care? She was just a whore from out of town. So what if she was slain? It was her fault, the bitch. More like her will come, in their own good time. So the task falls to her. She hunts the man down to a dark room on the far side of town and kills him in his turn. She talks to him as she kills him, about the wrong he has done to her and to all her sex. She sets him straight, while she cuts him slow and deep and good, right down through red flesh to white bone. She gifts him with as much pain as she can when she kills him so as teach him well, to help him learn the way he should act from here on. Do no more harm, she says, and puts down the knife, still wet. She strips the man and burns his clothes. She takes off her gloves and burns them too. Then she gets in the truck and sets off to find a new town. The place smells bad. A stain dries on the rug, drop by drop. This is what it means to die.

She will make a call in a day or two. The cops will swing by and take the man back to his wife, but Iris will be long gone. They will not catch her.

And each day, as she drives the truck through the shy glare of noon and the brash shade of night, Iris tilts her ear to hear the sky and blinks her eyes to see the wind. She sings a song they taught her when she was a child: The wheels on the bus go round and round, round and round. The tyres hum on the road, the signs strobe past one by one, and she is glad. The light and the dark enfold her equally, for she will never cease from her exploration; this is the new meaning of her life, this silent stream of polychromatic tintinnabulations.